THE COVEN

COVEN OF BONES
BOOK 1

HARPER L WOODS

ADELAIDE FORREST

LOTUS MOON PUBLISHING

Cover Design: Opulent Swag & Designs

Editing: Kaye Kemp Book Polishing

Chapter Headings & Scene Breaks: Etheric Designs

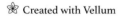 Created with Vellum

For those who love them villainous.

ABOUT THE COVEN

Revenge.

Raised to be my father's weapon against the Coven that took away his sister and his birthright, I would do anything to protect my younger brother from suffering the same fate. My duty forces me to the secret town of Crystal Hollow and the prestigious Hollow's Grove University—where the best and brightest of my kind learn to practice their magic free from human judgment.

There are no whispered words here. No condemnation for the blood that flows through my veins. The only animosity I face comes from the beautiful and infuriating Headmaster, Alaric Grayson Thorne, a man who despises me just as much as I loathe him and everything he stands for.

But that doesn't mean secrets don't threaten to tear the school in two. No one talks about the bloody massacre that forced it to close decades prior, only the opportunity it can afford to those fortunate enough to attend.

Because for the first time in fifty years, the Coven will open its wards to the *Thirteen*.

Thirteen promising students destined to change the world. If the ghosts of Hollow's Grove's victims don't kill them first.

TRIGGER/CONTENT WARNINGS

The Coven is a dark paranormal romance with gothic vibes and a dark academia setting. The male lead in this series is pushy, domineering, and manipulative. He goes beyond my typical morally gray antihero and is in my opinion an actual villain who gets his HEA.

Triggers include:
- dubious consent
- forced feeding
- graphic violence
- rough and explicit sexual content
- forced proximity
- betrayal
- references to past abuse & traumatic reactions to triggering stimuli
- knife violence
- graphic depictions of blood
- physical harm inflicted upon the main character
- ritualistic murder

PROLOGUE

ALARIC GRAYSON THORNE

In the 329 years since my making, I'd come to appreciate the finer things in life. The beauty of the meticulously cut colored glass in the arched windows and the prisms of light they cast over the dark stone tile of the halls at Hollow's Grove University was only one of those. It was not to be diminished by the tantalizing scent of witch's blood drifting from the messenger escorting me to the tribunal room.

The Covenant wouldn't wait long for any, not even the male they'd appointed as the Headmaster of their precious school. Cobwebs and dust lined the pathway before us, and I turned up my nose at the way the University had fallen into disrepair since I'd last set foot in it fifty years prior.

The witch at my side stopped before the tribunal gates at the end of the hall. She waved a well-manicured hand over the lock, watching as the iron and gold mechanism rotated until it parted. Gears turned slowly, the ripple effect sliding up until the rest of the locks followed suit. The bars latched across the seam where the two doors met finally retreated. The soft click of them opening a signal for the witch to grasp the handle.

"How many generations separate you and George Collins's

sister?" I asked, forcing the witch to pinch her lips as she looked over her shoulder at me.

"Nine generations separate *The Covenant* and I," she said with a sneer.

The witches were always so testy when discussing what had become of their leaders, of the two witches who'd commanded them through the centuries.

Susannah Madizza and George Collins were no longer— replaced by the two halves of The Covenant when the Hecate witches raised them from their graves.

"A shame," I said with a grin. "Sarah Collins was quite lovely before she died. It is unfortunate she wasn't able to pass that along to her descendants."

The witch's face fell with shock as I stepped through the gate she opened. I turned to the right and moved toward the tribunal room where The Covenant waited for me. My escort remained at the gates, the good little puppy her great-, great-, great- *whatever* grandmother had seen fit to raise her to become.

"You're one to talk, you undead bastard!" she called out behind me.

I adjusted the jacket of my suit, straightening the lapel as I grasped both the inner doors of the tribunal and swiftly pulled them open.

The Covenant sat in the gilded chairs they'd had fashioned centuries ago, skeletal fingers grasping the arms as what had once been Susannah Madizza leaned forward. Her hood shifted to the side, allowing some of the sunlight shining through the kaleidoscope windows at the side of the circular chamber to illuminate what remained of her face.

The flesh had long since rotted from her body, leaving only the gaunt shape of a skeleton to stare back at me. Her neck tipped at an unnatural angle where it had snapped when they hanged her, the slightest slant to the side displaying the manner of her death all those years ago.

Her eye sockets remained empty even as she somehow *saw* me. "Tormenting our children once again, Headmaster Thorne?" she asked, that eerie, ageless voice stretching between us. She tapped the tip of her finger bone against the arm of her chair in a steady staccato that I felt like a strike to my impatience.

The other half of her magic sat beside her, the masculine equivalent to her feminine.

George Collins had no descendants to his name to be defensive of—not with the rules that prohibited male witches from procreating if they chose to keep their magic. He was just as skeletal as Susannah, but his neck curved to the other side. What I could see of his bones revealed deep slash marks etched into them, lingering evidence of the torture he'd sustained in the hours before his death.

"I have to presume you did not summon me here to discuss my manners with your grandniece, Covenant," I said, gritting my teeth.

My kind were not meant to be subservient to any, but the magic that kept us bound to the flesh of our vessels made us reliant on the witches if we ever wanted to be freed from the bodies that trapped us.

We'd thought it a blessing to never need to possess a new form, to have a body that could hold us for an eternity.

We'd thought wrong.

"We have decided to reopen the University," George said, speaking before his female counterpart could interject. "We all need fresh blood. The attention we suffered as a result of that day has long since faded from memory."

"As much as I, too, would appreciate new blood to feed upon, I have to urge caution in opening our walls once more.

Rumors will spread the moment we announce our reopening," I said, looking between the two skeletons staring at me.

"Two generations of witches have been left to learn their magic in the privacy of their homes," Susannah said, rising from her throne. Her black cloak wrapped around her and hid her bones from view as she stepped down the dais stairs. "The time has come for them to be properly educated. We will only open our doors to twelve new students from outside Crystal Hollow every year, and we have personally selected those who will join us based on the power we've detected. There will be no formal announcement." She held out a list, her messy cursive writing displaying the names of those she'd selected.

"What assurance do we have that we will not suffer a repeat of last time?" I asked, thinking only of the safety of my kind. While we were difficult to kill, even some of us had been harmed in the massacre that had occurred fifty years prior.

"If we do not open our doors once again, the witches will have no one left to breed with. If we die out, so will your kind. Do not forget that you require the blood of our people to sustain you, Alaric," Susannah said, turning her back on me and making her way to the throne that waited for her.

I gritted my teeth, forcing my body into the shallowest of bows. "As if you would ever allow me to forget such a thing," I said, crumpling the list in my hand.

I turned my back on them, the muscle in my cheek jumping when they couldn't see it.

Fucking witches.

1

WILLOW

wo months later
Whispered words.

If I kept my eyes closed long enough, maybe I would convince myself that the last week had been a dream. A phantom of a nightmare, a figment of my worst imagination, the very day I'd been raised for.

And the one I wanted nothing more than to escape.

The whispers at my back existed within a bubble, as if I'd managed to separate myself from them. Even as all the people who'd murmured behind my mother's back waited for their turn to say goodbye to the woman they would never understand, I couldn't force myself to pry my eyes open.

I stood with my feet shoulder-width apart, a habit my father had ingrained in me all my life. Ready for anything, for a hunter to attack at any time—or something even worse. The tile beneath my shoes was unnatural, the separation it caused keeping me from touching the one thing that made my soul feel whole.

The dirt beneath my feet.

"Low," a small voice said.

A hand slipped into mine, much smaller fingers inter-twining in a pattern that we knew well. Ash stood at my side even after saying my name, giving me the chance to compose myself. To stop the force threatening to consume me. We'd kept my brother protected from the knowledge of what we were for his own safety, for what would await him if he ever discovered his magic and brought the coven down on us.

I should have been the one to be strong for him. After all, it wasn't only *my* mother who lay rotting in a casket for all to see, but his as well.

I forced my eyes open, staring at the pictures of our mother and our family. Smiling faces stared out at the crowd, looking deceptively human. As if we belonged here, when the only home we'd ever truly had wouldn't have embraced us if they'd known what we were.

Humans had only so much capacity for understanding in their hearts. They tended to shy away from actual witchcraft, if the trials that had nearly wiped out my ancestors were any indication.

A single, slow look down to my mother's face made me grimace, remembering why I'd closed my eyes to fight back my irritation.

Her lipstick was wrong. The color was far too red and brazen for my mother, who preferred to blend into the back-ground. It was readily apparent that the person who'd been responsible for preparing her for her services hadn't known her at all, covering the laugh lines she valued as a result of her happy, full life, free of the coven that would have dragged her back to Crystal Hollow kicking and screaming.

It was bad enough she'd need to be buried according to human customs—her remains trapped in a box in the earth that kept her from the elements—unless my father upheld his end of the bargain. He was meant to sneak into the cemetery in the middle of the night while the grave was still fresh, lay her to her final rest on top of the casket, and bury her all over again so that she could find peace.

I reached forward quickly, grasping the amulet she wore around her throat and pulling until the chain snapped. The amulet tore free as the whispering idiots behind me gasped in shock, but Ash was unbothered when I finally looked down to where he stood at my side.

His brown eyes were a perfect reflection of what I would have seen if my mother opened hers, so different from mine with our different fathers. He had the same deep mahogany hair that was so dark it was almost black, its warmth shimmering slightly in the too-bright lights of the funeral home.

"Let's get out of here," I said, nodding my head toward the entrance to the parlor. Ash nodded faintly, casting one last sparing look for our mother.

We both knew what came next. She'd given me very clear instructions on what to do with Ash when she finally succumbed to the illness that plagued her body, taking her from us bit by bit.

Ash released my hand, leading the way through the pews and carving his way toward the exit. He held his head high in a way that nearly made me smirk, his ferocity so reminiscent of Mom's. I repressed it as the people around me whispered of the death that followed us, of the fact that everyone who seemed to grow too close to my brother and I ended up in an early grave.

Magic had a way of burning through a witch's surroundings if they didn't satisfy it with use, and then eventually it would turn on the witch themself if ignored for too long.

As it had with my mother.

Mud covered the white tiles on the floor as we approached the exit, lingering on the bottom of the shoes of those who'd entered to bid farewell to my mother, Flora Madizza.

It was fitting in a way, I supposed. Soon enough, Flora would return to the earth from which she came. She would be placed into the dirt when my father fulfilled her last request. Finally, she would be at home in the place that gave her peace, her power absorbed back into the nature that called to us.

A hand wrapped around my forearm as I walked toward the exit, following behind my brother as he hurried to escape the stifling, suffocating oppression of being in a room with so many who didn't like us. He might not have understood the fear so many had of us, but he saw it no less.

My head snapped to the side, glaring at the man who grabbed me. His fingers tightened on my arm for a moment before he swallowed.

"It's customary for you to remain so that the town may pay their respects and offer you condolences," he said, watching as my eyes trailed down his chest and to the hand that touched me without permission.

He removed it slowly, feigning ease, as if he'd only released me because he was good and ready. I flicked my eyes back up to his, smiling crookedly when he flinched back from the eye contact with what he probably deemed to be a demon. I'd seen the eerie stare every time I looked in the mirror. The amber of one eye was natural enough, if not paired with the faint violet of my left eye. Most assumed it was an odd shade of blue, unusual but not unheard of. It was only in close proximity that people realized the truth.

A gift from my father's lineage—a trait that had faded away centuries prior.

"When have I ever cared for your *customs*, Mr. Whitlock?" I asked, pulling my loose gray cardigan tighter around myself as the wave of his distrust washed over me. I turned to face where my brother waited at the exit, pursing my lips as I took the first step toward him.

They would do what they wanted with my mother's body from here, and I would continue to exact her wishes as she requested. Ash pressed into my side when I reached him, then tugged open the door to allow him to walk through. I cast a lone glance back toward my mother's casket, knowing that soon there would be no turning back.

Without my mother's wards, the destiny my parents had chosen would come for me whether I wanted it or not.

"**G**et your things," I said, swallowing past the surge of emotion that seemed to clog my throat. The humans in town often called it a frog in the throat because of the hoarseness. I'd never understood the analogy, instead feeling as if it were grave dirt coming to claim me from the inside.

"I don't want to go," Ash pleaded, turning his brown eyes up to stare at me as I swung the front door closed behind me. It closed easily, so at odds with the way the wood swelled in the humidity of summer, making it difficult to squeeze into the frame. I spun, giving Ash my back as I clicked the deadbolt into place and drew the chain across the gap that let in far too much of the unseasonable air.

September wasn't usually so cold, even in our little town in the mountains of Vermont.

I kicked off the black flats I'd worn for Mom's service, nudging them to the side as I spun back to face my brother. Even with Mom gone, even knowing that soon enough this house would sit empty and forgotten, I couldn't bring myself to disobey her rules.

Rules that she no longer cared for.

Tears stung my eyes as I bent forward, touching my mouth to Ash's forehead. I felt him sigh beneath the touch, his gaze holding mine when I pulled back.

"You know we can't stay here," I explained, wrapping an arm around his shoulder. I tugged him out of the cramped entryway, heading toward the stairwell at the entrance to the living room.

He shrugged me off, rounding on me with his face twisted into a scowl. "Why not? Why won't you tell me where you're going?"

My eyes fell closed, knowing that the secrecy my mother had sworn me to was for his own protection. I just wished I could make him understand, that he could see just how little I cared for the duty they'd given me.

If I'd had it my way, destiny could kiss my ass.

"I'll tell you when you're older. I promise," I explained, heading for the stairwell.

I placed my hand on the old, walnut railing and glanced up toward my bedroom as I took the first step. The urge to bury myself beneath the blankets was all-consuming, wanting to hide away from the world; from the responsibilities and the expectations pressing down on me.

"You've been saying that for years! When?"

I ran my hands over my face, moving down from the step and squatting in front of Ash. "When you're sixteen, I'll tell you everything. I promise."

"Why not now?" he asked, his bottom lip trembling.

Our mother had never meant to have another child, not after the reality of what I was and what that would mean for those closest to me. The least we could do was protect him with everything we had—even if it meant abandoning him to people he barely knew in the process.

Living with his father's family was far better than dying alongside me in this stupid, foolish duty that I couldn't seem to escape.

"I wouldn't leave you if I had a choice. Please believe that," I said, taking his hands in mine. I squeezed them tightly, and I knew from the tears pooling in his eyes that he did. All his life, he'd been my entire world. He'd been the one my mother used to motivate me to practice the magic that felt so distant at first.

The promise of protecting him was all I needed to know to believe that it was worth it.

"So come with me," he said, sinking his teeth into his bottom lip. "My dad will take care of you until you find a new job. You know he will."

He would. Ash's father wasn't like mine. He was good and patient, loving and warm. He was everything a father should have been, and it was only due to our mother's need for secrecy that he hadn't been able to spend more time with his son.

But he couldn't protect me against what was coming, and worse yet, he couldn't protect Ash from the danger of being at my side when it did.

"It isn't that easy, Bug," I said, the term of endearment I hadn't used in months rolling off my tongue. It was the name Mom called him, but her illness had taken her ability to speak in the end.

Using it without her had seemed wrong.

Mom's coat seemed to sway on the rack as if a phantom breeze passed through the house, sending a chill up my spine. A reminder of how impossible it would be for me to go with him.

"It could be. Just promise me. Promise me that no matter where we go, we'll go together," he said, burrowing further into my chest. I pulled him tighter, swallowing past the burn in my throat and resisting the urge to sniffle.

I did the one thing I'd sworn never to do.

"I promise, Bug," I said, squeezing him tighter.

I lied.

2

GRAY

I rolled my neck to the side as I entered the Tribunal, casting my gaze around the circle. To either side of the dais where the Covenant waited, six witches sat in their colored ceremonial robes.

"Two summons in as many months. What has made me so fortunate to be deemed worthy of your presence this time, Covenant?" I asked, waving my arm in a mocking flourish as I bent at the waist.

"Careful, Alaric. While we find you entertaining most days, even our patience wears thin," Susannah warned.

I shrugged, looking at the witches, who watched me in disapproval. "I wasn't aware you could feel at all."

Susannah raised a bony hand to touch her face, running it over her skull as she swept back her hood to reveal the worst of her irritation. It was so difficult to determine a being's moods when they didn't even have skin.

There were no rolled eyes, no twitches in the cheek or pursed lips. Deciphering the Covenant's moods had become something of a game for me in the centuries I'd spent trapped in this half-mortal flesh alongside them.

"We have one last student to collect before classes begin in two days' time," George said, helpfully navigating away from my enjoyment of tormenting those who would rid the world of me if they could. Fortunately for me, they lacked the power necessary and would be stuck in this eternal misery with me.

I preferred the fires of Hell to the confines of the body crafted to trap me here.

"I was under the impression that we'd already collected two new students for each of the Houses. Am I incorrect in that assumption?" I asked, furrowing my brow. My men had successfully collected two whites, purples, grays, blues, reds, and yellows from outside the magical barrier surrounding Crystal Hollow.

"A new witch has made herself known to us," Susannah explained, sitting up straighter upon her dais. She looked to the lines of symmetry at her side, to the twelve witches who led each of the houses within the town. They were representatives of the original sixteen families that founded Crystal Hollow—all that remained of those noble lines in the centuries that had passed.

"Then surely, she can merely attend next year? If she's sixteen, she's far too young to begin at Hollow's Grove for another four years," I said, spinning in a circle slowly as I waited for any of those gathered to echo the sentiment. Hollow's Grove required all students to be at least twenty years of age, given the proclivities that happened within the school walls once a week when the Reaping came.

One of the White witches stood from her seat, tiny crystals sewn into the fabric of her gleaming robes as she held out a folder for me. I took it, flipping the manilla page open to glance down at the photo resting on top of a packet of information.

Shocking mismatched eyes stared back at me—the left a

faint, pale purple and the right sparkling like liquid gold. They were deep set and upturned at the outer corners, surrounded by deep olive skin. Her hair fell in full waves around her shoulders, a deep mahogany that was almost black, shining against the ebony leather jacket she wore to cover the first hint of fascinating curves.

I shifted the photo lower, the name at the top of the file making my brow raise in question. "Willow *Madizza?*" I asked, looking at what remained of Susannah. She was the last of the Madizza line, and I wasn't certain that she counted in any substantial way. Not when she wasn't really alive and existed alongside but separated from the rest of the witches.

"She's not sixteen, merely hidden from our sight for four years after her awakening. She is the last of a founding family, Alaric. Surely, even you can understand that it is of the utmost importance that she is brought to Hollow's Grove immediately," Susannah explained.

"How has she remained hidden all this time? Why didn't you know she existed before now?" I looked around the room.

For the witches, it was sacrilege to question the Covenant. I didn't pretend to care about such formalities, not when my soul was far older than they could dream to be. I'd existed since the dawn of time, since the creation of the Earth itself.

A few centuries was nothing but the blink of an eye.

"I have to presume her mother warded her from the sight along with herself after she faked her death over two decades ago. She truly passed last week," Susannah said.

There was no heartache over the descendant who should have been her great-, great-something granddaughter. Only the desire to see her bloodline restored within the town she presided over.

"I'll send Juliet. The girl may feel more comfortable if it is a woman who makes contact. Does she know what she is?" I asked, flicking through the file. She'd attended a human school, worked at a human newspaper. There was no sign of magical training in the documents.

"No. I want you to collect this one yourself. We have no reason to believe she has any clue what she is. But if she does, she possesses the magic of an entire lineage within her, Alaric. She's unpredictable at best—more than likely dangerous if she feels cornered. Take Juliet with you, as well as Kairos, at least. See that she's unharmed but make it clear that her attendance at Hollow's Grove is not optional in this case," Susannah instructed, standing from her seat.

The other witches followed, bowing their heads in respect as Susannah approached me in the center of the circle. She laid a skeletal hand upon my shoulder, the dark magic that animated her rippling through me. It called to me, as like called to like, recognizing that we weren't so different after all.

Immortal souls trapped within something not quite alive and not quite dead.

"You want me to force her to come here?" I asked, the whisper echoing between us.

I possessed no morals. I cared nothing at all for the girl I'd never met or the free will most would say she had a right to. But the Coven cared about such things. They mandated that nothing could happen in Crystal Hollow unless a witch gave permission.

From breeding to feeding, they consented every step of the way. Even if they had to twist circumstances to gain that consent, they did what they had to do to ease their guilty conscience with lies.

"No matter the cost. Do you understand me?" the Covenant asked, and even without the flesh of eyeballs to gaze back at me, I felt the press of her intentions. She would not allow her line to die out, not when she, at last, had a chance of seeing it replenished. "For the good of the Coven, the girl must return with you."

"And if that only makes her hate my kind? What then?" I asked as her hand left my shoulder and she swept past me, heading for the private rooms at the back of the tribunal where she and George kept themselves isolated except to speak with their flock.

"Then there will be another witch to hate you when you feed from her. I should think you would be used to it by now," Susannah said, barking something that almost resembled a laugh as she pulled open the doors and retreated from sight.

I spun on my heel, going to gather Juliet and Kairos for our journey across state lines. At least she was only a few hours' drive away, and we'd reach her quickly enough.

One of the Red witches caught my eye as I passed, smiling sultrily as she looked at me as if I were her next meal and not the other way around.

They hated us, but that didn't stop them from wanting the hate sex that so often came with feedings. Centuries of disdain couldn't stop the fact that a witch and a Vessel were *very* well suited in some ways.

My fangs throbbed with the need to feed, but I pushed them back. It could wait until I returned.

There was work to be done first.

3

WILLOW

J stood from the table, leaving Ash to finish his dinner as my cell buzzed in my hand. Stepping out of the kitchen and heading for the stairs, I answered with a quiet murmur.

"You know it's too dangerous to be calling me right now."

"Why haven't you disposed of your phone or your brother yet?" the male voice on the other end of the line asked.

"I am not *disposing* of my brother," I snapped, glancing back toward where he remained in the kitchen as I kept my voice hushed. My black jeans hugged my legs as I ascended the stairs slowly, trying not to draw attention to the urgency I felt. "Ash made it clear that he doesn't want to go without me. His father is meeting us at the bus stop tonight, so he'll be there to help if he refuses to go alone. I can't risk being the one to drive him to Maine. Not now."

"You should have sent him away days ago. What were you thinking?" my father asked, his voice dropping low with the scolding tone that I was far too familiar with.

I'd have been more concerned to have him speak to me *without* it.

"I was thinking he deserved to attend his own mother's fucking funeral," I whispered, swinging my bedroom door closed and leaning against the back of it. I'd packed a small bag, mostly to convince Ash I had every intention of joining him at his father's house. But I'd filled it with the small pieces of my life that mattered to me.

I wouldn't be allowed to wear the clothes I preferred, the gray and black tones that covered me from head to toe not suited for a Green. My boots scuffed over the carpet in the bedroom as I moved toward my bed and sat on the edge, hanging my head in my hands.

"You're playing with fire, girl. If they find out about him—"

"I know." I sighed, rubbing at my eyes. My fingernails were painted a matte black, the polish chipped at the ends. I frowned at them as I pulled them away from my face.

"If he wanted to attend the funeral that badly, then you should have left and gone elsewhere. His father could have taken him," my father, Samuel, said.

"You're demanding I give up my entire future for your revenge. The least you can do is understand I would want to attend my own mother's funeral," I said, dropping onto my mattress with a sigh.

"It is not just my revenge. She was your aunt, Willow," he argued, and his voice went quiet in the way it only did when talking about *her*. The older sister who had given everything to protect the knowledge of his existence. The one who had stolen her baby brother from his crib and sent him to grow up somewhere far away from the Coven.

So no one could make him choose between his magic and his ability to sire children.

What a loving relationship he'd fostered with that gift, turning his only daughter into a weapon designed to do the one thing he couldn't...

Find his sister's bones.

"I know she was," I said.

Even if I'd never met her, I couldn't help but want to avenge the young woman they'd murdered fifty years ago. I just didn't want it enough to never see my brother again. As much as I wanted to earn my father's approval and do the *one* thing he and my mother had raised me for, I'd have walked away from all of it if there had been even a chance of Ash and me finding a safe place to hide.

"She deserves to find peace, Willow," my father said, his voice softening before he continued on. "And you deserve to have what is yours by birthright."

"I don't give a damn about my birthright," I said.

The confession hung between us. Collecting the bones was a means to an end, a necessity for my aunt and all those who came before her to find their way home.

Most of the witches of the Coven drew their power from nature. The Greens, like my mother, from the earth; the Whites from crystals; the Yellows from fire.

But the Blacks had been different.

We drew our power from the bones of our ancestors, from the magic that only existed within our line. Without those bones, we were nothing, and they were tucked safely within the boundary of Crystal Hollow somewhere.

I felt them—knew that they existed. Any wise person would have burned them with salt when they killed off the last of us just to be safe, but someone had kept them instead.

A perverse collector's item, I was certain.

The last of the necromancers.

I scoffed as my father spoke, his words a regurgitation of everything he'd said over the course of my life. I'd been too young to remember when he taught me the principle of summoning, of how to use my blood and wear the bones of my ancestors to raise the dead.

"Do you have any idea what I would give to be the witch our ancestors chose to wear the bones?"

"I have some idea," I said, letting the bitterness come through in my voice. I knew exactly what he would give to be chosen.

He would give them me. He would sacrifice me in a heartbeat if he thought the bones would fall to the only remaining member of the Hecate line. It was why he'd only had one child, so that there would only be one person standing in his way.

The sacrificial lamb.

He didn't feel their call. Didn't hear them whispering to him in the night when there should have been silence.

For Ash's sake, that couldn't happen. I'd grown up knowing that one day, I would either have to kill my father or allow him to kill me.

The ringing of the doorbell saved us from having to acknowledge that reality, making me sit up quickly as I glanced toward the door.

"Fuck," I hissed, hoping for the first time that it was just a pesky, nosy neighbor coming with a casserole to pry into our business and my plans for how I would support the two of us.

My father hung up without a word. There was no touching goodbye—even knowing that if that was who I feared it may be, he might never see me again. There was a very good chance I wouldn't survive Hollow's Grove University.

I hurried for the door, sprinting to the stairs. My relief pulsed through the air when Ash remained safely tucked inside and out of sight. He'd been forbidden from answering the door years ago in an effort to protect him, leaving me to huff a breath as I adjusted my gray sweater and hurried down the stairs.

"Go into the kitchen and stay out of sight," I whispered, shooing him as far from the front door as possible.

He did as he was told, tucking himself into the kitchen, though he lingered near the doorway so that he could listen to what might be said.

His curiosity would be the end of me.

I drew in a deep breath, trying to convince myself that it would just be Mrs. Johnson waiting on the other side. That she'd thought to see if we'd eaten already and brought us *another* lasagna. Placing a hand on the gold-plated doorknob, I glanced down at the amulet I'd already fastened around my neck. The chain was irrelevant, but the black tourmaline nestled safely within the rose-gold wire cage would protect against compulsion. All witches in the Coven wore them when they came of age, and I'd be damned if I risked facing one at my door without it.

With my free hand, I reached up and unfastened the chain and deadbolt. Twisting the knob as I confirmed with one last glance behind me that Ash had remained hidden, I pulled the door open a crack and peeked outside.

I swallowed as my eyes landed on the male standing on the front porch. He was alone, his lips twisted into the faintest of smiles. I had no doubt it was meant to be reassuring, softening his full lips from the tense set that seemed to linger beneath the unfamiliar gesture.

Definitely not Mrs. Johnson.

The power rolling off him confirmed he not only wasn't my nosey neighbor, but that he also wasn't even human, let alone truly alive. His eyes flashed as they connected with mine, the blue steel of them darkening for a moment before he lowered them down to the amulet at my chest. My breath caught at the sensation of those smoldering eyes running over my body, of the way I could feel it like claws dragging over the surface of my skin lightly.

He was beautiful and infuriating—a disaster waiting to happen.

"Miss Madizza, I presume?" he asked, his voice deep and raspy as he slowly tilted his head to the side. His gaze continued to rake down my body, sliding over my stomach and thick thighs until his smile broadened when he took in the combat boots on my feet.

"Are you talking to me? Or my feet?" I asked, pulling my sweater tight across my chest. His gaze came back up in a slow, languid path. He didn't hurry to meet my eyes once again, in spite of the fact that I'd called him out, the arrogance of centuries of life allowing him to behave in ways that defied manners.

"I am most definitely talking to you," he said, crossing his arms over his chest. He leaned his shoulder into the iron column that supported the roof of the open porch, looking far too comfortable in the space that was meant to be mine.

"What is it that you want from *Miss Madizza*?" I asked, resisting the urge to wrap my fingers around my amulet. My best chance in getting Ash out safely, even though they had already found me, lay in pretending I knew nothing of who they were. If I feigned innocence, maybe I could sneak him out.

"I represent a prestigious university. We have a unique opportunity for her to study alongside the best and brightest students of her year. Perhaps I could come inside to discuss it?" the male asked, pushing himself off the railing with a nudge of his shoulder. He took a step toward me as I stepped through the door, pulling it mostly closed behind me and blocking his path.

"No," I said, my tone brokering no argument.

Too quickly.

He raised his brow at me, his mouth parting lightly as he ran his tongue over his bottom teeth. I smiled to soften the urgency in my voice, swallowing down my terror at having a predator so close. He took another step toward me, stopping when he was near enough that I had to tip my head back to look up at him.

"A girl can't be too careful these days. I'm sure you understand," I said, focusing on the rhythm of my heartbeat.

A deep breath in, then another one out.

My amulet warmed against my chest as he looked down at me, holding my stare as he attempted to force his compulsion on me. I pretended I couldn't feel it, pretended that the crystal didn't confirm everything I'd already suspected about his unnatural beauty.

Vessel.

He studied me intently, his steel-blue eyes flashing. This close, I found myself mesmerized by the ring of gold surrounding the pupil of his eye, a spark of warmth in the otherwise cold of his stare.

"Of course," he murmured, spreading his lips into a carefully controlled smile. He'd had centuries to practice, to avoid showing the fangs that would send a panic through even the most foolish of humans.

"Hollow's Grove University would like to welcome you to attend in two days' time." He glanced over my shoulder at the house. My mom would have never allowed it to fall into disrepair, caring for it even if it was no Buckingham Palace, but the disdain with which he studied the aging siding made my neck prickle with rage. "It's the sort of opportunity that a girl like you would be foolish to reject so carelessly."

I shifted, turning my gaze down as I smiled in disbelief. "A girl like me? What does that mean, exactly?"

"An orphan," he said, not missing a beat as the word rolled off his tongue. There was no sympathy or pity for my recent loss, only a matter-of-fact statement that made angry tears threaten my eyes.

"Don't you need to be a child to be considered an orphan?" I asked, sinking my teeth into my cheek. I leaned forward, putting myself in his space. His nostrils flared as I got closer, the scent of my blood undoubtedly filling his lungs. "If I'm a child, then what does that make you with your lingering gaze?"

"You're not a child," he said, his jaw tensing as I held his gaze in challenge. "I shouldn't have used that term. I only meant that you are suddenly on your own in this world. Having a place to start over may be to your advantage—"

"I'm going to make this very simple so that we do not waste any more of one another's time," I said, cutting him off. "I'm not interested in attending any university that sends a seedy, sketchy man to the doorstep of my home. Any reputable university would allow me to apply myself. If you'd like to leave me an application and save a stamp, my mailbox is right over there." I pointed behind him to the end of the driveway in the distance—to the little red mailbox that sat there.

"There are no applications for Hollow's Grove University. It's invitation only," the man said, taking a step back. He held out his hand for me to shake, staring at me intently as he willed me to take it. I raised my chin, ignoring it pointedly while he continued. "I should have introduced myself. I'm the headmaster of Hollow's Grove, Alaric Thorne. This is your formal invitation—"

"Then leave my *invitation* in my mailbox," I corrected.

"I *am* the invitation," he said, clenching his back teeth as he glared down at me.

He pulled his hand back, sliding it into the pocket of his trousers. The three-piece suit he wore was far too distracting for my tastes, a complete and utter distraction. I had a feeling that was the point, as if his very being was sin wrapped up in the finest suit.

I reached behind me, grasping the doorknob so that I could pull the door open just enough to wedge my body into it. He couldn't enter without an invitation, and I'd be *damned* to the nine circles of Hell before I ever gave him one.

I smiled as I maneuvered myself into the house, peering out at him as he watched me like a wolf. "Then I am definitely not interested."

4

GRAY

I moved quickly, surging through the distance between us and wedging my shoe in the crack in the door before the witch could pull it closed. The door hit the side of my foot, springing back to open slightly as her fingers scrambled to keep hold of the knob. Her eyes widened slightly at the speed, blinking as I appeared in front of her suddenly.

Reaching up, I rested my forearm against the siding next to the door and leaned into her face as my upper lip pulled back, revealing the faintest hint of fang. Her heartbeat increased, pulsing faster in spite of whatever training she'd had to try to disguise her nerves.

"Why don't you come outside and lie to me again, love?" I asked, smiling down at her as those odd, mismatched eyes blinked up at me. They were fanned by natural, long black lashes. The circles beneath them reflected just how tired she must have been, and I had a moment where I wondered if it was her norm or because of her recent loss.

"I'm surprised you can fit on that porch with the size of your ego," she said, smiling that fake, saccharine grin that made her appear older than I knew her to be. It was the look of a cynical woman who had lived long enough to experience the ugliness the world had to offer.

It made her seem ageless.

Movement behind her distracted me from the way her lips curved around her next word, preparing to deliver me with some doubtlessly clever, enjoyable line that would both infuriate and entertain me. It had been so long since someone readily offered me a challenge. Her refusal reminded me of the thrill that had once been in the chase of predator and prey.

A boy of maybe six stood in the hallway behind her, glaring at me as he clutched a fire poker in his hand. He hefted it awkwardly, showing that he knew nothing of what to do with it.

It was a drastic difference to the way Willow held herself, to the steadfastness and stillness in her body. Every movement served a purpose, every twitch of her finger was intentional.

She'd trained, I realized with certainty. Whereas the boy had not.

Willow turned her head to look at the boy over her shoulder in the same moment she thrust her free arm out and covered my mouth with it. Any doubt I'd had fled, her hand cutting off the command to allow me entry into their house.

He did not possess an amulet to protect him from compulsion.

I grinned against her palm, letting my fangs touch her skin and reveling in the shudder that went through her body.

"Get back in the kitchen. Now," she ordered. The boy glared at her but did as he was told, swinging that fire poker at his side as he stalked out of sight.

It was almost cute that he wanted to protect her. I imagined she didn't agree when he'd revealed the deception she'd tried to create. She released my mouth when she felt certain I wouldn't speak, wouldn't use my compulsion against the boy I had to presume was her brother.

"That's quite the secret you're keeping, *Witchling*," I said, staring at the side of her face as she watched him disappear from view. The carefully constructed mask she'd donned for me slowly slipped away, the faint hint of a pleasant but blank smile dropping. Her face hardened, her cheekbones appearing sharper as her gaze glimmered, and she slowly turned it up to look at me through those long lashes.

"I don't know what you're talking about," she said, pressing her lips into a flat line. Her sweater parted to reveal the faint glow pulsing around her tourmaline amulet, shimmering against her olive skin.

"If you come with me quietly, I won't tell the Coven about the male witch in your house," I said, making an offer that she wouldn't have received from any of the others. I was the only one who cared so little for the laws of the witches that I would dismiss them so carelessly.

"You expect me to trust a blood-sucking parasite?" she asked, her eyes flashing in defiance. With the walls dropped between us, the depths of her hatred for my kind became clear in the endless gaze she leveled me with.

"You can't hide in that house forever. I'm offering you a way to save your brother from making the Choice. Call someone to get him and come with me, and no one needs to know," I said, raising my hands placatingly. I didn't back away, didn't give her the opportunity to close the door as my foot stayed wedged in her way.

She took her eyes away from mine, turning to look back in the direction her brother went one last time before she made the choice we both knew was her best option.

But when she turned her attention back to me, her scowl shifted into a satisfied grin. "Watch me," she growled, her nose crinkling with the almost animalistic snarl that consumed her face. She released the door entirely, stomping her boot down on my foot in the same moment she jabbed the side of her hand into the front of my throat.

My breath cut off. Sharp pain erupted through my throat as she crushed it. Her second strike went to my balls while I was still reeling from the fact that the vicious thing had attacked me. I covered my groin with both hands to protect myself from the foot she raised, leaving my chest open as she used it to shove me back a step.

I didn't go far, but it was enough.

She retreated with speed I rarely saw in even the most well-trained witches, grabbing the door and pulling it closed while I gaped after her. My throat pushed out, uncrushing and healing, as I rotated my head from one side to another.

Fucking witches.

The curtains on the front windows pulled closed even though she was nowhere to be seen in them, leaving me to turn to face that Hell-damned mailbox at the end of the driveway. I pulled my cell phone from my pocket, dialing Juliet's number.

I descended the three steps that led to the ground in front of the porch, pressing it to the side of my face as I stared at the too-quiet house.

"Do you have her?" Juliet asked, and the sound of the SUV starting came through the call.

"No. She knows what we are. I want eyes on every exit point from the house," I snapped, grinding my jaw as I walked around to the backyard and forcing myself to listen for any sound of escape. I'd be damned if she snuck out while I was alone.

"Got it," Juliet said, undoubtedly shifting the car into gear.

With no need for discretion any longer, she'd floor it down the road to close the minimal distance in no time.

"And Juliet? When she does surface, she's *mine*. Is that understood?" I asked, wincing as I took a step and my balls throbbed with pain.

Juliet was silent for a moment, thinking before a harsh chuckle bubbled free. "The witch got the jump on you, didn't she?"

"I underestimated her," I admitted, staring at the closed curtains on the back of the small, green house. "I won't make that mistake twice."

5

WILLOW

"*G*et your bag," I ordered, glaring at Ash and hurrying toward the small pantry closet off the kitchen. I hauled open the door, kneeling in front of the panel in the floor. My fingers felt along the edge, searching for the tiny groove where they would *just* slip in, and lifted the wood to reveal the rough, shabby staircase my mom and I had built ourselves when I'd turned sixteen.

"Low, what is that?" Ash asked, hiking his backpack up on his shoulders. I stood, placing a hand on the small of his back and pushing him into the dark. I flicked on the light to the hidden basement, illuminating the dirt floor at the base of the steps.

"Down you go," I said, trying to keep the urgency from my voice. I didn't want to frighten him—not when there were so many things he didn't know. But with the Vessel waiting outside and plotting a way to force us out of the house, we needed to *move*.

He descended the stairs quickly, leaving me to slip into the narrow passage and pull the wood panel closed above me to cover our tracks. Every moment would count when it came to getting Ash out. With his powers bound, he would be safe from the Coven until I died at the very least—the ropes of his binding forged with grasses summoned by my magic.

I moved to one of the paneled walls of the basement, sliding the wood to the side to reveal the massive tree roots that had grown and spread beneath the passage that would lead us to freedom. It was why Mom had chosen this house, this place, as our sanctuary. The trees here went deep underground, making it easy for us to create tunnels beneath the surface.

"What are you doing?" Ash asked as I ran a palm over the first tree root. I grabbed the knife and sheath off the shelves of supplies in the basement, strapping the holster across my thigh and forcing myself to ignore the confused pain on my brother's face.

This was the day I'd dreaded, the day that all our deceptions came to light.

I watched his face, his little forehead creased in confusion as I pulled the knife from the sheath.

"Willow," he said, stepping forward as if to stop me when I drew the sharpened edge of the blade against my palm. A thin line sliced through, blood seeping through too slowly as I clenched it and pressed my fingertips into the wound. I held Ash's horrified stare as I reached out with my palm covered in my blood, touching it to the tree root.

"Sanguis sanguinis mei, aperte," I murmured, allowing my eyes to drift closed as the tree drank from me. As it took the blood I offered in exchange for safe passage to the woods. The magic of the Greens flowed through my veins even if the bones of the Blacks eluded me.

The root beneath my hand shifted, drawing my attention to it as it staggered and pulled itself through the earth. Dirt rained down from where the root moved, falling to the floor and finding a new home there. As it shifted to the side and rose, a tunnel appeared in the space it had once blocked.

I sheathed my knife, grasping Ash by the hand and tugging him toward it.

"I'm not going anywhere until you tell me what's going on," he said, snatching his hand back as he left me glancing between him and the tunnel that offered us our only chance.

"There isn't time," I protested.

I went to the shelf of supplies we'd kept tucked safely away down here all these years, away from his prying, nosy eyes. My aunt's journal rested on the top shelf, collecting dust since I'd finished reading through her experiences at Hollow's Grove University years ago.

Stepping around to his back, I unzipped his backpack and deposited the journal into it. "This will explain most everything, and when you're older, I'll find a way to tell you more."

My aunt wasn't his aunt, and he wouldn't have the same magic she did. She'd had the magic of the necromancers, not the earthen magic of Ash's and my mother. But he would understand the basic notion of what it meant to be a witch.

Of the dangers lurking in Crystal Hollow that I needed to protect him from.

"Did Mom know?" he asked as I moved around to the front and guided him into the mouth of the tunnel.

Grabbing a flashlight quickly and turning it on, I grasped the wood panel, pulling it closed as we moved inside.

It was always so dark underground, the lack of stars shining in the sky making this tunnel some of the truest darkness I'd ever known. Panic threatened to consume me, the reminder of the other true darkness lingering. I shoved it down for the sake of my brother, pushing through with a deep, steadying breath.

"*Claudere*," I murmured, instructing the tree to resume its natural positioning. It moved, sealing us off from the basement once again as I took Ash by the hand. My skin was wet with blood as I gripped the flashlight in my injured palm, nodding until I realized he probably couldn't see me well.

"She was a Green Witch too," I said, glancing over at him as I moved us through the tunnels slowly but steadily. The ground beneath our feet was uneven, the dirt dug out slowly over the course of years, magic chipping away at it bit by bit to avoid overuse. "As are you."

His lips parted in shock, staring down at his hand as he lifted it to look at it with new appreciation.

I didn't tell him that I'd bound his magic to keep him hidden, choosing instead to leave that conversation for when he came of age. Until that day, until he could make the choice of what he wanted for himself, I wouldn't allow the Coven to take it from him.

"But I've never—"

"And you won't be able to until you're older," I answered, pausing my steps to turn and look at him with the stern set to my lips that he knew all-too-well. "You can't tell anyone. You understand that? Your father isn't like us. His family is not like us, and revealing what you are will just mean that creatures like that man outside find you and take you."

"What was he?" Ash asked as I tugged him forward more quickly. Once we reached the cave, we would have to run through the woods. We'd have to hope that the Vessel couldn't scent us.

"Something called a Vessel," I explained, contemplating how much I should tell him. He was so young, so impressionable. I still remembered my first nightmare of the creatures who survived off witch's blood when I'd been too young to know the horrors of them. "They work with the Coven of witches and live together. We want to avoid going there alto-gether," I said instead of giving him the truth.

That they were bodies crafted by the Hecate line, designed to live forever and house the *things* inside them. Without those Vessels, they burned through human bodies within a year.

What had once been allies serving the same higher power had become tentative enemies trapped together—an animosity that grew over generations.

Light shone faintly in the distance, the sun setting not quickly enough for my taste. The cover of darkness would have helped us blend in even slightly against the Vessel's strong senses.

I stopped as we emerged from the tunnel, climbing up toward the cave entrance in the woods. I knew if we continued away from the house, we would eventually reach the bus station. We were blissfully close, given how far apart things tended to be in our town, particularly after our traipse under the yard and beginning of the woods.

In the distance, I could see the faint movement of people around our home. Of those who would seek to chase us out of the place where we'd lived for as long as I could remember. I kept us tucked safely within the mouth of the cave, squatting down in front of Ash and taking his hands in mine as I tossed the flashlight back into the tunnel.

"No matter what happens, no matter what you see, you keep going," I said, ignoring the way his eyes widened. "You run as fast as you can, and if you keep going straight, you'll end up at the bus stop. Your dad is meeting us there. You just have to get there, okay? Promise me you'll get there, Bug."

Ash nodded, blinking rapidly. "What about you, Low?"

I cupped his cheek in my hand, forcing myself to smile as I pressed my forehead to his. So many lies in so few hours. "I'll be right behind you," I said, nodding as I stood and patted him on the back. I moved him behind me, positioning myself between his body and the Vessels. I pointed him in the direction he needed to go.

"Go!" I whispered harshly, giving him the little shove he needed to stumble into the woods. He was short enough that he blended in with the brush of the unkempt forest, the green clothing he and Mom favored helping him blend in. He'd worn her favorite color for her funeral, and I suppressed the quiver to my lip as I knelt and touched the surface of the dirt.

Pressing my fingers into the earth itself, I didn't wince when the grains wedged themselves beneath my nails. It was packed on the surface, leaving me to claw my way through until I reached the soft, fresh soil beneath.

I waited, sending my magic out in a wave through the earth of the forest. I felt each tree, every root, where it connected to the very dirt that surrounded my fingers. Planting myself as if I was one of them, I closed my eyes and drew in a deep, fortifying breath. When I flung them open, I knew that my eyes pulsed with a thread of green lacing its way through them at the center.

I waited still, giving Ash time to put a healthy distance between us before I created a distraction. Time passed as if it had slowed, the call of the Vessels striking me in the chest as they tried to call to Ash. To convince him to just open the door for them, that they could offer him a new life away from this place. I hoped he was far enough that he couldn't feel the press of it, that it wouldn't tempt him to return.

Only when one of the Vessels turned his attention toward me did I send my power out in a ripple through the forest. The words left my mouth as I called to the trees that surrounded me, to the ones closest to the house. The Vessel closest caught sight of me as my lips formed them, his head snapping to the side as he tried to warn the others.

"*Adiuva me,*" I said, asking the forest for help.

A thick branch from the tree closest to the Vessel snapped out, creaking as it struck him in the chest and sent him flinging back. He screamed as he flew through the air, colliding with the side of the house and bouncing off it to fall in a heap.

The other male, the one from the porch, spun to look at his fallen friend. His attention snapped to me as I stood, raising my chin as I met his gaze. He took the first step toward me, cracking his head to the side. When I didn't move, I smiled, knowing that even with his heightened senses, he would hear me.

"You wanted me to come outside. What now, Headmaster? Do you need an *invitation?*"

He took another step forward, his second foot poised to move. I knew it would come more quickly, that he would cross the distance between us with speed I didn't have a hope of keeping up with.

I dropped to my knees suddenly, slamming my palms down on the ground. The earth rose in a wave, a ripple shuddering through the forest as it moved toward the house and the yard. The Vessel, *Headmaster Thorne*, must have cursed as he surged forward. The forest met his advance, trees crossing their branches to block his path as the ground lifted and knocked him off his feet.

I watched the first tree roots rise from the ground, grasping him by the ankles and wrapping around his arms. They pinned him to the earth as I turned back to the forest.

And I ran.

6

GRAY

I snarled, thrashing what little I could as the tree roots tightened. One wrapped around the front of my throat, pressing against the same windpipe Willow had crushed on the porch only an hour before. Even with it already healed from the attack, the familiarity of the moment struck me in what would have been my heart if I'd had one.

I tugged at one of the roots, freeing my arm as they tried to pull me into the ground itself. My ribs cracked, my body caving with the force of them as the one that had wrapped itself around my torso yanked. As soon as I freed that hand, I clawed my way through the root at my throat, tearing the mangled, menacing thing and ignoring the scream that seemed to come from the bark as I tore it off.

A shadow appeared above me, blocking out the last of the sun as darkness descended on us. My skin tingled with irritation, the healing my body had needed burning through the witch's blood in my body far too quickly. Without it, the sun would become more than just a minor irritation.

It would burn me alive.

Juliet swung her sword down, hacking at the thick root on

my stomach. I resisted the urge to flinch back, trusting her not to cut through me. The piece of Willow's tree shuddered, its ends trembling as it fought against the pain.

She swung her sword to the side as a tree branch swayed toward her, meeting it with a blow that sent it rippling back. Another struck for her in the very same moment, leaving her to defend herself rather than trying to free me. I clawed at the root on my torso while the trees were distracted by the greater threat, tearing through the wood slowly.

Juliet glanced down at me, raising a brow in mockery as she watched me struggle. "You underestimated her again," she said, scoffing.

I growled my warning, even if she was right. I hadn't expected her to be *this* in control of her magic. Even with her being the last of her line, as her brother hadn't yet come into his power, I'd expected to find a half-trained witchling in need of serious educating about what she was capable of. I should have known better.

Flora Madizza had been a stubborn, defiant brat of a witch before she faked her own death to escape the Covenant. She'd spent far more time in the gardens than with her Coven.

Kairos joined the fray, the back of his neck marked with blood from where he'd cracked his head against the side of the house. If he caught Willow before I did, there would be very little I could do to control his rage. He dealt in absolutes. It didn't matter to him if Willow was fighting for her brother's life; he would seek to harm her in retribution, regardless.

Juliet cut through the rest of my binds quickly, leaving me to get to my feet and crack my neck as all my bones settled back into place, my body healing itself as the sun pressed down on me more firmly with each and every passing moment.

Part of me wanted her to bleed for what she'd done, for the

humiliation of being felled by a single witchling. But the other part of me knew there were fates in store for her that would make for far more entertaining revenge.

I took a step toward the woods.

"You can't seriously be thinking of following her *in there*?" Juliet asked as I spun and grabbed my sword from the backseat of the car she'd parked in the side of the yard.

I glanced at her over my shoulder, noting the way she studied the slight reddening of my skin. The sun would set soon enough, but who knew if we'd be safely back within the boundary of Crystal Hollow before morning?

Besides, I didn't want one of the witches who waited for me there.

I wanted *her*.

"I'm hungry," I said, listening to the sound of Willow as she raced through the woods. They seemed to move with her, rustling in her wake as if they worked to cover her path.

"It's rude to play with your food," Juliet said, crossing her arms over her chest.

"Just find the boy," I ordered, and I followed my dinner into the woods.

7

WILLOW

a branch brushed against my arm as I ran, the gentle touch of the leaves making me pause for a moment as I looked back toward the house. I was far enough that I couldn't see it any longer, but I felt what the trees wanted me to know.

He was coming.

I looked to the right, knowing that I needed to buy Ash more time. His small legs hadn't been able to cross distance as quickly as I could, and he didn't have the woods at his command to bend and shift to ease his way.

Ten minutes. If I could buy him that against a Vessel, it would be a miracle.

I grasped the thickest part of the branch where the tree had reached out to touch me.

"*Me paenitet,*" I murmured, apologizing for the pain the tree would feel—for what I needed to take. I pulled my knife from the holster on my thigh, using it to saw through the branch. The tree didn't shudder, didn't show any sign of the pain I knew it felt.

Of the pain that struck me in the chest with every slice.

It seemed to wrap me in an embrace, comforting me even as I hurt it. It couldn't speak, couldn't give me the soft assurances as my mother once had as I did whatever I needed to do to protect Ash.

But it could hug me, wrapping its branches around my body.

I resisted the urge to cry when I finally managed to hack through the branch. Pressing the end between my thighs, I quickly worked to shave the other end into a pointed tip, breaking the smaller branches off the sides so that I would be able to grip it. I didn't have much time. The earth sent a ripple toward me when he got too close for comfort.

Each step of his feet through the woods rang through them like a vibration, the fight the forest gave him minimal to keep him on my trail. I couldn't risk him deciding to go after Ash instead.

He would be easy prey.

I returned my knife to my sheath, hefting my handmade stake fashioned from the hawthorn tree and testing its weight.

He moved out of the clearing, his body traveling at a speed I had no hope of really seeing. He emerged in a swirling black mass that was stark against the setting sun. Bats fluttered as they left him, flying around his body in a vortex that must have protected him from the worst of the damage the forest could cause.

A single gash sliced across his cheekbone, cutting through the ethereal beauty as he bared his teeth at me. A trickle of blood stained his cheek. His eyes fell to the stake clutched in my hand, the animalistic look in his eyes making them seem darker when he raised them to mine finally.

"Careful, Witchling. At some point, this will all cease to be entertaining," he said, taking a step toward me.

The trees reacted before I did, a root swiping for his feet.

He jumped over it without taking his gaze from mine, advancing as those bats fluttered protectively.

A branch lashed out, aiming for his throat, but the tiny creature blocked it, taking the blow meant for him with a screech.

I held out my free hand, signaling the trees to stop their attack. While the Vessel might have been willing to sacrifice them to the fight, that was something I couldn't tolerate.

The Vessel turned his head to look at where the branches withdrew, studying me curiously. "It's just my kind you want to kill then?" he asked, laughing as if the thought was ridiculous.

It made me want to prove that I could do it, but unless I got the *perfect* shot, it would be next to impossible. A Vessel could only be destroyed by a Necromancer, their magic sending the *thing* within back to the depths of Hell. A stake could do the job, technically, if a witch managed to slip their magic into the chasm where the heart might have been.

Mine was a stake carved from wood. A Blue needed to find a way to slip water within their heart chasm, a Yellow fire.

But it wasn't *just* the element itself that needed to fill the hole in their existence, but the essence of magic it would take to *unmake* the Vessel. Only a Black could do it without great personal sacrifice. It wasn't a sacrifice many witches were willing to make.

Not when it drained them of everything and left them powerless. A fate worse than death for a witch of the Coven.

Humanity.

"I'm not stupid enough to think I can kill you," I said in answer, spinning the stake in my hand dramatically, distracting him, stalling for time. "But that doesn't mean I can't maim you."

The Vessel moved so slowly, acting as if he could sneak up on me before I realized what he was doing. I waited until he was within my grasp, letting him get far too close for my comfort. The scent of him washed over me, filling the woods with it. It was the scent of wet soil after a light summer rain, earthen and fresh all at once.

When his foot struck the leaves that the trees had gathered around me, I leapt forward. A tree root raised beneath me, shoving me forward and giving me momentum as I flung myself toward him. I drove the stake toward his heartless chest, screaming as I channeled my magic into the wood in my hand.

The forest around us went silent, my magic leaving it to focus on that stake. Headmaster Thorne caught my wrist just as the tip touched the fabric of his suit. He fell backward as the rest of my body followed, crashing into him so that he landed on the forest floor.

I fell on top of him, scrambling to get my legs around his hips even as his grip tightened on my wrist. He held me with ease, squeezing at the joint until I felt my bones grind together.

"Release it," he ordered. I pressed my other hand to his chest, pushing myself up so that I sat astride his hips and put all my weight into the hand he seemed determined to shatter.

"Fuck you," I snarled, pressing harder. His eyes widened as it indented the fabric, the stake slipping just slightly closer to his chest.

He grinned, a cruel laugh sliding over my skin as he wrapped his free hand around the front of my throat. He squeezed, cutting off my breath as the webbing between his thumb and index finger pressed against my windpipe.

"Gladly, Witchling. Though I must admit, I thought I'd need to buy you dinner first."

He used it to flip me to my back suddenly, and I might have lost the air in my lungs if he hadn't already stolen it. His body covered mine immediately, slipping between my thighs and holding me still. With his body pinning my hips, his hand on my throat and the other grasping my wrist, I did the only thing I could do.

I used my other hand to grab him by the hair, tugging his head to the side as he glared down at me. His fangs gleamed in the darkness. His eyes drifted closed as I pulled, trying to yank him back so that he would release my throat. Instead, he only laughed again, running his tongue over his teeth before that haunting blue stare met mine.

"You're quite the little demon, aren't you?"

"Do not insult me by comparing me to your kind, blood-sucker," I hissed.

"I wouldn't dare to insult you, love. It's a compliment," he said, his thumb pressing harder into the side of my neck where he gripped it. He tipped it to the side, baring my neck to his gaze as my eyes widened with realization.

I released the stake, attempting to push my hand into the dirt beneath my body to connect to the forest once more. He dropped his head toward me too quickly, his mouth approaching my exposed neck.

"No!" I screamed, thrashing my legs as I fought against the way he held me pinned.

Lips touched my skin, a twisted sort of pleasure blooming as I broke out in goosebumps. He smiled against me as he held me still, ignoring my fight as the tips of his fangs touched me.

They broke through the skin brutally, a gentle pop resounding through me. I felt every drag of them through my flesh, felt them plant themselves as deep as they could as a strangled whimper escaped me.

Then the pain came, the deep burning that stemmed from my throat as he drew my blood into his mouth. He groaned into me, the sound tightening something in my stomach even as the burning spread through my veins. His toxin worked its way through me, and the bastard did *nothing* to ease the pain, even though he could have.

He could have transformed that pain into pleasure, instead he left me to *burn.*

"Get. Off. Me," I snapped, releasing my grip on his hair and thrusting my hand into the dirt. His head snapped up from my throat, his teeth sliding out of the puncture wounds they'd created.

"Fuck," he grunted as a branch slid between us and flung him back.

His weight left my body. One of the tree roots from beneath my body lifted me, sliding against my spine and guiding me to my feet. I touched a hand to my neck, peering down at it as it came away stained with blood.

"That was rude," I said, bending down and gathering dirt from the forest floor. I rubbed it into the wounds, my skin warming as my magic worked to heal them slowly.

Thorne stood from the ground, adjusting his suit as he ran his tongue over the blood gathered at the corner of his mouth. "Worth it," he said, eying the trees around him as I contemplated how to proceed. It seemed we were at a stalemate, deciding how best to proceed. We both knew what the other wanted, but *getting* it seemed to be another challenge.

The scream that tore through the night saved me from all thought, making my head snap toward the direction of the bus stop.

No.

I ran, bursting through the woods. The forest cleared a path for me as I sprinted, lifting my feet and giving me more speed. A dip in the ground would have slowed me down had a tree root not raised, creating something for me to slide along and cross it with ease.

No. No. No.

"Not fast enough, Witchling!" Thorne called out, his voice surrounding me. I couldn't see him as he bled into the darkness that had encompassed the woods during our fight, focusing all my strength on getting there.

Ash screamed again, the sound of a male's laughter following as I burst out of the woods and sprinted across the pavement at the bus stop. Each step took me away from the place that bolstered me, that offered me my only chance at fighting.

Three figures surrounded my brother's small form where he stood at the center of the parking lot, perfectly positioned to weaken me.

Thorne rested a hand on my brother's shoulder, his unnatural speed having allowed him to reach Ash and the others more quickly than I could. He looked down at my brother as I skidded to a stop in front of them, my gaze darting over Ash to make sure he wasn't hurt.

Thorne's voice drew my attention to him, his free hand reaching up to touch his bloodstained mouth in a wordless threat.

"Hello again, Witchling."

8

WILLOW

*P*eople loaded the bus in the distance behind them, and I could just imagine that the person who stepped off was Ash's father. He'd been so close to freedom.

"Let him go," I whispered, pushing the words past the burn in my throat.

Vessels were unpredictable, and the one with his hand on my brother was just as likely to tear out his throat as he was to send him back to the Coven.

What they would do to him, what they would make him choose...?

"Now, why would I do that?" Headmaster Thorne asked, tilting his head to the side as he studied me. His eyes dropped to the dirt smeared on my neck, as if it disgusted him to see the mark of his feeding healed beneath it. "I already gave you the chance to come quietly to save him. You rejected my offer rather rudely."

"Please," I murmured, holding Ash's brown-eyed stare with mine. His eyes were wide with fear, the faintest tremble racking his body as he silently pleaded with me. "Is there anyone you love? Anyone you would do *anything* to protect?"

His hand tightened on Ash's shoulder as I turned my gaze to his, meeting the cold blue of his stare. The gold seemed to flash at my question, studying the tears that pooled in my eyes. "No," he said, shaking his head subtly. "Vessels do not have hearts, Witchling. You'd do well to remember that in the coming years."

"Then I feel sorry for you," I said, and the words had no malice. They weren't intended to hurt, only to offer sympathy. "That you'll never know that feeling."

"Even though it leads to this?" he asked, turning to glance at Ash for a moment. "Even though it weakens you?"

"Yes," I said, nodding in confirmation. His eyes flashed at my answer, studying the path of a tear on my cheek. "I would feel this pain one hundred times over before I gave him up."

Thorne released my brother's shoulder, sliding his hand into his pocket as Ash spun to stare at him in shock. "Go," Thorne said, nodding his head toward the bus waiting at the end of the lot.

"Gray," the female Vessel warned.

The breath rushed out of my lungs, my body swaying forward as my shocked relief made me stare at Thorne with wide eyes.

Gray, she'd called him.

I pressed my lips together, nodding and looking at Ash. He couldn't stop his oscillating stare, looking back and forth between the two of us in shock.

"I love you, Bug," I said, giving him the only goodbye we would get. I didn't dare to cross the distance between us, didn't want to risk doing anything to make Thorne change his mind.

"Low," he said, shaking his head as his little face twisted with tears.

"Go," I said, nodding and encouraging him on.

"But what about you?" he asked, his voice breaking as the reality set in. That I wouldn't be going with him.

That I never had been.

He shook his head, planting his feet as if he planned to stay with me.

Thorne took that chance away from him. "Look at me, boy," he commanded, the magic of his compulsion rolling over my skin. My amulet warmed against my chest in response, but Ash followed the order. His eyes widened as they connected with Thorne's, the gold at the center of his iris brightening as he held my brother captive with his stare. "Run. Get on the bus, and do not ever look for Willow again."

Ash didn't hesitate to leave me. He couldn't, not with the Vessel's compulsion controlling him. He spun on his heel, racing forward across the parking lot. He rushed into his father's embrace, the other man watching us briefly before he turned and led Ash into the vehicle.

I collapsed to my knees on the concrete, an ugly sob tearing out of my throat. I hung my head forward as I listened to the sound of the bus, of the tires rolling across pavement as it left the parking lot.

As the last sight of my brother's face haunted me.

The side of a bent finger hooked beneath my chin, raising my gaze until I looked up into the stare of Thorne. "Why?" I asked, even though I was grateful for what he'd done. I couldn't understand it, couldn't make it make sense.

"One day, you will owe me a favor for this. You will give me anything I ask of you," he said softly.

A chill spread from where his finger touched me, and I reeled back to claw at my throat. Tendrils of darkness spread over my skin, moving down the front of my throat and chest. They curved, dancing over my flesh as they burned a sigil of black into my skin just below my collarbone. It was a pattern of crossed lines, impossible to make sense of while I looked at it upside down. The dark tendrils vanished once they'd marked me with the physical manifestation of my worst fear.

A deal with a demon.

"What of the Coven? They'll be furious to hear you sent a male witch away," the other male Vessel muttered, interrupting my horror as I knelt on the pavement.

"What the Coven doesn't know won't hurt them. Neither of you are to speak a word of this to anyone. As far as the Coven is concerned, Willow is the last of the Madizza line," Thorne answered, and there was no hesitation as they nodded their assent. He held out a hand for me, and I swallowed as I studied it. As if it were a snake that might reach out and bite me.

He already had.

"Come, Witchling," he said as the female Vessel disappeared in a burst of speed. "There are things we must discuss." I ignored his proffered hand, pushing myself to my feet as he sighed in irritation. "Are you going to make this difficult *every* step of the way?"

"Most likely," I said, trying not to think of how weak my voice sounded. I couldn't muster the energy to give him the snark he deserved, not when everything within me felt raw.

The Coven had taken everything from me. I would make them regret it.

"Hollow's Grove thrives on structure and order. It is very important that we find a way to maintain those things at all times, even with your rather unwilling addition to our school," he explained.

A car sped into the parking lot, going far too fast as it skidded to a halt just in front of where we stood. Neither Vessel so much as flinched as Thorne moved toward the rear driver's side door, grasping the handle and pulling it open.

"Are you going to be a problem for me, Miss Madizza?"

I moved toward the car, stepping close to him as I mustered all that remained of my energy and glared at him. "If it is order that you value, then I will bring you nothing but chaos."

I smiled, then rolled my eyes at the grin he gave me in return.

I got in the car.

9

WILLOW

The woman driving turned off the main road that led into the town of Salem, Massachusetts, according to the signs. I'd never been there, obviously, having needed to stay as far away from Crystal Hollow as possible. My mom had told me the stories of what had become of the town that had once been the home to our ancestors, how the stories of the witches hanged there had become what the town was known for, and the way tourists flocked there during the entirety of October.

Somehow it felt like the perfect karma to me that the town was known for the people it had tried to rid itself of, the persecutors fading into history. It felt like something that would have brought me peace from beyond the grave.

The Headmaster of Hollow's Grove sat beside me, typing frantically on his cell phone. His thumbs flew over the screen with speed that should have been impossible, a blur as I swallowed down the surge of unease in my gut.

His face was set into a stern expression, as if whoever waited on the other side of the conversation had annoyed him to no end. His inky, dark hair was subtly swept back from his face, revealing his square jaw and the well-trimmed facial hair that framed it. With a straight nose to fully define his profile, I knew just how difficult my father's plan would be with him at the helm of the Vessels.

If he knew what I was or what I'd come to do, he'd close the distance between us and tear out my throat before I even had time to beg for my life. The fact that I wasn't loyal to the Coven any more than I was the Vessels wouldn't save me.

Not when he discovered I was the one who could Unmake him.

He glanced toward me, forcing me to turn my stare out the window. I swallowed down my irritation that I'd been caught studying him, staring at what I could only assume was a face he was used to using to get his way. Where he probably thought I was interested, I'd only been sizing up the task ahead of me.

Seduce the Vessel.

Find the bones.

Nausea churned in my gut at the thought, at the task my own father had laid out for me. There had to be another way to find them, because the thought of me being able to seduce an immortal creature who looked like *that* was laughable. Especially when all he really wanted was to eat me.

And probably not the fun way.

"The Covenant has requested I present you to them as soon as we arrive," he said, tucking his phone into the pocket of his suit jacket.

I leveled him with a glare that must have conveyed exactly what I thought of being brought to the very remains of the woman who had made my mother so miserable she left the only home she'd ever known. She'd faked her own death to buy her freedom, killing a woman who looked like her and burning her corpse until it was unrecognizable.

Even though she'd chosen someone that the world would be better off without, a woman who abused her own child, the death and what she'd done had haunted my mother until the day she too died and joined the afterlife.

I didn't bother to pretend I didn't know of the Covenant. Doing so when I'd clearly known what Thorne was the moment I saw him on my doorstep would be futile.

"What interest would the Covenant have in me, Headmaster Thorne?" I asked, shifting my gaze away from the road that quickly shifted from pavement to dirt. A muscle twitched in his jaw, and I couldn't decide if the formality of the address irritated him somehow.

"You are the last of their living descendants. I think the better question is what *won't* they want from you, Miss Madizza," he said, his voice turning mocking as he said my name.

"And what happens when I have no interest in being their pet witch?" I raised my brow, flinching back when he finally met my heated stare. The gold surrounding his pupils seemed to burn as he studied me, flaming with the warning he wanted me to heed.

"You are not the only one who thinks of Crystal Hollow as a prison, but the world isn't yet ready for us to exist in the open. You endangered us all by living outside the wards for as long as you did, with the kind of magic you possess. There is an entire line of magic trapped within your veins until your brother comes of age and claims what is his. Any other witch would have gotten rid of him before he could do so," Headmaster Thorne explained, picking a strand of my deep red hair off his suit. It swayed in the breeze from the flowing air at the front of the vehicle as he dropped it beside me, the only sign of him being remotely affected by our scuffle in the woods.

"Perhaps that selfish greed is why only I remain of the Greens. Maybe the witches deserve the fate that awaits them without connection to the magic that formed the wards," I snapped, staring up at him.

His face was so close to mine as he twisted in his seat, his lips curving up into a little grin. "You'll get no argument from me that the witches are selfish, greedy creatures. Do not forget, your ancestors came into their powers by selling their souls to the devil himself. The magic that flows through your veins may be green, but your heart is black like all the others in the end."

I scoffed, laughing as I reached between us and poked him in the space where his heart should have been. "At least I have one," I said.

His gaze dropped to the finger against his dress shirt, to the place where only fabric separated us from touching. It trailed leisurely over my finger and hand, up my wrist and sweater-covered arm until it jumped up to meet my gaze.

"I believe the humans have this saying that may serve you well," he said, reaching up to grasp my hand. He squeezed it tightly enough that it felt like my finger bones ground together, lowering it into my lap. "Don't poke the bear?"

"What do you know of humans?" I asked, refusing to look at where he still held my hand.

"I know they don't taste as good as witchlings," he said, bringing my hand to his face. He bent it back, exposing my wrist as he placed it beneath his nose and inhaled my scent.

I drew it back sharply, struggling against his grip as I growled a feral warning. "They're also much less likely to slit your throat while you sleep."

He released my hand finally with a small, crooked smirk—revealing a hint of a single fang. I couldn't tell if it was a threat or a promise, if he meant to instill fear or hoped for something more carnal.

"Does that mean you intend to be in my bed, Witchling?"

"Over my dead body," I hissed, turning back to face the window.

Trees surrounded both sides of the road, curving over the gravel to form a canopy. Mist filled the woods around us, stretching toward the sky and casting an eerie presence over the forest that surrounded Crystal Hollow.

"I'll have to come to yours then," Thorne said, making me snap my gaze away from the window and back to glare at him. The arrogance in those steel-blue eyes was everything I dreaded, and I decided it wasn't a matter of threat *or* sin.

It was both.

"I will—"

"Would you two just fuck already?" the woman from the driver's seat said with a groan. She rubbed her chin on the steering wheel as she drove along the winding road, climbing up the subtlest of inclines. "You'll feel better once you get it out of your system."

"I'm not sure I could live with the shame," I said, giving her a saccharine smile.

She raised her head, looking at me in the rearview mirror as she grinned. "Don't knock it until you try it, baby girl," she said, lifting her chin. "I've got a friend—"

"No, thank you," I said, swallowing back the surge of nausea spinning in my gut. The Vessels were a symptom of the disease I'd been raised to hate, bodies created to exist alongside the Coven. Housing something nefarious and sinister.

Even knowing that it would likely be part of what I needed

to do to achieve what I'd come here to do... I couldn't stomach it yet.

I wasn't ready.

"I'll bet Kairos would be more than willing to give you a soft introduction when you're ready," she said, turning the steering wheel to go around a particularly harsh curve.

I swallowed back my nausea, leaning forward in my seat. The belt stretched to accommodate me as I lifted my hands, touching them to the man's shoulders from behind. He didn't so much as twitch as I moved them toward the side of his neck, trailing my fingers over his skin gently. He shuddered at the touch, at the warmth of my body against his cool skin.

If he was the chilled air of autumn, I was the warmth of deep earth that kept out the frost. Reminiscent of the mud from which he'd been formed, calling his physical form home.

A low, subtle growl vibrated through the car, bringing a smile to my face as I pressed the side of my cheek against the back of his headrest. My eyes went to Thorne, finding his cold stare watching my every move. I held it, putting every bit of challenge I felt into the glare I gave him as I spoke.

"Do you want to fuck me, Kairos?" I asked, watching as Thorne's upper lip twitched.

The other man didn't answer, remaining wordless as his body was perfectly, unnaturally still. I pressed two fingers into the front of his throat, gripping him slightly and placing my flesh directly beneath the path of his nose. I didn't take my eyes off Thorne's as Kairos grabbed my hand, lifting it to his nose as if he might scent me.

Thorne's growl made him stop dead, dropping me as if I'd burned him. "That's enough," the headmaster ordered, sighing as if it pained him to admit that I'd made my point.

"I'm the last of the Madizza witches who gave their blood to the formation of your Vessel. Not only will the Covenant be eager to *breed* me with a male witch of their choosing, but I could have my pick of your kind if I so chose," I said, crinkling my nose as I sat back in my seat and glared at the man across from me. "You know, for *fun*. So do not disillusion yourself into thinking that I would ever choose you."

"That sounds like a challenge, Witchling," Thorne said, grinning as if he'd won something. "I very much look forward to reminding you how much I hate you when I bury my cock between your thighs."

I flushed, my mouth dropping open as I fumbled for words. Thorne's steely blue eyes burned with cold as he studied me, his smile broadening when I didn't have a quick enough response.

"Called it," the woman said, saving me from having to come up with a response. I shifted my gaze toward her, trying to quell the racing of my heart. It was all according to the plan my father had decided would be the most likely to produce results, so why couldn't I squash the dread sinking into my stomach?

"Are we nearly there?" I asked, swallowing as I looked out the window once again.

The trees seemed taller, more ominous, the farther we got from the main road. The mist seemed to spread, thickening and becoming more difficult to see through. The brush and dead leaves on the forest floor were lost to it, and I realized how startling the forest was without that. It was something I'd become so familiar with, something I needed to feel rooted.

I didn't like it when I couldn't see the earth at my feet.

"Nothing to say?" Thorne asked, and I didn't bother to glance at him. I knew the exact expression I would find if I did, could hear the smug note of satisfaction in his voice.

"I learned long ago that sometimes silence is louder than words. I see that is a lesson you've somehow managed to avoid in your centuries haunting our world," I said, keeping my eyes trained on the unnatural stillness of the woods.

There were no birds to be found in the trees or squirrels climbing up the trunks as the woman took the bends slowly. We were going up a slow, steady incline, but even looking behind me, I couldn't see any movement in the treetops.

I returned my gaze to my window, studying the mist as it shifted and moved. A black streak darted through it, appearing for only a moment before it was gone again.

"Did you see that?" I asked, turning a shocked stare back to Thorne once again.

"Creatures far worse than witches call these woods home. You'd do well to remember that should you get thoughts of running off," he answered, and I tried not to think of the massive black thing or the glimpse of glowing eyes.

What manner of beast was that large?

The slope of the hill grew sharper, creating a steady, winding bend that seemed to go on and on forever. It reminded me of the on-ramp for the interstate when Mom and I had taken Ash to the aquarium in New York. A continuous circle that made my stomach twist with the curve. I had no doubt that if it hadn't been for the belt strapped across my chest, I would have slid toward Thorne unwillingly.

As we climbed and came to the top of what I'd assumed to be a hill, I realized it was, in fact, a cliff. The school jutted up out of the cliff side, arches and spires reaching for the sky. It was built in light gray stone, with arched windows and doors covering the face of the building. The window atop the main doors was enormous, half the height of the school in its entirety, with detailed windowpanes that laid out Hecate's maze.

My skin throbbed at the visual symbol of the Goddess who'd created us all. The first witch who'd led to all of our creation, forming an alliance with the devil and leading to the witches serving him.

She'd been the first necromancer, the first to summon the other clans of the Coven for each to be bestowed with magic. The condition of her being the first witch had meant that she and her descendants would be the only ones to have power over the dead, reserving that ability for herself.

Reserving it for me.

The car came to a stop in front of the main entrance, and I didn't hesitate to shove open my door and stand before the school. The steps leading up to the doors were six in number. Six steps, six doors, and six windows surrounding them. I turned to look to the other side of the car as the Vessels stepped out, my eyes landing on the memorial stone over-looking the sea. I made my way to it, sidestepping Thorne as he reached for me.

It was a simple granite slab, with the names of the dead carved into it. "They're the witches who were lost in the massacre," the woman answered, her voice solemn. "They say their ghosts still haunt the school."

I forced myself not to let any emotion show when I found my aunt's name.

Loralei Hecate.

"It's a shame there aren't more names here," I said, twisting my lips into a scowl. It was, in a sense, a horror that the Vessels could rarely be killed alongside the witches, and that those who had corrupted the Coven hadn't been the ones to die.

My hatred ran deep, but it didn't run quite *that* deep.

The woman blinked at me as I turned my back on the memorial, giving no indication that I knew any of the names found there. None could suspect I was aware of any of the events that transpired in more than a vague sense, or that I had any personal connection to them.

My mother hadn't been related to Loralei, and my father, well...

He wasn't my father as far as the Coven knew.

The Hecate line had died with my aunt, and for now, that was how it needed to stay.

10

WILLOW

*T*horne appeared at my side, lacing his arm through mine as I made my way to the doors.

"Will someone go and fetch my things from my mother's house?" I asked, trying to pull my arm free from him.

"Is there anything in particular you require?" he asked, and I felt his gaze on the side of my face. I didn't bother to look at him as I waved my free hand toward the closed doors.

They creaked open slowly, each of the six doors parting to give us our choice of entrance. It might have been an unnecessary show of magic, but it served as a reminder for me.

Stone. Earth. Nature.

Those were my elements. Those were the things I had an affinity for. The souls trapped within the Vessels were none of my concern as far as anyone else knew.

Neither was the cemetery that I could feel pulsing with the bones of the dead at the edge of the tree line. If I followed that thread, followed that instinct, it would feel as if I plunged myself underwater. As if touching it would require the ability to breathe in the depths of the ocean, and I had always been far better suited to the land beneath my feet.

"No. Just clothes," I said, knowing that my father would sneak in now that we were gone and get rid of any evidence that I might be anything other than the Green I pretended to be.

Thorne looked down at my clothing, his gaze taking them in with a languid sweep. "You'll be provided with clothing suitable to a Green and expected to wear your House colors to classes. I will arrange for some clothing to be provided for your downtime as well."

"Shouldn't that be the Covenant's responsibility?" I asked, allowing him to lead me through one of the open doors. The Covenant cared for the witches—saw to their needs. Students and teachers lingered in the entryway to the school as we entered, leaning into one another to murmur.

"Are you fond of the color green, Miss Madizza?" he asked. There was no mistaking the shift in energy when my surname left his mouth, the way those around me paused their conversations to stare.

"Was that really necessary?" I asked, gritting my teeth as I raised my chin in the face of their scrutiny.

"Better to face the vultures with your head held high and the truth in the open than attempt to hide a secret The Covenant will never allow you to keep. What you want became irrelevant the moment you stepped through the doors of Hollow's Grove," he said, guiding me to the left.

Before me, an arch supported the top of two sets of stairs that curved out to the entryway. From that arch, two more columns of stairways went to the upper floors and a spiral labyrinth of floors and levels overhead. It was all crafted in the lightest gray stone, reflecting the light and somehow calling to the shadows all at once.

"The Covenant wishes to see you immediately, Miss Madizza," a young man said, stepping toward us. He bowed his head lightly, as if in respect that I hadn't earned as he held out a hand. I smiled hesitantly, trying to hide my discomfort with the formality as I lifted my own to accept.

"I'll take her," Thorne said, tugging on the arm he still held captive.

"I'm more than capable of escorting her," the other man said, but he drew back his hand as Thorne swept me toward the hallway.

"She would eat you for breakfast, Iban," Thorne said, not bothering to look over his shoulder at the younger man as he guided me down the hall.

Iban's footsteps weren't nearly as quiet as the Vessel at my side as he followed behind us. The stone of the pathway in front of us was freshly polished, glimmering in the moonlight trailing through the massive arched windows to either side of us. On Thorne's side, they overlooked the drive and the memorial at the front of the school. To the other, I looked into a courtyard at the center of the building. It housed what looked as if it may have been a garden at one point, but the plants within weren't flourishing in the way they should have.

Even with the Madizzas being absent from Crystal Hollow, House Bray should have been using their magic to maintain the land if it required assistance. The trellis that should have been covered in vines of roses was nearly barren, even the thorns weakened and brittle. I resisted the urge to answer their call, allowing Thorne to guide me down the hall until we stood before the legendary doors of the Tribunal rooms.

The surface was covered in black iron, gold laced throughout it to form mechanisms. I could barely see through the gaps in the metal to the entry room beyond.

Iban stepped up beside me as I raised my hand, jerking to a stop when I waved it before the lock. The gears turned, rippling through as the rest of them followed. The bars retracted with a soft click, and when the last one moved out of the way, the doors parted open toward us.

"I see your mother has told you more than I thought," Thorne said, tugging me forward as he stepped into the Tribunal rooms. Iban followed behind us silently.

"Fortunately for all of us, you know nothing of my mother," I said, ignoring the weight of his gaze on the side of my face. If he'd known her, she'd have done her best to have him imprisoned in the earth. She'd have summoned the roots from the trees to do her bidding, ridding the world of him in the only way she had any ability to do.

She might not have had the blood of the Hecate line flowing through her veins, but she was the fiercest, bravest woman I'd ever known. She held the magic of all the Madizzas within her body, controlling it in a way I now understood took immense control. Even as we walked through the entryway to the Tribunal room, I felt mine pulsing beneath my skin. Writhing and twining within me as if it had a life of its own, just waiting to be unleashed upon the world.

It took everything in me not to allow it to erupt like a volcano, spraying rock and molten lava over the surface of the earth. Using my magic felt more like taking a tiny breath after years of suffocation than trying to reach for anything. It was always there.

Always waiting.

The doors to the inner Tribunal room were open wide, and I forced my chin just the slightest bit higher as I drew in that breath. Air filled my lungs, the scent of the stone surrounding me washing over me and calling to that Green magic of the Madizza line. I answered the call, feeling the hair on my arms rise as my magic awakened from the miniature slumber I kept it in.

Thorne stiffened at my side, the slightest hitch in his next step alerting me to the fact that he felt it. I squeezed his arm lightly as I glanced up at him from the corner of my eye, his steely eyes darkening as he recovered and strode forward.

If I had to face the Covenant, if I had to stare into the empty, hollow bones of the beings who had made my mother's life such a misery that she fled the only home she'd ever known, I would do it with her magic coating my skin.

With her death, I'd inherited all of it until my brother came of age and some of it passed onto him. Susannah Madizza might have been the greatest witch of her age, but the power that had made her so was no longer hers to command.

It was mine.

We stepped through the magical barrier that waited just inside the Tribunal room, keeping what was spoken within a secret from any who might have snuck into the entryway. It sunk into my chest as I passed through, formed from a representative of each of the original houses. Only the Madizza and Hecate lines were missing, but that barrier seemed to recognize something within me. It lingered, holding me trapped in the center as it swirled around me. At my side, I was vaguely aware of Thorne stepping through, of him tugging at my arm as if he could pull me along with him.

I held his gaze as I raised my free hand, turning my palm to face the sky. The shimmering, translucent power of the barrier washed over my bare skin, sliding beneath my nails deep enough to draw a single drop of blood. I let out a startled gasp as it pulled from that spot.

Red floated amidst the barrier, intertwining with the shimmering mist. There was a flash of light as it released my hand finally, spitting me out the other side. I caught myself on my next step, only stumbling for a brief moment as Thorne tightened his grip on my arm and offered me an odd sort of support.

I couldn't resist the slightest urge to lean into him as I clenched my free hand into a fist, hoping that whatever the barrier had sensed, the magic hadn't revealed it to any of the witches staring back at me. Thorne guided me to the center of the circle, passing between the gap in two of the chairs. They were each marked with symbols of their house, the witch perched within wearing robes the color of their magic.

Two of the chairs were empty. A quick glance at the Hecate throne revealed twisted black iron carved into elaborate spires of darkness. At the top of the throne rested a single skull forged in iron, the bones of a spine sliding down the center and skeletal arms draped over the top.

I didn't allow my gaze to linger as I moved it to the other empty throne. Where Hecate's seat on the Tribunal had been crafted from darkness itself, the Madizza throne was formed from vines that still moved. They lived where it was not possible, sprouting through cracks in the foundation to form the empty seat of my ancestors.

At the top of the throne, a single rose bloomed back to life as I watched. Whereas before, it had been nothing but a withered husk, the petals spread wide, and color returned. Red tipped in black, as if the edges were tainted by death itself.

We stopped in the center of the circle, and it was only then that I turned my stare toward the two figures waiting on the small dais. The cloaks that covered their forms were black, an affront to the memory of the Hecate line. The forms were near identical, and I knew it was because there was nothing but bones left beneath them. The Covenant had no flesh to cover their skeletons after centuries of life after death, and anything that had made them human was long gone.

They swept their hoods back in unison, revealing the

skeletal faces within. Susannah Madizza and George Collins rested upon their gilded thrones, with their necks crooked to the side as the only indication of how they'd died.

"I present Miss Willow Madizza to the Covenant," Thorne said at my side.

I didn't allow my stare to break from the figure staring back at me, from the intense, eyeless gaze of my ancestor upon me. She searched my face, probing for any sort of information she could glean as her skeletal fingers grasped the arm of her throne. She pushed to her feet, walking forward as the bones of her feet tapped against the floor with a lightness that shouldn't have been possible.

I heard each bone connect with the stone tile, from her heel to her smallest metatarsal, with each step. I refused to allow the nerves I felt to show as I stood beside Thorne. Part of me wanted to force him to release my arm, but something in that contact felt like it grounded me.

I hated him. Hated his kind with every fiber of my being, but he was predictable.

Familiar.

His motives were clear. His intentions simple.

The ancient witch who stepped toward me was a mystery, the bones of her neck grinding together as she tilted her skull to the side. She stopped only when she was a breath before me, her figure taller than mine as she stared down at me with empty sockets.

"You look nothing like your mother," she said, the first words she'd spoken to me washing over my skin with disapproval.

She raised a hand, grasping the ends of my hair between her finger bones as I turned my attention to the way her skeleton rolled the strands as if she could feel them. My mother's hair had been brown, the color of the earth.

As had her mother's before her.

Mine was a distinct, deep auburn, like the darkest merlot. Or as my father liked to call it, hair the color of old blood— like what pulsed in our veins.

"Neither do you," I said, my voice remaining calm and casual. One of the witches in the thrones about the room gasped, and Thorne fought back a chuckle at my side.

But the Covenant's lipless mouth twisted into a wry smile. "No, I suppose I do not, child," she said, dropping my hair and clasping her hands in front of her.

"I'm not a child," I said, even if the words felt futile when faced with an immortal being such as Susannah.

"I suppose you're not. We were robbed of the opportunity to know you when you were. And it does not seem lost on my headmaster that you have very much come to us as a woman," she said, turning that eternal, empty stare to where Thorne still held my arm. There was no movement on her face, no shift in her bones, but I somehow could still sense the way she raised her brow at him.

If she'd had one, anyway.

"I am merely her escort into an unfamiliar life," Thorne said with ease, the words rolling off his tongue. If I hadn't heard all his promises of being in my bed for myself, I might have believed them.

"Good. My granddaughter is very much off-limits to you and your kind, Headmaster Thorne," she said, reaching forward to unwind my arm from his. He didn't fight when she guided me toward the dais, stopping as I stood just before the two thrones.

"That's not entirely true," he said, and even without looking back at him, I heard the smirk in his voice. But my mother had warned me that my seduction would need to be a secretive one—that the Covenant forbid relationships between witches and Vessels.

"We both know I am not speaking of that *unfortunate* exception." The Covenant sneered at him over my shoulder, taking the first step and releasing me.

She returned to her throne as I stood, allowing silence to permeate the room. I would not be the first to speak, wouldn't reveal my discomfort with the way they watched me.

"It is customary to kneel when presented to the Covenant," one of the witches said, forcing me to turn my gaze to her. Her voice was not unkind, as if she understood that I had been uninformed of their ways. Her pretty face was partially hidden behind a white cloak and hood, the slightest hint of gem tone purple hair peeking out from beneath.

I smiled, taking some of the sting out of my words. "Do I look like I care about your customs?"

"You will kneel," another witch said. This one was male, his cloak green as he swept it back to reveal his angered face. His throne was crafted from the wood of a birch tree, leaves sprouting as he pushed to stand.

He moved forward with a hand extended as if he meant to touch me, and I watched from the corner of my eye as he took three quick steps toward me.

"I wouldn't do that, if I were you," Thorne warned, taking a single step forward as I turned my gaze toward the Bray witch. I didn't speak an incantation or so much as twitch my fingers.

I let loose a single breath, the tiniest bit of magic erupting through the room. The Bray throne grew, branches snapping forward to wrap around the front of his chest.

"Please have a seat, Mr. Bray."

He glanced down at those branches in shock, his mouth parting as he leveled me with a dark stare. In the next moment, they snapped back to the throne, taking him with them. They tightened around him as he struggled, holding him firmly seated. As the other line of Green witches, the Brays were always destined to have some animosity for my return.

"You've been trained," the other Covenant said. His voice was deeper than Susannah's, a single remnant of the fact that he'd been a man when he was alive.

I didn't answer him as I shifted my attention to him, letting him feel the weight of my magic in the air before I drew it back to myself. Only when Bray settled in his chair did I speak. "Just because my mother hated all of you doesn't mean she hated what she was."

"To be a witch with no Coven is to suffer unnecessarily. We should not be alone in this world," George Collins said, forcing me to laugh.

"She was far more alone here than she ever was in her life amidst the humans, and that's saying something since they feared her half the time. At least there she was more than just breeding stock," I snapped, knowing fully well what fate would wait for me if I remained too long.

"Saving an entire lineage is an honor that your mother never understood," Susannah snapped, her fingers squeezing the arm of her chair.

"Not if she believed that the lineage needed to die," I answered, smiling serenely, as if I hadn't issued a grave insult. It was nothing against House Madizza. The entirety of Crystal Hollow was corrupt.

They all deserved to die.

"Is she always this difficult?" Susannah asked the headmaster. She pinched her nose bone between her fingers, sighing in dismay.

"Given what I've seen since meeting her, she's being fairly cooperative at the moment," he said with a chuckle.

I turned to him, glaring, but I didn't bother to fight it when a grin took over my face instead, and I giggled in acknowledgement. "Think of it as something to look forward to," I said, spinning back to where the Covenant looked irritated.

"Iban, would you show my errant granddaughter to her room, please?" she asked, ignoring Thorne's growl and pushing to stand and moving out of her throne. "Do try not to eat him on the way, Willow."

I refused to look at Thorne to see his reaction, refused to acknowledge the way his hand clenched at his side in the corner of my eye. Let him think I was wholly uninterested in his ridiculous jealousy.

"Eww," I said, pressing a hand to my chest as I feigned disgust. "I would never do such a thing. Burying him alive is much more my style."

The Bray witch blanched as I smiled at him, reaching up to pat his cheek and leading the way out of the Tribunal room.

The woods seemed like a good place to hide a body... or ten.

11

WILLOW

The man at my side wore trousers the color of a deep forest, so dark they were nearly black. His shirt was white, strikingly bright against the green of his tie, which he worked to loosen as we left the tribunal room.

"I'm not going to bury you alive," I said, glancing at him.

He chuckled beneath his breath. "Generous of you," he said, placing a hand on the small of my back and guiding me through the entryway.

I felt eyes on my back, and where I might have protested the touch from a stranger under normal circumstances, I allowed it. Glancing toward Iban, I blinked up at him through my lashes and pursed my lips lightly. I might not have been able to fake a blush, but I caught a glimpse of Thorne watching us from the corner of my eye.

My ancestor spoke to him as he glared after us.

I smirked, shifting the slightest bit closer to my escort as I walked.

He laughed, his chest shaking as he shook his head from side to side. "You're trouble," he drawled, the deep baritone of his voice draping itself over my skin.

I smiled up at him, showing all of my top teeth in a rare moment of lightness.

"You have no idea," I said, raising my brows at him. If he knew, he'd encourage the Covenant to kill me and be done with it. Last of the Madizza line or not.

The doors to the Tribunal rooms parted, iron spreading wide as we approached. He guided me through. The dark of the hallways seemed to penetrate everything, surrounding me completely. Only in that courtyard did the moon seem to shine, illuminating the dying ivy and rose bushes attempting to scale the building, even though they were nothing but withered husks of something that had once been beautiful.

"What happened to the plants?" I asked, stopping beside one of the open windows.

The air outside was cool, the night air of Massachusetts in September drifting through. There were no windowpanes on this side of the corridor, and I could smell the damp earth of the soil from which the plants should have grown. While the Madizza line might have fizzled out for a few decades, the Brays should have been more than enough to maintain the balance of nature.

It shouldn't have required much effort at all, as the earth was fully capable of thriving without us in all other parts of the world.

"No one knows. The magic here isn't as potent as it used to be," Iban answered, rubbing a hand over the back of his neck. He frowned at the dying plants in the courtyard as I paused my steps. He kept walking a few paces, his arm slipping off the small of my back. Without our audience, I allowed the touch to fade away without encouragement.

He'd served his purpose for the moment.

Turning fully toward the courtyard, I sat on the window ledge and swung my legs over. Sliding across the stone beneath the arched window, I dropped into the courtyard itself.

"Your room is this way," Iban said.

I didn't look at him as I strolled toward the trellis and the ivy there.

"It will still be there in a few moments," I called.

Even the trellis itself was aging, uncared for and neglected. I wondered if it had to do with the closing of the school, if they'd stopped caring for the grounds during the fifty years since students had roamed these halls.

I reached up a single hand, running my finger over a single dried, dead leaf of ivy. It crumbled to pieces, falling from the vine and dropping to the ground at my feet in bits. My brow furrowed as the vine swayed toward me, as if it was starving for life of any kind. I allowed it to wrap around my finger, squeezing as if it could drink my magic down.

"When was the last time someone made an offering?" I asked, my finger slipping through the vine as I knelt before it. My hands touched the dry, infertile earth, watching as it sifted through my fingers. New England soil was fertile; it was potent for growth and sustaining life.

This was anything but natural.

"Offerings are forbidden by the Coven," Iban answered, crossing his arms over his chest as I stood.

I gaped at him, my mouth opening and closing as I shook my head in disbelief.

"Forbidden," I repeated, hurrying through the motions as I shrugged my sweater off.

My arms were bare beneath it, the crisp air cool against my skin. Iban ran a muscled hand through his well-groomed and tousled sandy brown hair, his jaw clenching beneath the short beard that framed his oval face. He sank his teeth into his bottom lip as his green eyes widened, staring at the tattoos that covered my right forearm. The black outline of flowers with some delicate white shading within curved up to my elbow where there was a gap before the dahlia flower covered my shoulder and biceps, curving up to the side of my neck and reaching down beneath the fabric of my tank top to cover the side of my breast.

I reached up with my bare hands, touching both of them to the brittle vines that hungered for replenishment. It wasn't about needing magic to keep them alive. It was about them needing to receive back a portion of what had been taken from them.

The vines wrapped around my fingers, creaking as they extended to cover my hands. There was a caution within the movement that horrified me, as if the plant itself was struck in disbelief that anyone could want to give rather than *take*.

"*Accipere*," I murmured, pressing my hand more firmly and encouraging the vines to take what they needed.

They slowly stretched farther up my arms, wrapping around my skin and twining around the tattoo of flowers. They stopped when they reached my elbow, shifting their energy from spreading to squeezing.

I gasped as they tightened painfully, my skin bulging around the spots where the vines touched.

"Willow," Iban said, stepping toward me.

"Don't," I said when the vines retracted slightly.

He didn't touch me as I let my eyes drift closed. My skin broke in the places the plant touched me, blood seeping out along the edges as tiny barbs sank into me. The moment the vines drew blood, the tang of magic filled the air. It was metallic and earthy, with the scent of flowers and pine needles lingering. The vines shuddered with each drink, with each pull as they fed what they had been denied.

What was theirs to begin with.

"Blood magic is forbidden. If the Covenant discovers what you're doing—" Iban protested.

My eyes fly open.

"What are they going to do? Expel me?" I asked with a harsh laugh.

All of us knew I would willingly leave if given the choice, but that choice had been taken from me before I'd even been born. There was only one purpose to my birth, to my existence.

The Covenant was too stupid to recognize the viper waiting in the flowers, prepared to strike at this first opportunity.

I fell to my knees as the plants continued to drink, taking only enough blood to carry the magic they so desperately needed. My offering didn't go without notice. The dried leaves covering the vines reawakened. Green burst from the vine where it touched me, a fresh shock of color spreading its way up in a wave from my elbows to my hands. It continued toward the trellis as life began anew, until the wood support behind it was hidden by the lush green plant.

I hung my head forward as exhaustion threatened, determined to give everything the plant needed. The grip loosened as if the plant realized it dared to take too much, that if it put me at risk, it may never be given another offering again. As it released me, a single leaf swept across my cheek, and I leaned into the touch.

Into the soft and subtle thank you it seemed to offer.

The vine slid along my skin gently, leaving distinct, bloodied welts behind as it returned to the trellis it called home.

"Let's get you to a healer," Iban said, stepping toward me.

I slid my fingers into the earth beneath me, gathering up a

single handful of dirt that now felt soft and ripe. I spread it over my injuries, covering my arms and hands in it.

It gave me the relief I'd earned with my offering, glowing with a soft green light as my wounds stitched closed. Iban's eyes grew wide as he studied them, watching as I brushed the dirt from my arms to reveal smooth, unblemished skin.

I pushed to stand, swaying on my feet as a wave of dizziness filled me. A vine stretched out, catching me around the waist and stabilizing me without being asked.

"It helped you. Of its own accord," Iban said, the shock in his voice disarming. Whatever he was, whatever the Brays had become, they were as far from what my mother had taught me of Greens as possible.

"Our magic is about balance. You cannot take more than you give and still expect nature to answer your call. It's a dance, a relationship like no other. If all we do is take and use, how are we any better than the humans who poison the earth?" I asked, running a gentle finger over the vine that had stabilized me.

When I felt able to stand on my own, it pulled away once more and returned to its slumber, now satiated.

"No wonder my mother hated it here. You've all become so corrupted by your own selfishness, they don't even teach the old ways anymore, do they?" I asked, shaking my head and taking a step toward the window I'd slid through to get to the courtyard in the first place.

The ground rushed up to meet me, pressing into the bottoms of my feet and helping me keep my footing. It sprang beneath me, helping my weakened limbs find the energy to move. It wasn't my magic that motivated it to do so, not when I'd depleted so much of it in offering to that vine.

It was the symbiotic relationship that a witch was meant to have with her affinity. Harmony, rather than theft.

I leaned against the edge of the stone, touching my hands to the ledge and attempting to lift myself up. Before the earth could help, Iban's face filled my vision as he stood before me. He placed a hand on each side of my waist, lifting me up until I rested fully, and drew in a deep breath.

"What you just did—"

"Was forbidden. I know." I sighed, shaking my head as my eyes drifted closed with exhaustion. If I hadn't feared for my life in this place I'd needed to come, I might have gone straight to sleep. It had been a long time since I'd needed to give that much of myself at once.

"It was beautiful," he said, his deep voice shocking me. He wrapped my sweater around my shoulders, giving warmth to my chilled skin as he stared down at me. "I've never seen anything like it."

"You aren't going to run and tell the Covenant that I broke the rules?" I asked, laughter bubbling up as I glanced back toward the Tribunal room.

"No," he said, his brow furrowing as he grasped my hand in his. He turned it over, looking at my uninjured skin and wiping away grains of dirt. "You make me wish I hadn't given up my own magic. I think maybe that's something worth protecting."

The smile drifted off my face as I met his gaze, staring up at him. My shock took over, consuming every waking thought. Of all the things he could have said, *that* hadn't been what I'd expected.

To exist without my magic felt like losing part of myself, like losing the most important part of what made me, *me*. I didn't know who I was without the whisper of the earth in my veins or the scent of the woods filling my lungs.

Even now, knowing what I'd given would return with time and rest... I felt like nothing. Like an empty shell of myself.

Of all the things the Coven had done, I was fairly certain the Choice that male witches were required to make was the most cruel. Family or magic.

"This doesn't look like her room, Mr. Bray," Thorne's voice said from behind me.

I groaned as I hung my head forward, my forehead pressing against Iban's white dress shirt. His tie tickled my cheek as I tried to ignore the weight of the headmaster's gaze pressing into my spine.

"We got distracted," Iban said, helping me to maneuver my legs up onto the stone. He climbed up beside me, moving through to help pull me along the stone as gently as he could manage.

I giggled as I stumbled into his arms, the delirium of my exhaustion making me feel half-drunk. It had been so long since I'd allowed myself to feel such things, the risks far outweighing the benefits most of the time. To be depleted of magic so suddenly was a shock to the system, making me crave some sort of stability.

I knew the moment Thorne realized what I'd done, his body tensing as Iban wrapped an arm around my waist and supported me as I stumbled through the first step.

"Here," Thorne said, raising his wrist to his mouth.

He brushed his suit jacket up his arm, unfastening his cufflinks so that he could roll his sleeve up and out of the way. He sank his fangs into his flesh slowly, holding my gaze with his burnished steely stare. Blood coated his lips when he pulled it away, stepping toward me and raising it to my mouth.

I reared back.

"Drink. It will help replenish your magic."

I shook my head as I frowned, disgust rolling through my gut. If his blood was inside of me, he'd have certain... access to me, and I would be less able to fight. His compulsion would be stronger. He'd be able to sense me wherever I went; my emotions would be easier for him to *feel* as if they were his.

"Don't be stubborn," Thorne growled, reaching forward to grasp me around the back of the neck so that he could hold me still. He pressed his wrist against my mouth, his nostrils flaring when I kept it clamped firmly shut. "Open your fucking mouth and drink, Witchling."

"She doesn't seem to want it, Headmaster Thorne," Iban said, and something about the caution and disbelief in his voice made me believe it wasn't something that the Vessels offered often.

"Must you be so impossible?" Thorne asked, finally withdrawing his wrist.

I waited until the puncture marks healed over before I let my lips part enough to speak. I carefully wiped the blood off my face with my forearm, not allowing a single drop or smear to touch my tongue.

"Must you be such an asshole?" I asked, ignoring the choking sound Iban made as I took a step away from Thorne. The younger male was quick to step with me, supporting me as I did my best to walk on my own. My legs felt like Jell-O beneath me, trembling with each and every step.

"At least have the decency to carry her if you want to pretend to be chivalrous," Thorne barked, and I felt the way Iban twitched in response.

"I'm not pretending to be anything," he protested, but he made no move to pick me up. That suited me just fine, as having him assist me with walking was embarrassing enough. I didn't need him to realize I was too heavy and drop me.

"For Hell's sake," Thorne groaned behind me.

I took another step, and nausea swirled in my gut when my foot never touched the stone. My world went upside down as Thorne swept my feet out from under me, catching me beneath the knees and placing his other arm around my back.

I squealed as I flung my arms around his neck without thought, the blueness of his stare far too piercing when we were this close.

"Put me down," I whispered, swallowing down my unease.

Greens were not meant to be off the ground entirely. Even stone tile was better than this Hell.

"Do shut up, Miss Madizza," he said as he strode forward, making his way down the corridor and toward the entry hall we'd entered the school in. There were no remaining students to mingle, and all was quiet as he headed for the stairwell.

"Rude," I snapped, squirming in his grip.

"All that will do is make me more inclined to drop you," he said, his gaze pinned on where he was going as he carried me. He was careful not to jostle me too much as the ache of my depleted magic settled into my bones.

I scoffed. "As if you aren't already inclined to do that."

The corners of his eyes crinkled at the edges as a deep rumble began in his chest. It was a rare, genuine smile, and I stared in shock as his lips spread into a wide grin.

"Do you ever get tired of your own attitude?"

"I do not have an attitude!" I protested, my eyes wide. If I hadn't been too terrified to release him for fear he may drop me, I might have slapped him for the incredulous way he glanced at me from the corners of his eyes.

I could *feel* the silent, "really?" in that look.

"Is that so?" he asked after a moment. He climbed the stairs as if I were weightless in his hold, even though he and I both knew that wasn't true.

I was average height with an hourglass figure. My body had a decent amount of muscle packed onto it, all lingering beneath a certain love of chocolate and sweets that softened my curves. I loved my "mid-size" figure, but I'd never met someone who could carry me up several flights of stairs.

"You seem to bring out the worst in me," I admitted, seething as I had no choice but to admit that while he was difficult and inherently evil, perhaps I wasn't exactly cooperative either.

He chuckled, shaking his head as he rolled his eyes to the ceiling. "Likewise, Witchling."

"Do you call all the Hollow's Grove students *Witchling*? Is it because you can't be bothered to remember their names?" I asked, curiosity driving me as he rounded the corner at the top of the third flight of stairs. The farther we went from the earth below, the more I hated this damned place.

"Just you," he grunted, not offering any further information as to why I was so fortunate to receive a nickname I hadn't asked for.

"Lucky me," I groaned as he kicked open a set of doors. The hallway before us consisted of only a single door on either side of the corridor, and he lowered me to my feet in front of the one on the right.

"Key," he said, holding out a hand.

Iban deposited an antique-looking brass key into his hand, and I blushed as I realized that I hadn't even noticed he'd come up the stairs with us. His eyes snagged mine as if he knew it too, and my blush deepened.

Headmaster Thorne was dangerous in all the worst ways if I couldn't even notice my surroundings when he held me in his arms.

Hell's sake, I was damned.

Thorne slid an arm around my waist as I swayed, trying to reassure myself that my exhaustion was the cause of my distraction. His other hand slid the key into the lock on the door, turning it until the old wooden door swung open. He deposited the key into the back pocket of my black jeans as he reached around me, his mouth only a breath from my own.

"This is grossly inappropriate," I muttered, watching as his lips twitched into a smile.

"So is calling your headmaster an asshole," he murmured, patting the key with two swift but firm taps that made me twitch in his arms.

He guided me through the door into a common area with four chairs and a sofa lingering by the fireplace in the corner. There was a small kitchenette with a refrigerator and sink beside the door. On either side of the room, two doors waited. The one on the left was open, revealing a small, but pretty bedroom.

"I assume that's mine?" I asked, peeling myself away from Thorne's grip. The room swayed as I walked toward it, but I lingered in the doorway to the private room as I glanced in.

The walls were painted a light gray, the sage-colored drapes opened to reveal a view of what I felt certain were meant to be gardens. The headboard of the double bed was upholstered in a fabric the color of sand, the linens a light, natural cream. The chandelier that hung overhead had pink and yellow interspersed through it in the shapes of delicate flowers. A single wood nightstand rested beside the bed, with a bouquet of roses in a vase set upon it.

"Does it meet your standards?" Thorne asked, knowing it was far more elegant than the home I'd shared with my mother and brother.

"It's lovely," I admitted with a hesitant sigh. I bit my lip as I stepped in slowly, glancing toward the gardens that needed my attention. I was already tired just thinking about it.

"Good. Classes begin in the morning. I'm sure one of your roommates will be happy to show you the way," Thorne said, retreating back into the role of Headmaster.

My thoughts scattered, scrambling frantically for a way to bring back the man who'd carried me up the stairs. Love didn't exist for a Vessel, but the lust he showed was something I could work with. Something I *needed* to work with if I wanted to find my aunt's bones. I opened my mouth to speak, dread filling me at the thought of what I needed to do.

Of how horrible it had once seemed.

"Goodnight, Miss Madizza," he said, shoving his hands into his pockets as if he didn't know what to do with them.

I swallowed, clamping my mouth shut as I nodded. "Goodnight, Gray," I murmured, the words soft enough that a human wouldn't have heard them. My cheeks warmed as I chewed on the inside of my lip.

Thorne froze, his head tilting to the side slightly as he held my gaze for a moment. He nodded once, pressing a hand to Iban's shoulders as he stood looking between us as if he was dumbfounded.

Thorne—*Gray*, I forced myself to correct even my thoughts—nodded once.

Then they were both gone.

12

*M*y nights were always restless.

I wandered the halls of Hollow's Grove, choosing to forgo the offer of nighttime companionship from one of the female Vessels who had warmed my bed in the past. Gemma had done nothing to deserve the angry response she'd gotten when she made herself available tonight, but that hadn't stopped me from flinching away from her touch.

Even hours later, my reaction infuriated me. The girl was nothing. Just another witch who would soon be groomed into whatever the Coven wanted her to be, with a heart filled with nothing but hatred for my kind. The witches made me feel nothing but gratitude for the fact that I did not possess a mass of beating flesh within my chest.

Better to not have one at all, then to have one that rotted beneath my skin.

But it had been decades since someone arrived in Crystal Hollow, looked the Covenant in the face, and defied them at every turn. She was obstinate and difficult, rude and ill-tempered.

But as I stared at the trellis where her magic had brought the courtyard back to life, there was no doubting one truth.

The witchling had gotten under my skin.

Life had spread from those vines, rippling across the courtyard in the hours since I'd delivered her to her bed. The rose bushes pulsed with life, fresh buds appearing from the vivid, green leaves and sharp, pointed thorns. Where before everything had been nothing but the ghost of a reminder of what had once been, now the courtyard thrummed with life. With vibrancy that had been missing from the Coven for a very, very long time.

My hands clenched at my sides as I turned away from the sight of what she had given. The Coven didn't deserve the sacrifice she was willing to make to bring the land they'd used and abused back to life. Susannah and George had led the witches away from everything that had once motivated them, sinking further and further into the selfishness that drove the politics within the families.

The good of witchkind didn't matter to them any longer, when it had been all the original families cared about in the beginning. We'd built this town, sheltered it from the fearful humans of Salem in order to protect the magic Lucifer had granted to the witches for their agreement to serve him.

The doors to the Tribunal rooms glowed with golden light as I turned my back on them, heading for the stairs to the student dormitories. It wouldn't be long before the first Reaping would be upon us, and I would move through the dormitories along with the other Vessels, taking my pick of witches for the night.

I took the stairs quickly, luxuriating in the empty halls. It was so rare that this school was not bustling with activity, where staff and students alike didn't mingle and get to know one another while they prepared for the coming school year.

With classes beginning the next day, at this late hour, they'd all retired to their rooms to rest.

I pulled my copy of the key to Willow's room from my pocket, turning it in the lock quietly and stepping into the darkened room. The moon and stars shone in the sole window at the other end of the common room, the massive circle off-center thanks to the fireplace that lingered in the corner opposite to Willow's door.

The knob to her door turned easily as I pushed it open, stepping into the darkened room. She hadn't bothered to pull the curtains closed before she lay down on top of the bedding. In her exhaustion, she hadn't even changed her clothing into the set of sleep shorts and tank top I'd arranged for Juliet to bring to her room as soon as we'd arrived.

Her sweater was tossed over the end of the bed, leaving her in nothing but a tank top and a pair of jeans that looked horribly uncomfortable to sleep in. I strode to her side, where she slumbered peacefully in the center of the bed. Her head was tipped slightly to the side where I stood, giving me time to study the soft lines of her face.

The edge of her personality was gone in her rest, her sharp thorny words and scathing looks missing. It made her look younger somehow, less hardened by a life in hiding. I didn't understand why I'd come to her room, having never violated the privacy of a student's dorm in the past. While I didn't need to be invited into any place within the school, given my name was one of those on the documents of legal ownership, handling the school was a delicate dance of balance.

My alliance with the witches could tolerate barbed comments and passive hatred. Sneaking into their rooms at night would be a different story.

Yet here I stood, at the bedside of the granddaughter of Susannah Madizza, of all people. I lowered myself to the bed, perching on the edge carefully. Willow didn't stir, her breathing and heartbeat remaining steady and slow.

Reaching out with a single hand, I brushed a line across her cheek that was marred by the faintest trail of her dried blood. The scent of it was a distraction I didn't need, a temptation driving me to do things I hadn't intended when I'd come here.

I didn't know what I'd intended by coming here.

The old evidence of what remained on her arms and hands was the only indication that she'd used the forbidden magics, that she was aware of the innate power of witch's blood. Her mother hadn't practiced the old ways when she'd lived in Crystal Hollow. Flora had been raised by her mother with Susannah's constant input and interference until her mother died. It was on that night that she'd faked her own death, escaping the possibility of having Susannah as her sole guardian even though she'd been a teenager.

I hadn't known her well. Hadn't known any of the fledgling witches at the time, with Hollow's Grove already having closed down after the massacre six years prior. My interactions with them had been as limited as possible to begin with, and she hadn't even come of age when she'd left.

So what had happened to Flora Madizza after she left Crystal Hollow, and why had it motivated her to return to the lost ways of magic? I suspected the little witchling sleeping peacefully knew far more than she wanted to admit, and I wished I could take her amulet and demand the answers I needed.

Instead, I watched her shift positions, rubbing her legs together as if she desperately wanted to get more comfortable. I sighed, glancing toward the stack of pajamas on her dresser on the opposite wall. I lifted her shirt slowly until it revealed the thinnest line of skin on her stomach. I slowly unhooked the button on her jeans, keeping my eyes on her face. I felt confident her magical exhaustion was too much, and she stood no risk of waking, but I wanted to know at the first sign if I needed to flee before she found me in her room.

The witchling would never let me hear the end of it.

I unzipped her pants next; the sound echoing through the silence of the room. She still didn't stir, not even as I curled my fingers into the waistband and carefully peeled them down over her hips. Her skin was soft against my fingers, the curve of her thighs coming into view as the jeans pulled down slowly.

I paused when I reached her knees, shifting myself lower on the bed so that I could carefully maneuver the tight fabric over her calves and ankles, taking them off her feet and tossing them to the floor beside the bed.

Her underwear were black, a lacy boyshort that curved down her stomach in a low V before resting higher on her hips. They were the perfect pair for her body, drawing my stare to her curves and the softness of her figure.

I let my fingers drift over the slight swell of her stomach, enjoying the sleepy little moan that came from her throat in response to my touch. She rolled her head farther to the side, arching her back so that she pressed into my touch.

"Fuck," I hissed between gritted teeth, forcing myself to stand from the bed and put distance between us as my cock hardened in my slacks and my fangs throbbed with the need to feed.

I couldn't risk putting Crystal Hollow and my ability to cohabitate with the witches at risk, especially not for a witch-ling I didn't even know.

One thing was clear. I wanted to fuck Willow Madizza.

She'd just have to be awake when I did it.

13

WILLOW

I tugged at the bottom of my green and black plaid skirt, wishing I could close the gap between the hem and the top of my thigh-high stockings. Wearing a skirt was so impractical if I was going to be burying bodies in the woods.

Even if my plan was to try to keep the violence to a minimum, I wasn't known for my lack of impulsivity.

My reflection in the mirror was something I didn't recognize. I'd left my hair down, falling around my shoulders. The color was glaring against the white of my dress shirt. My forest green blazer rested over the end of the bed, the black shoes they'd set out for me forgotten and tucked under the edge.

My combat boots didn't look quite right with the thigh-high socks and the absurd little ribbon that knotted into a very loose sort of bow in the place of a tie. I'd deal with the skirt without a fight, but I'd go to war over footwear.

I lifted the blazer, shrugging my arms into it and settling it to rest over my shoulders comfortably. There were no buttons down the center, leaving it to drape open and leave the high waist of the skirt where the shirt tucked in visible.

I rolled my eyes as I moved to the door to my bedroom, pulling it open to find three faces staring back at me. They were all somewhere around my age, and I knew they were probably all descendants of the original families.

At least before the school had closed fifty years ago, legacies roomed together. It didn't matter that I was one of the thirteen students taken from outside the barriers of Crystal Hollow. One of thirteen students who showed magical promise and could offer some diversity to the bloodlines.

I'd been born a legacy. I would die one as well.

"You must be Willow," the first of the girls said, breaking from the other two to approach. She took my hands in hers as she beamed at me, her energy radiating off her in waves. "I'm Della Tethys." She confirmed my suspicions of being a legacy, the name of one of the two original lines of Blue witches rolling off her tongue.

I slowly pried my hands out of her grip. Her skin was cool to the touch. Her turquoise eyes swirled like sea water as she relented, turning back with a flip of dark hair to smile at the other girls and motion them forward.

The one wearing a gray and black plaid skirt with a gray blazer stepped forward, wringing her hands more shyly. "I'm Nova Aurai," she said, and something about her felt unsettled. Her eyes were devoid of all color, the lightest of grays staring out from a remarkably beautiful face. Her dark hair was set in stunning ringlets, her lips naturally dark and lovely against her deep brown skin. "That's Margot Erotes," she added, gesturing to the blonde in the background.

The Red witch made no motion to come closer, studying me thoughtfully as her blonde hair framed her face in a long bob. "Pleasure," she said, her voice practically a purr. The hair on my arms rose in response to it.

"Don't mind her. She doesn't like to be touched," Della said, crooking her arm through mine. "It's nothing personal."

I raised a brow at the Red witch, noting the slightest tinge to her checks. A sex witch who didn't like to be touched.

"That sounds absolutely torturous given your magic," I said, the words slipping free before I could stop them.

Margot breathed a sigh of relief, her shoulders sagging forward when I didn't pass judgment or mock her. "You have no idea."

Nova moved to the kitchenette, grabbing four granola bars out of a jar on the counter. She tossed one to each of us. "We missed breakfast, so these will have to do."

I tore open my package with my teeth, taking a massive bite. After the energy I'd expelled the night before, I needed *more*. I needed protein and food from the earth.

Nova smiled as she pulled the front door open, jerking to a halt when she found someone standing on the other side. Iban smiled somewhat shyly, running his free hand through his hair. "Headmaster Thorne thought you might need this, Willow," he called over Nova's shoulder.

I stepped forward, my brow furrowing as I took in the sight of the plate. An English muffin with eggs, Canadian bacon, and melted cheese was half wrapped in foil, and the plate was otherwise filled with fresh fruit, cherry tomatoes, and sliced cucumbers. I took it from him with a soft laugh, grabbing a grape and popping it into my mouth.

"That was thoughtful of him," I forced myself to say as I chewed. It was considerate, suspiciously so, and I imagined the younger witches didn't have any clue what a witch needed after that kind of offering to a source.

He might have been one of the only ones who did.

If any of them thought it odd that the headmaster had

done something of that nature, they didn't say it. The looks they silently exchanged communicated it clearly enough.

I stepped past Iban into the hall, pausing when I realized I hadn't the first clue where I was supposed to go. I smiled sheepishly at him as I picked up my breakfast sandwich and took a bite.

"Where's my first class?"

"Ah, I think Della may be the best to help you with that," he answered, running a hand through his hair.

"Iban has no magic, Willow. What need would he have of classes meant to teach him such things?" Della asked. The words weren't spoken cruelly, but Iban's whole body flinched regardless.

"Then what are you doing at Hollow's Grove?" I asked, my brow furrowing.

I hadn't realized that those who made the Choice attended the school even after they'd given up their magic, but I should have realized it the night before.

"I serve the Coven in other ways," he said, nodding down to the plate of food I held in my hands. "Besides, given my age, the best place for me is here now. I'm not going to find my mate anywhere else, am I?"

"You're willingly looking for your mate? Aren't you a little young?" I asked, my voice hitching. The thought of having children at our age was horrific to me. I'd barely even begun to *live*.

I hadn't at all, if I were honest with myself.

"I gave up my magic in the hopes of finding a suitable match that the Covenant would approve of, and I could fall in love with. I'm not going to risk missing her," he said, smiling.

I shoved a bite of melon in my mouth to buy time to push down the discomfort I felt over needing to answer. With the way he was staring at me, unease settled in my gut.

The Coven would approve of him as a match for me. He was a Green, keeping the bloodlines as pure as possible. While a witch only inherited the power from their mother, as the father was powerless by the time of conception, they still prioritized keeping the Houses pure when they could.

I had a feeling, with the closing of the school, they'd been forced to be less selective without fresh blood coming in every year for breeding. But neither of my parents were a Bray, nor were my grandparents, to my knowledge.

Beyond that, I didn't know. I didn't want to think about it.

I swallowed loudly, linking my arm through his. "Whoever she is, she'll be a lucky woman," I said, smiling as I took another bite. Iban's cheeks heated, and I knew I would need to squash whatever this was sooner rather than later.

He'd given up his magic to have a family.

I didn't intend to have one at all—even if I lived long enough.

It was far more likely that I would die trying to find my aunt's bones—far more likely that *Gray* would drain me of blood and leave me to die when he discovered the truth of who I was.

I forced myself to smile through the stark reality, letting Della and the other girls lead us to our first class of the day. Iban seemed happy enough to go with us, so I let him walk beside me as I tried to gain a little of my strength back from my breakfast.

The faint hum of magic pulsed in my veins with each bite of fruit as the cycle of life rejuvenated me. I'd sacrificed, so now it did the same, but what was taken by force would never be as powerful as what was freely given.

I felt my eyes pulse with warmth as I looked up from my plate to the classroom my roommates led me into. Headmaster Thorne stood at the front of the room, a chalkboard behind him. He'd rolled up the sleeves of his dress shirt and tossed his suit jacket over the back of the chair at the desk. His cold stare met mine as my escort guided me into the room, and I flushed as that knowing look dropped to the plate of food in my hands.

"Thank you," I forced myself to murmur beneath my breath. I wasn't sure if even his hearing was strong enough for that, but he smiled just slightly.

Iban stopped me by the door, spinning me subtly and smoothly until my back struck the stone of the wall just inside the classroom. I giggled as he leaned into my space just slightly, keeping a respectable enough distance. He didn't crowd me, didn't put an arm above my head or make me feel trapped. Guilt swelled in me as I did what I shouldn't, using the opportunity he'd given me.

I reached up, brushing a stray strand of hair away from his temple as his green eyes darkened in response. He leaned his head into the touch. "You're playing with fire," he said with a grin, his teeth shining and perfectly straight.

"I have absolutely no idea what you're talking about," I said, fighting back a smile of my own. The fact that he saw through me settled some of my guilt.

He hummed, placing his hand above my head now that I'd made the first move to touch him. "Soon enough, you'll realize that the Vessel isn't a possibility for you," he said, leaning in to whisper the words so softly I knew he was aware of our audience. I smiled up at the cooperative, playful man. "Maybe then you'll see me the way you seem inclined to pretend you do."

The smile drifted off my face slowly, leaving me to gape up at him as the meaning of the words struck me in the chest.

Iban leaned in, touching his lips to my cheek sweetly. "Enjoy your games, Willow, but just know I play to win."

14

GRAY

*S*he surprised me, taking the seat next to Margot in the front row. She smiled at the sullen woman, keeping her distance and not crowding her—giving her space that most didn't afford to the Reds.

Willow picked up a grape, popping it into her mouth and chewing slowly as she held my gaze. I'd never in my life thought that a woman could even make eating feel like a sultry game, but knowing she hadn't rejected the food I'd sent for her soothed some of the irritation at seeing her flirt with the Bray boy.

She was the worst kind of danger, a temptation that would push me to do stupid, foolish things just to get my cock wet. Because that's all it could be. With my true body and heart locked in the pits of Hell, I had no interest in anything more.

The Covenant would attempt to take my balls before they let me pursue something more than the Reaping with Susannah's precious granddaughter, anyway. I scoffed at the thought, settled in the knowledge that witches and Vessels would never willingly come together in such a way.

Willow crossed her legs beneath the table, drawing my

attention to the combat boots on her feet. She'd ignored the shoes I *knew* had been provided, since I'd seen them in her room the night before when I stripped off her pants. I wondered if she knew someone had been there, or if she'd convinced herself she'd taken them off the night before and just forgotten it.

Her face was calm, her heart rate settled. While she'd proven to be a gifted liar, I didn't think she would be able to disguise the symptoms of her fear if she realized someone had entered her room while she slept.

I smirked as I raised a brow at her, lifting the textbook into my arms and approaching her table. The rest of the students had already been given the necessary items they'd need for their education, but Willow hadn't been present for orientation.

"We have a dress code, Miss Madizza," I said, placing the book in front of her.

She leaned forward, taking it from me. Her fingers brushed against mine as I released it, and I knew the contact hadn't been unintentional. How quickly she'd gone from telling me she would never allow me to touch her to hinting it was what she wanted. The suspicion that had sunk inside me only grew with every lingering gaze and flirtatious comment.

"Are you going to give me detention, Headmaster?" she asked, cocking her head to the side.

Margot swung her head to look at her as Willow flipped open the textbook, thumbing through the pages absently.

"We don't have detention here," I said, crossing my arms over my chest as I tried to decide exactly what sort of game she was playing.

Her eyes met mine once more, and beneath the false bravado, I saw it lingering there. *Uncertainty*. I pursed my lips, nodding in understanding. Willow was using her flirtation as a way to hide her discomfort, sinking her teeth into anything familiar.

Me. Iban Bray.

We were the only two males she'd met, aside from Kairos, and she'd flirted with him as well.

It wasn't about *me*. It never was, but that wouldn't stop me from taking *exactly* what I wanted from her.

"That's a shame," she said, her mouth dropping into a pout that was somehow cute.

"Not particularly," I said, not bothering to disguise the sting I didn't want to feel. Her lack of specific interest shouldn't have mattered to me. Who she fucked wasn't my concern as long as I was one of them.

But somehow, it did matter.

"If you're in need of personal attention after class, I'm sure Mr. Bray would be more than willing to accommodate your needs, Miss Madizza," I said, allowing my eyes to rove over her figure.

Her mouth dropped open just slightly.

"Excuse me?" she asked, her flush confirming what I suspected. She didn't even *want* to take someone to bed, but for some reason she just couldn't keep herself from taunting me.

I called her bluff. "If you need to be fucked," I said, dropping my voice low. Only the students closest to her could hear my words, but her cheeks darkened and highlighted the dark spots of her freckles all the same. "I'm certain Mr. Bray would be happy to service you."

She clamped her mouth shut, her embarrassment fading away and fury taking its place. Her jaw hardened. It was gone only a moment later before she struck me with a smile that felt as sharp and dangerous as a belladonna plant.

"You're right. I'm sure he will be."

I glared at her, my smirk dropping as she leaned back in her chair. She crossed her arms over her torso, highlighting the swell of her breasts as she turned to Margot and smiled as if she hadn't been affected by my harsh words in the slightest.

Fucking Hell.

"Turn to page three," I snapped, turning back to my chalkboard. My mood had sufficiently plummeted, and Willow only continued to taunt me as she slowly ate the rest of the fruit I'd had delivered to her.

All men enjoyed a challenge, but Willow was something different. She was something worse.

She was *impossible.*

15

GRAY

I cleared the board of all my notes, focusing on the task as my room full of witches shuffled their belongings and prepared to head to their next class. Forcing myself not to look at Willow, I couldn't stop the growl that vibrated my chest when she spoke to Margot. Where the blonde witch had spoken quietly, murmuring at an appropriate level for speaking to someone who stood directly beside her, Willow carefully calculated her next words.

"Do we have any classes where Iban will be present?" she asked, and I could practically hear the threat in her voice. I didn't know her well enough to know if she intended to follow through on it or if she planned to just continue to use him to push my buttons.

The Coven would do their best to entomb me if I killed off a male witch who'd sacrificed his magic to breed. They weren't common, and as such, they were rewarded in other ways. Iban would be provided for by the Covenant until he made an appropriate match, given luxuries that even the other male members of the Coven weren't afforded.

A private room at Hollow's Grove so that he could entertain all manner of company if he chose. His pick of witches to mate with.

There was no doubt who he'd set his sights on. I just didn't know if the Covenant had pushed him to make the match or if the interest was genuine. I supposed it didn't matter, as Susannah would agree to it, regardless.

I smirked, realizing I wouldn't need to risk her wrath to rid myself of the boy's interference.

Willow would do that for me if she suspected that was his intention.

"Why do you teach history to witches?" Willow asked.

I turned to find her standing behind me. Her roommates lingered at the door, watching her cautiously as if she were a ticking bomb. I suspected her behavior was rather odd to them, given that they'd all been raised the same way—a way that was very much different from what I suspected of Willow's upbringing.

"Who better to teach history than someone who was alive to see it?" I asked, dropping the eraser to the ledge at the base of the chalkboard. I crossed my arms over my chest, waiting for the next inevitable question.

"It seems an odd choice, given your obvious bias against the Coven," she said, her bottom lip twitching ever-so-slightly. I noted the act, realizing she'd done it whenever she considered something that didn't make sense to her. A twitch when she attempted to solve a riddle.

Whatever Willow's life had been, one thing was clear. She was not purely driven by whatever her mother had taught her. She was not indoctrinated in the same way the witches of the Coven were from the time they were born.

There was an element of justice within her. A desire to know the truth that couldn't be denied. I had a feeling whatever her mother had raised her to believe, she'd also given her the gift of thinking for herself.

It was a gift many were not afforded.

"Name me one person who would not have a bias in teaching history," I said, laughing as her mismatched eyes glimmered with malice. She knew I was right, and she smiled to confirm it, turning her gaze to the window at the side of the room.

"I merely meant that it is interesting that the Covenant allows you to teach—"

"The Covenant does not control me. I do things for the good of Crystal Hollow, because seeing it preserved serves my purpose. Whatever you were told about the hierarchy of power here, consider the *bias* of the source. Of course, witches would believe they sit at the top and run the show," I answered, grinning at the way that bottom lip twitched again.

"Maybe you should consider that history is always written by the victor. I find it *very* hard to believe that Susannah is okay with you sharing history and implying that perhaps you got the better end of the deal that was struck between the devil and Charlotte Hecate," Willow said, her brow rising in challenge.

"Perhaps, but I've given her no reason to take issue with my method of teaching. I stick to the facts and do not embellish. It is better for all of us involved that way. Allows witches like Susannah to continue to think herself the victor, while my kind know how to be patient," I said, approaching my desk. I leaned my ass against it, reaching down to grasp the edge as Willow's gaze dropped to my revealed forearms.

That lip twitched, and I suspected this one had nothing to do with how to unravel a mystery and everything to do with how to get what she wanted.

"You don't seem particularly patient to me," she said, tipping her head to the side as she approached my desk. None of my other students would have dared to come so close, and her friends at the door exchanged a quick look and scampered off accordingly. She stepped between my spread legs, reaching up and adjusting my tie with a casual ease that shouldn't have been there.

"A witch's life is a blip compared to mine. I have watched countless of your kind wither and die. When this generation of witches I'm teaching is dead and gone, I will still be here," I said, grasping her wrist and slowly pulling her hand away from my tie.

"Not all witches die," she said with a shrug, not fighting to loosen herself from my grip. I held her carefully, cautiously. I didn't want to hurt her, even if the idea of seeing her skin covered in bites and bruises from more pleasurable endeavors did fill me with an odd warmth.

"I hardly think we can consider the Covenant *alive*," I argued, staring at the way her mouth parted slightly when she smiled. The strong bow of her lips was enticing, drawing my gaze down to the pink of them every time they moved.

"I wasn't talking about them," she murmured, biting her lip as if she could feel the heat of my stare.

Disbelief flooded my veins, forcing me to turn my attention back to those strange, mismatched eyes. "What was your mother doing teaching you about Charlotte Hecate?"

The witch who had first struck the bargain with the devil had been granted immortality to oversee her Coven, to rule over them, but she hadn't wanted the authority. She'd given her leadership role to the Covenant, raising them from the grave as they had been her mentors in life.

A mistake that had cost her greatly when they tore the flesh from her bones and buried it. Somewhere in the gardens, her flesh had been buried—unable to rot because of the immortality that had been granted to her.

Her spirit, and her magic, lived on in the bones that had been passed down to her descendants. It was why the keeper of the bones, the chosen of the Hecate line, guarded them with her life. Why her relatives had done everything in their power to protect her, where other houses were embroiled in competition.

"She did not die," she said, and the solemnity in her voice told me that she knew that had not been a blessing. That she'd spent an eternity unable to heal herself; her body separated and scattered. The finger bones that remained in the pouch the Hecate line had carried with them were but a fragment of her, and even those bones could not allow her to be with her family in death.

It was cruel, perhaps the most heinous of acts committed by the Covenant in their thirst for power.

"You are not Charlotte Hecate, Witchling," I said.

The warning hung between us, unspoken. There was no point in reminding her that she should not endeavor to be like the witch who had suffered endlessly.

"No," she said, leaning forward.

I gripped her wrist harder, feeling her fingers flex beneath the strength of my grip as she pushed it to the side and bent her head back, staring up at me. I leaned toward her, meeting her halfway, drawn in by the mischievous glimmer in that stare. Her tongue ran over her bottom teeth lightly as she paused with her mouth just a breath from mine.

"But I am brazen enough to make a deal with the devil like she did."

Her words sent a chill through me, understanding that the young thing didn't have the first clue what she was dealing with. What kind of horror those words and that promise could bring upon her life. I held very still as she brushed her lips against mine, huffing a slight laugh as her scent filled my lungs.

"You're very easy to seduce for someone who has such patience," she said, and my eyes drifted closed as the hum she emitted seemed to sink inside me.

Like a siren calling me to the sea, there was something unnatural in that noise. In the voice that was more of a song than spoken words.

"Patience has nothing to do with us."

She raised her hand at the same moment I did, touching the side of my neck with her open palm. The heat of her skin was like a brand, thriving and *alive* in ways that my Vessel had never been.

It had been an eternity since I'd felt that warmth inside of me, since the warmth of any bedmate seemed to penetrate the cold of my flesh.

Yet one touch from her and my eyes drifted closed.

She pursed her lips against mine, the lightest kiss I thought I'd ever received. I felt the touch down to my toes, as if she could breathe life into me, when the one who'd formed this body had been in charge of the dead.

If Charlotte Hecate was death itself, Willow Madizza felt like life.

She pulled back just enough, her point made when it felt like she'd turned me to Jell-O in her hands. My eyes fluttered open slowly, staring down into her eyes that I had the distinct feeling she'd never bothered to close.

"There is no us," she said, her voice the softest of murmurs. Something cruel lived in that whisper, the harsh edges hinting at the rejection I'd given her earlier.

I thrust my hand into her hair, gripping it and tugging her

head back as I bared my fangs at the sudden change in her expression.

"This feels like there is," I growled, grinding forward until she could feel my cock straining against my slacks.

She shuddered, a ragged breath leaving her as she glared up at me.

"I am not a toy. Why would I settle for the scraps of your attention when I could have another on his knees and ready to give me anything I asked for with nothing more than a word?" she asked, but her body swayed forward, pushing into my touch rather than moving away from it.

"Then why are you here?" I asked, tugging her head to the side so that I could lean forward, dragging my lips over the side of her throat. She shuddered, and I smiled against the skin, letting her feel the press of my fangs.

"To show you exactly what he'll have that you won't. So that when you next come into my room while I'm sleeping, you might at least hesitate before you decide to pretend you do not want me the next day," she said.

Every bone in my body stilled.

I pulled back, staring down at her in surprise. "You were asleep," I said, not even bothering to pretend I didn't know what she was talking about. There was a confidence in her words and the way she spoke them, leaving me with the reality that she had no doubt I'd been there.

"I was," she agreed, not offering any more information as I studied that guarded stare of hers. "That does not mean I could not smell you all over me when I woke. The roses confirmed what I already suspected."

"The roses? They spoke to you?" I asked, wondering when the last time I'd heard of a Green communing with nature had been.

"They'll speak to any Green. Most are just too ignorant to listen," she said, twisting her head in my grip as if she could pull free, but I refused to release her. "I wonder what the Covenant would think if they were to discover you violated me in my sleep."

"I did no such thing," I argued.

"Right. Taking off my clothes while I slept was entirely innocent—"

"You looked uncomfortable, but I did not touch you beyond that. Make no mistake, I want you to scream my name the first time I fuck you, not sleep through it, Witchling," I said with a snarl, dropping my head back to her neck. The need to feed on her was overwhelming, growing with each moment she spent pissing me off. I wanted to remind her what I was.

Who I was.

"If you ever touch me, I'll be sure to think of anyone but you. I won't be able to enjoy it otherwise," she said, making me snap at her throat. She shuddered in my hold as my teeth grazed her skin, and a callous chuckle slipped free as I raised my mouth to her ear.

"Then be sure to scream his name for me. I'd like to know who I need to hunt down the next time I'm hungry," I whispered, reveling in her shocked gasp as she shoved both her hands against my chest and pushed.

"Headmaster Thorne!" The cold voice came as a reprimand, striking across the space between us. I pulled my head back from the curtain of Willow's hair, raising my glare to the door where the Covenant stood with an apple clutched in her bony hand. "Need I remind you that you are not to feed on the students outside of the Reaping?"

"She's willing," I said, turning my glare to the witchling held in my grasp.

She smirked, holding my stare and knowing she held the

power in that moment. While Susannah couldn't get rid of me, she could make my pursuit of Willow far more difficult.

"Is that true, Miss Madizza?" Susannah asked as Iban stepped around the corner. He rubbed the back of his neck, looking sheepish. I wondered what he'd seen that had driven him to seek the help of the Covenant.

I hoped he'd seen Willow writhing against my cock with my mouth at her throat.

All traces of arrogance fled from Willow's face as she turned against my hold, glancing back at her ancestor.

"I didn't give him consent to feed from me," she said, pushing against my chest once more.

With the audience watching, I relented and released her.

She turned her back on me, striding toward Susannah and plucking the apple out of her hand. The Covenant couldn't eat it, but they'd been her favorite in life, and she could often be found with one in her grip, as if it reminded her of life.

She turned an eerie stare toward Willow as the younger witch raised it to her mouth, sinking her teeth into it slowly as she smirked back at me. I dropped both hands to the edge of the desk once more, the wood cracking beneath the force of my grip. It was all that offered me any control, all that stopped me from finding out what those little, *vicious* teeth felt like at my throat.

Then she strode forward, walking through the doors as Iban followed at her heel. Only when he was through the doors did she raise her free hand, flicking her wrist and sending the doors slamming shut without looking back once.

Her exit was slightly dramatic, but I had to give her points for flair.

"That one is trouble," Susannah admitted, dropping her arm to her side now that she possessed no apple to look upon.

I nodded, not bothering to argue the point. I'd thought the same more than once.

"All the more reason for you to stay away from her. Keep your teeth to yourself and your dick in your pants where my granddaughter is concerned. Whatever this is between you two ends here," she snapped, turning her back on me as if that was the end of it.

"And if I don't agree?" I asked, crossing my arms over my chest as I stood from my perch on the edge of the desk.

The Covenant froze, turning to face me as her jaw clenched. "You know the rules."

"I can wait until the Reaping," I said, shrugging as the heat of her stare struck me. There was a warning there, one that I chose not to heed.

"You intend to invoke *dominium*?" the Covenant asked, clasping her hands in front of her. "I have plans for Willow. I will not tolerate you getting in my way."

"*Dominium* is my right. You cannot stop me," I answered, grinning as I approached her. If anything, knowing how vehemently she opposed my claim of ownership over Willow only drove me to enact it more.

"A right which you have not claimed in centuries! Why her? Why now?" she asked, her fury rising. Her magic might have been taken from her in its natural state, but she still possessed raw magic that had been given by all the houses of the Coven to bring her back.

Combined with Charlotte's magic to reanimate what was already dead, it enabled her to be more than just a shell.

"I like the way she tastes," I said, shoving my hands into the pockets of my slacks.

"This is a mistake," the Covenant said, backing away a step. She didn't try to dissuade me, just moved toward the doors, which she blew open with a burst of air.

"Susannah?" I asked as she stepped over the threshold. "She's not to know."

"You don't *want* her to know that you've invoked *dominium* over her?" she asked, her brow furrowing as she tried to work out exactly what game I was playing.

She'd never know, or if she did, she'd already have one foot in a grave she wouldn't escape a second time.

"I'll inform her when I'm ready," I said, waiting until she gave her nod. She couldn't argue with me, not in this.

Willow was mine.

16

WILLOW

*D*ays passed where I didn't speak to Gray. Where I didn't see him outside of his class, and he didn't send breakfasts to my room. I refused to acknowledge the sting in my center that felt like disappointment, chalking it up to the fact that my duty would be far more difficult than I'd anticipated.

How was I supposed to find out where the Vessels had hidden my aunt's bones if I couldn't be in the room with the fucker for two seconds without wanting to tear out his throat?

It felt like a pointless waste of time, and I would have much rather been back in my home with Ash at my side, finding a way to cope with the loss of Mom. At least we would have had each other to lean on. Instead, I was trapped in a school I didn't want to attend, contemplating all the ways I'd already failed.

I couldn't push past my father's teachings, his reminders that men preferred women to be seen and not heard. To seduce the headmaster, I'd need to be quiet and demure instead of brazen. I felt fairly certain I'd fucked that seven ways to Hell and there would be no backtracking now.

Besides, I'd seen the way the other witches watched him during class. My attraction to him, as much as I wanted to deny it existed, wasn't unusual. Even those who had grown up in the Coven and learned to hate his kind still felt the pull to him.

His Vessel was unusually handsome, even in comparison to the others. The Vessels were all unnaturally beautiful, but his was just somehow... more.

That was how I'd found myself in the library after class under the guise of studying. The curved windows in front of me were covered with the fine mist of rain, making the woods outside the school appear hazy and distant. The room was too dark to be practical for reading, but I preferred the calm, muted atmosphere of this library to the fluorescent lights at the public school I'd attended as a child. The library walls were covered in wooden shelves. Books far older than I lined them and were organized in a fashion that probably only made sense to the woman in charge of the space. It had embarrassed me to need to ask her for books on what I was looking for, with no digital search function to enable me to seek out a topic.

But she'd helped, giving me a small stack of books and telling me to just leave them on the desk when I was finished.

Iban had offered to join me, to keep me company as I tried to "catch up" on material that I already knew objectively. Nothing could replace the fact that I hadn't grown up in the culture of this place in the same way the others had, but I knew my facts.

The male witch had only sighed at me sadly, his expression holding no traces of anger I'd come to expect from the men I'd turned down. Somehow, the disappointed set to his features was worse, reminding me of the impossibility of what I had set out to do. I hadn't felt a single twinge from the bones since arriving at Hollow's Grove, and I wondered if they were even here.

They existed. I knew that from the magic that pulsed within me occasionally, hovering just out of reach. I couldn't grasp it and knew I wouldn't be able to until I fulfilled the destiny I'd been chosen for and held the bones in my hand.

I flipped through the book in front of me, determined to find any trace of answers. It should have been the location of the bones that I searched for, a registry of any type that had followed the massacre. Instead, I buried my face in the lore of the Vessels, trying to determine why Gray had so much clout within his kind.

The words on the page were an echo of what my mother had taught me, that the Vessels had adopted new names upon entering the Vessels created for them. Nobody knew their true identities, whether the demons the Hecate line had given flesh were lesser demons or even if one of the seven demon lords walked amongst us. There were rumors that the first of the Vessels had been one of them, perhaps sent by the devil himself to supervise his new colony of worshipers on earth.

But in all the centuries since the witches and Vessels had come together to form Crystal Hollow, I could find very little record of actual worship. Whatever the purpose of the experiment with witches and Vessels, it hadn't made itself known yet, at least not to me.

I wanted to know, but I knew it didn't matter to me. It couldn't, not when finding those bones had to be my priority. But Gray's thinly veiled words rang in my head as I stared at the next page, not seeing the words written in front of me any longer. His kind knew how to be patient.

But patient for *what*?

"Miss Madizza," a stern voice said.

I spun, slamming the book shut and draping my forearm

over the cover so he couldn't see the title. The last thing I needed was for the arrogant fuck to know I was spending my free time researching him.

"I'd like a word."

I picked up the book, shoving it into the pack that hung over the back of my chair. The strap went across my chest as I hoisted it up onto my shoulder, creating that line through my cleavage that I detested more than anything.

Seat belt boobs were hardly attractive.

Gray's eyes dropped to it for the briefest moment, his stare remaining entirely impassive before it returned to mine. There wasn't a single flicker of even remote interest, and I squashed the irritation that made me feel. The way it made me feel less somehow, when what men thought of me rarely mattered.

I didn't need them, not when I could achieve anything I wanted on my own. They were nothing but a distraction from my purpose, except he *was* that purpose. He was the only one I couldn't allow to distance himself from me.

Fuck.

"So speak," I said, pursing my lips as I shrugged.

I hadn't meant for the irritation to slip through, wanting to retreat back to the more reserved version of myself I'd been taught to be. But the other witches were all cooperative. They did as they were told and paid attention in class, hanging on his every word as if it was a lifeline.

Maybe the key to standing out against that backdrop was to be the mouthy thing who pissed him off. He was standing in the library seeking me out, after all. Not them.

Even if he seemed entirely uninterested, I could work with having his attention on me for whatever reason. I couldn't work with being ignored.

The librarian tutted from her corner, her glare settling on

me as she didn't dare to give it to the headmaster. He smiled slightly, turning and holding out an arm to gesture me forward.

"Let's go to my office," he said.

I rolled my eyes as I stepped around him and left the books behind me.

He was silent as we stepped into the hall and made our way up the next flight of stairs. I trailed behind him, trying not to think about the last time we'd been on the stairways together. Of the way he'd carried me when it was entirely unnecessary, when he could have just left me to Iban and allowed me to stumble into my bed.

I'd thought he wanted to fuck me, but the interest in that had seemed to wane.

He turned the knob on a door that stood alone on the landing just below the dormitories, pushing it open to reveal a massive, bright space. His office was easily the size of the entire bottom floor of the house I'd shared with my mother and Ash, with three floor-to-ceiling arched windows that came to a point at the top to fill a single one of the walls. They overlooked the cliffs, the faint, misty image of the ocean outside sparkling in the distance.

There was a seating area in front of them, a camel-colored sofa and an oversized chair framing a coffee table. Books remained stacked on the table, despite the shelves that lined the wall behind his desk, which was off to the other side. His chair was a bright red, the back arched and severe as he approached it. The door to his bedroom remained open, as if he cared very little for the fact that anyone could see into his private space.

"You live here?" I asked, following him toward his desk and prying my gaze off the dark gray paneled walls in there and the fourposter bed that was elaborately crafted from iron and entwined with gold filigree detailing.

"I have a house in the village, but I remain here when the school is in session," he answered smoothly, leaning against his desk and gesturing to the single chair that waited in front of it.

I stood beside it, refusing to sit and feel as if I were a chastised student. Whatever had made him summon me here, I highly doubted it had anything to do with my coursework.

"What did you need to speak to me about?" I asked, folding my hands in front of me. The bag hanging over my shoulder was weighed down with books. I wanted nothing more than to set it down.

But until I could figure out exactly what Gray's story was, I suspected it may be better to bide my time until I had more answers about what may drive him.

"Are you really going to stand? You cannot even do what you're told when it is as simple as sitting in a rather comfortable chair?" he asked, raising a brow at me incredulously.

I returned the look, not bothering to voice my answer. He didn't need the words as his eyes drifted closed in frustration, his hand raising to pinch his brow as if I gave him the worst kind of migraine.

"Impossible," he muttered.

"I take that as a compliment," I mumbled, looking away from him and taking in the rest of his office. I ignored the luxury that seemed so unfair, focusing on the smaller items in the room and allowing that twinge of magic within me to sweep out... looking for the bones.

"You shouldn't," he barked, distracting me from my endeavor.

"What's your name?" I asked.

His head jerked back, eyes widening as a stunned smile

curved up the edges of his lips. "Alaric Thorne. You truly do not remember my *name*?" he asked, scoffing as if it was totally believable I would forget such a thing. That was quite stupid of him, as I remembered *everything*.

"Not that one," I said, rolling my eyes to the ceiling. "Your true name."

"That," he said, crossing his arms over his chest as a scowl claimed his face. "Is a very rude question."

"It's only a name," I answered, lifting the bag from my shoulder and placing it on the chair he was determined for me to take.

"Names have power. Names are how demons are summoned by witches, and I have no intention of being summoned anywhere," he said, his voice dropping low with warning.

"It would still work? Even with you in a Vessel?" I asked, considering what I knew of the creation.

The demons had been granted an immortal form that needed blood to continue functioning, but their soul had been bound to it. They couldn't come and go freely as they once had, inhabiting people and burning through their bodies.

These lasted, but they were a prison.

"Would it pull your soul from the Vessel?" I asked, my head tilting to the side in curiosity. The idea had merit. If Vessels could be torn from their Vessels, they could be sent back to Hell.

"No," he said, his lips curving up into the slightest of smiles, as if he could read the path my thoughts had taken. "I would be forced to answer, but I would have to travel the long way."

"Interesting," I murmured, trying to quell my disappoint-ment. The Vessels weren't my priority, but if I happened to manage to rid the world of them in the process, I wouldn't be mad about it.

"I brought you here to discuss a truce between us, and you stand there plotting my demise," he muttered, but the twitch of his lips was more amused than angry.

"A truce?" I asked, watching as he stepped around his desk and took his chair.

He gestured toward the one waiting for me once he was settled, seeming to realize that if he was sitting, it would put us on even footing. I sighed, lifting my bag out of the chair and depositing it on the floor as I waved my arms dramatically.

I might do it, but I'd make it clear I thought it was stupid.

"There is no reason we need to be at odds during our time here," he said, answering my question.

"Of course there is. You are a Vessel, and I am a witch," I said.

Simply put, our kinds had hated one another for centuries. The Vessels had never forgiven the Covenant for what they'd done to Charlotte Hecate, and I couldn't blame them in the end. She'd given them life, been as holy to them as the devil was.

"Are you really, though?" he asked, steepling his hands on the table in front of him. He leaned toward me; his steely gaze intense on mine as he continued with the one thing that would always remain true. "You have magic flowing through your veins. There can be no doubt about that, but you are as much a part of this Coven as I am an angel."

"I've only been here a few days," I said, sinking my teeth into my bottom lip. I'd never intended to hide my hatred for the Coven, so I didn't know why his words disarmed me so much. But they did, making it feel as if he'd stripped me down and revealed every last vulnerability.

I'd be alone. For the rest of my life, whether it was here or in another place after I fled, I would do so with nothing but the clothing on my back and hopefully a bag of Hecate bones.

The life of the necromancer was a lonely one. The pulse of death was far too much for most to tolerate being near.

"You have no intention of joining the Coven in truth. You use magic they've forbidden—magic that you and I both know needs to be restored in order for the world to come back into balance," he said, leaning back in his chair.

The motion dragged my attention up to the portrait at his back. The morbid image of Lucifer's fall from grace stared me in the face. Where the feathered wings of an angel had once been, there was only the open, gaping wounds where they'd been torn from his flesh.

A single tear dropped down the figure's face, his stunningly beautiful features twisted in pain. His eyes glowed bright gold, the harsh set to his features betraying every moment of his rage.

He was like nothing I'd ever seen before, emitting such power from a painting that the breath caught in my throat. *That* was who I risked the wrath of if I somehow managed to undo the Coven and the Vessels. Sending Lucifer's minions back to Hell if He didn't desire it would bring untold danger upon myself.

"It's there to serve as a reminder," Gray said, his words both sympathy and accusation all at once. "That no matter how pretty the shell may be, we are all capable of great and terrible things."

"That sounds like it came from a fortune cookie," I said, turning my stare back to him. I shifted my face back to that emotionless blank canvas I had spent years perfecting, running my damp palm over my skirt to hide the only remaining sign of the fear that the portrait had given me.

"My point," he said, his voice becoming far less patient as

he stood from his desk, "Is that you are capable of thinking for yourself. You know as well as I do that the Coven has fallen to ways that are not natural, and that for whatever reason, the Covenant is determined to encourage that corruption. Two family lines have nearly been erased as a result of it. Perhaps you are exactly what this school needs right now, Miss Madizza."

"How so?"

"You're brave enough to make a deal with the devil? Take me instead," he said, holding out his hand. He raised it to his mouth, nicking his thumb with a fang until a drop of blood welled there. "Help me bring the Coven back to the old ways and restore the balance before it's too late."

I paused, considering as the scent of earth and vanilla filled the air. "What's in it for me?"

"You don't wish to see the Coven restored to what it was meant to be?" he asked, his lips parting. The center was stained with blood, making it look poutier than normal.

The irrational urge to lean forward and lick it from his mouth rushed through me. "I care very little for what happens to the Coven." It was true, though what happened to the earth as a result of their behavior was a different story. I couldn't restore every plant on my own.

Even my magic was not that vast.

Gray nodded, shifting that thumb closer to me. It approached my mouth, but never touched. The deal with a demon had to be made with consent in mind, and he could do nothing until I was active in making it.

"My protection against the Covenant. I will make sure she cannot follow through on her intent to see you wed and bred as soon as possible without your explicit and voluntary agreement."

My heart stopped beating, skipping in my chest as it

squeezed. I had known my time here would be limited before they tried to do just that, but the way he made it sound...

"Have they already started discussing suitors?" I asked, turning my eyes away from him.

"I believe they started discussing them before you'd even arrived in Crystal Hollow. The moment they discovered your existence, you had one purpose to them," he said, and even though I'd been ready for it, I couldn't shake my disgust.

I was more than a womb.

"How will you protect me from that?" I asked. Even with the suspicion that he had more authority here than my mother had been aware, I didn't think it extended that far.

"I have my ways. For now, all you need to do is trust that I will keep to my end of the bargain."

"Does that protection extend to other things? Will you keep them from killing me if I piss them off too severely in the process of restoring the old ways?" I asked, pursing my lips. I couldn't find the bones if I was dead.

"You are of no use to me dead. I have a vested interest in seeing you survive long enough to assist me, so yes. My protection will extend to other aspects of your life if I deem them dangerous to your body or your overall wellbeing, be that emotional, mental, or physical," he said, staring down at the welling blood.

"And who is going to protect me from you?" I asked.

A grin consumed his face. He took a step closer, moving until his thumb was only a breath away from touching my lip.

"I've a feeling you'll do just fine on your own, Witchling," he said.

I grasped his wrist, guiding his hand away from my face. Leaning forward, I gave into the desire to lick the blood from his mouth. Drawing his bottom lip into my mouth, I ran my tongue over the surface until the sweet taste of apple covered my tongue. I drew back while his eyes were still half-shut, raising his hand to my mouth and sucking his thumb as deep as I could, consuming his blood and taking it as part of me.

His eyes opened as I drew back on his thumb slowly, releasing it finally as he leaned forward. The standard custom was for him to pierce my thumb the same way he had, but he mimicked my actions. His eyes held mine as his mouth lingered just a breath from mine, his teeth pinching my bottom lip pointedly until it bled. He groaned as he covered the wound with his mouth, sucking on the flesh and taking the blood he needed for the deal.

I was breathless by the time he pulled back, my eyes closed. I opened them to find his arrogant, steel eyes burning with desire, threads of magic laced through his irises like stars in the sky.

"I still don't like you," I muttered, stepping back as I tried to compose myself. I braced myself, keeping a damper on my emotions. With his blood fresh in me, he'd have greater access.

But not if I didn't feel.

He grinned, a soft chuckle leaving him as he stepped around his desk. "And I still intend to fuck you, Witchling."

"Then I guess we remain at odds in some ways," I said, lifting my bag from the floor and placing it on my shoulder.

"But these odds are so much more fun," he said.

I couldn't help the hint of a smile that took me as I shook my head at him. Turning on my heel, I fled the office and the odd warm feeling climbing up my throat.

Just the blood, I reminded myself.

17

WILLOW

Susannah paced back and forth at the front of the room. In the days since I'd begun attending Hollow's Grove, I'd learned to tune out the tipping and tapping of her bones on the floor. She'd taken to pretending I didn't exist, and I suspected it was out of the knowledge that she didn't know what might come out of my mouth at any given moment.

That *might* have had something to do with calling her an overconfident lesson in bone density when she'd insinuated that I wasn't paying attention.

Sometimes the truth hurt.

"Where does magic come from?" she asked as she paced, her gaze scanning over the faces in our group.

I'd learned that the legacies attended classes together, dependent on age. That the small group of students who surrounded me in every one of my classes came from one of the original bloodlines. Most of them had survived the centuries without issue.

It wasn't lost on me that I seemed to be descended from the only two bloodlines who didn't procreate fast enough to outlast the murders within families. That was just fine with me.

It meant my uncle wouldn't be putting a knife in my back, simply for the fact that I didn't have one.

"The source," Della answered proudly.

"And what is the source, Miss Tethys?" Susannah asked, stopping her pacing to level the Blue with a studious glare.

"It's... it's where magic comes from," she said, shrugging her shoulders as if the why didn't matter.

"It comes from the world around us. It exists in everything. That's why there are so many different manifestations of that magic," I said, kicking back in my chair. I relaxed where the others were too occupied taking notes or staring at the member of the Covenant as if she might grind her bones down on their flesh and make them into her dinner.

"Then how do you explain the Reds?" one of the male witches asked. His blond hair was long, swaying in a single straight layer as he whipped it over his shoulder. His brown eyes were hard on mine as his posture went rigid.

"If you think that sex is unnatural, that's a circumstance of your own self-loathing that I cannot help you with," I said, smiling at him as his jaw clenched.

"Enough, Willow," Susannah snapped.

I didn't say another word, not because she'd told me to be quiet, but because I'd already made my point. I let my lips tip into a smug smile, waiting for the confirmation I knew she would give.

"Desire, lust, and sex are all part of nature, Mr. Peabody."

The Red didn't look my way, his hand gripping his pen a little tighter.

I wasn't certain what the legacies had spent their child-hood doing in the town of Crystal Hollow, but it certainly didn't seem like being even remotely educated was on the list.

"The exact number of houses among the original families was determined by the elements, not us. There were other families that we were forced to leave behind in Salem, even though we understood that it would likely mean they'd suffer the injustice of the witch hunters. Balance is of the utmost importance, and there was only the opportunity for two of each color to come with us. The crystal witches and cosmic witches, the water and fire witches, the air and earth witches, and the life and death witches. We've commonly come to know of them as the sex witches and the necromancers, but they were created to establish balance to Hecate's line," Susannah explained, tossing the apple she held in her fingers into the air. She caught it, and I could just imagine the flesh bruising beneath her hard grip.

Just as she'd done to what the Coven had been meant to be.

"Why was the Hecate line only one family?" I asked, seeking the answer my mother had never been able to provide. Each of the other manifestations of the source had been given two bloodlines, except the original.

"Charlotte Hecate was too strong for her own good. Her ability to channel death and give a twisted sort of life could not be replicated. That kind of power multiplied could have been catastrophic. So we gave her two points of balance to her one, hoping that she would be managed that way," she said, and the words felt like a lie as she spoke them. I didn't doubt there was *some* truth in them, but something else lingered at the back of my mind.

Something I couldn't seem to grasp fully. The Hecate line had already been at a disadvantage with the way she seemed unable to pass her magic onto her family members, even in her life. There was strength in numbers among the other houses, but the Hecate line had only ever had one witch.

When she died, the magic passed on.

Until my aunt. The only possible source for the magic had been my father, and he should have *felt* it even with the bones out of reach. But it wasn't until I came of age that those bones started calling to me.

My father had suspected. He'd sadly been right.

"As dangerous as Charlotte Hecate was in life, the death of her final descendant was a tragedy for the Coven. Her death enabled the Vessels to gain power, making it impossible for us to be rid of them permanently. How do you punish something that does not die? How do you keep it in line when they're too strong to fight and there is no threat to be had that wouldn't take the witch's magic along with it?" Susannah asked, glancing around the room.

"You could burn them," one of the Yellows said, snapping his fingers and forming a tiny flame.

"The Vessel will repair itself, even from the ashes," Susannah said.

"What if you trapped it in a rock?" a White witch asked, toying with the crystals she held in her palm. Her dark lashes fluttered nervously, as if she already knew the answer.

"It can work for a time, but there is very little that can entrap a Vessel for long. They're strong enough to break rock," Susannah answered, and I found my mind wandering to what Gray would think of this conversation.

Of her educating his students on how to harm him.

"I think maybe you're the best one to answer this question, Covenant. After all, you cannot kill that which is already dead," I said, raising a brow as she spun to glare at me from those creepy, empty sockets. I thought I might have seen her bones tip into a smile, if such a thing was possible?

Could you smile when you didn't have a mouth?

I shuddered when Susannah spoke. "The only way to

weaken a Vessel is to deprive it of its food source. Only then can you entrap it in the earth long enough for it to slowly fade into nothing. Without witch's blood to maintain the Vessel, it simply ceases to be, eventually."

"And how do you convince a Vessel not to simply take the blood it needs?" Della asked.

"You can't," I said, turning my gaze to her. There was nothing on this earth that would convince a Vessel not to feed.

I smiled when Susannah kept quiet, but we shared a knowing look. For once, she understood that I knew something that her vows to the sanctity of the Coven had kept her from revealing. She could not incite violence between the witches and Vessels outright.

The only way a witch could keep a Vessel from feeding was to invoke the price of a broken bargain. The price was servitude—the inability to reject the other's demands.

If Gray failed to protect me from harm as promised, his life would belong to me.

Whether I found the bones or not.

18

GRAY

I strode down the stairs of Hollow's Grove, aiming for the Courtyard. One of the witches trailed at my side, her face carefully controlled as she wrung her hands in front of her. Her nerves pulsed off her, and I knew it wasn't unfounded.

Fifty years ago, I'd nearly strangled a witch for delivering similar news.

The witch moved out of the main entryway, not even glancing at me as I followed. I'd not even bothered putting on a shirt when she knocked on my door, needing to see the evidence for myself. It was impossible for such a thing to be occurring all over again.

We'd found the person who'd confessed to the crimes and brought him to justice accordingly.

The Covenant stood in the courtyard, side by side, as they stared at the ground just in front of the trellis that Willow had made an offering to. Fresh life filled the entirety of the space at the very center of the school, leaving absolutely no doubt that *something* had transpired. If Willow hadn't already admitted what she'd done, Iban likely would have.

Especially when I saw what rested on the ground.

Her eyes stared at the skies above, blank and unseeing, as I maneuvered my body over the edge and went through the window. The witch who'd come to inform me of the death stayed behind, pressing her hand to her mouth.

The body of the young witch was half-wrapped in thorny vines. Her arms and legs covered by roses as if the plant could claim her body for itself and pull her into the earth in that very spot. They moved over her skin, writhing and alive in ways I hadn't seen in decades.

I stepped closer to her, recognizing her as one of the students we'd brought from outside Crystal Hollow. She was one of the Thirteen—one of the few students in attendance who did not have a family history within the boundaries of the town.

Few knew the truth of the events that had predated the massacre that killed so many of our numbers. Even fewer knew the gory details of the reality the Thirteen students of that year had faced.

I couldn't recall the witch's name, but I bent down at her side. Reaching forward, I touched a finger to each of her eyelids—drawing them closed. It horrified me to think that none had bothered already, and I looked up to glance at the gathered crowd.

Willow caught my eyes immediately, staring at the body in confusion. I suspected the young witch hadn't seen much death in her life until her mother left her.

"We should close the school. Now," George said, voicing a thought I knew Susannah would not agree with. The Covenant made eye contact with one another, and even Susannah sighed as she shook her head. Her chest fell, her boney body sagging even when there was no air in her body.

Or you know, lungs.

"We will not allow whoever is responsible for this to deter our students from the education they deserve. It must be a copycat, someone who thinks to joke by instilling that terror in the students once again," she said, and I wondered what it would take for her to see the reality.

If this happened once again, there would be no new blood for her to mix with her witches.

"What of Willow? She isn't safe here," George said, glancing toward where the Witchling watched our interaction closely. She growled, the sound rivaling the fiercest of Vessels as she lifted herself over the ledge and into the Courtyard.

She passed by the Covenant, ignoring them entirely as she touched a hand to the vines that had wrapped themselves around the young witch. She pulled at them, muttering beneath her breath in Latin and commanding them to let go of the bounty they'd discovered. The vines obeyed, retreating into the ground slowly, as if they no longer wanted to cause the witch further harm.

"They wouldn't listen to me," a male voice said, and I looked up to stare into the brown eyes of the Bray elder. Suspicion lurked in his gaze as he looked at Willow, as she lifted dirt from the ground and rubbed it into the welts on the dead witch's body. "Interesting that they will listen to you. Almost as if they recognize you."

"That's because they do," Willow said, looking over the rest of the witch. She searched for wounds, I realized, looking for the cause of her death. "I made an offering to this Courtyard when I arrived at Hollow's Grove." She pushed the other woman's blazer away from her chest, wincing when the fabric stuck to her skin.

The blood from the hole in her chest had begun to dry,

sealing the fabric against her. She must have lay here undiscovered for quite some time for that to happen.

As it had been fifty years ago, something had been taken from the witch—something vital. Where her heart should have been was nothing but a gaping hole, and Willow stared into it. The other students who had gathered reacted far differently than she did, shocked gasps filling the courtyard.

But Willow just stared in silence, her gaze remaining fixated when others were driven to look away from the blood and gore. As if she couldn't take her gaze off it. "There's no sign of her heart anywhere," she said, rocking back onto her heels as she finally turned that inquisitive stare away. "What happened to it?"

She touched a gentle, probing finger to the slash marks across the witch's chest, the grooves far too deep to have been made by anything human.

"We haven't found it," Susannah answered, snapping out of her trance and stepping forward. She grasped Willow by the forearm, attempting to drag her to her feet as I fought against the urge to tear her bones off the Witchling.

"Why don't you tell us what you did with it, girl?" Bray asked, crossing his arms over his chest.

"You think I did this?" Willow asked, her voice rising as if she couldn't stop the ripple of shock that stole through her body.

"You made an offering and days later, a witch is dead in the same spot. I do not think that a coincidence," Bray said, glaring at Willow.

She quirked her brow as she rose to her feet, tipping her head to the side in a way that was far more primal than any witch I'd ever seen. Something about the angle made my spine tingle with awareness, with the knowledge that Bray had made a grave mistake.

"If I wanted to kill someone, it wouldn't be a witch I didn't even know," she said, and I watched as she clenched her jaw. "If I kill, I won't be stupid enough to leave the body lying around."

"Enough," Susannah said, sighing as she glared at Iban's uncle.

The elder Bray didn't hesitate to clamp his mouth shut, silencing whatever retort he'd been prepared to deliver. It entertained me greatly that Willow was destined to sit on the Tribunal with him upon completion of her studies at Hollow's Grove, that as the only remaining Madizza witch, she would become his equal immediately upon graduation.

It would serve him right.

"Willow has no motivation for killing one of the Thirteen," Susannah said.

"Perhaps she's killing off those she is in direct competition with, getting rid of anyone who may pose a threat to her interests," Itar Bray said, and the smirk that came over his voice was nothing short of cruel. "Iban was quite cozy with Miss Sanders before you arrived at Hollow's Grove."

He watched Willow, waiting for the moment when her hurt showed, where she crumpled like the jealous schoolgirl he clearly thought her to be. Instead, she jerked her arm away from the Covenant, stepping toward Itar until she stopped directly before him and glared up into his smug face. He had the common sense to falter in that look, his mouth twitching as she smiled.

"What on earth makes you think I give a single fuck who Iban spent time with before he knew me?" She pressed up onto her toes, leaning closer as I fought back the rumble of laughter that fought to break free from my chest.

I didn't know what I'd expected when the Covenant sent me to retrieve the sole remaining Madizza witch, but it definitely hadn't been Willow with earth in her heart but *fire* in her blood.

"Are you not jealous that your prospective mate was cozy with another woman so recently?" Bray asked.

"I think I'm far more concerned with your preoccupation with my love life," Willow said, backing away with a grimace. She turned away, leaving his question unanswered for a moment as she moved to pass Susannah and George. "But to answer your question, no. I am not bothered. Unlike some here, I know it's far more fun when you're willing to share."

I choked. The look on Bray's face as she strode past me was nothing short of incredulous, and Willow left us behind without a second thought.

"Follow her," Susannah ordered, and it took me gathering myself for a moment to remember to swallow before my sharp laughter followed after the Witchling. "The school is no longer safe for Willow. Maintaining her safety is now our greatest priority."

"Shouldn't you be concerned about the other *eleven* students remaining who may be slaughtered and harvested for organs at any given time?" I asked, but I'd already turned to follow after Willow. The Covenant didn't need to know of the bargain we'd struck, or that I had a very vested interest in keeping Willow safe from harm because of it.

"The other eleven students are not the last of an entire bloodline. You know what happens with each one that is lost." Susannah's voice followed after me. It was not lost on me that Willow would not welcome my presence in her room.

It also wasn't lost on me that Willow could do whatever she wanted. She could commit nearly any crime within the walls of Hollow's Grove, and she would survive the aftermath.

The Coven's desperation to restore her blood had created the perfect weapon to bring about the downfall of everything they'd created—corrupted. She would either be their undoing or our salvation, and the most satisfying part of it all was that they wouldn't be able to do anything to stop her when she took everything from them.

She wouldn't settle for anything less.

19

WILLOW

I shuddered. The voice that surrounded me was so unfamiliar. It took me moments to realize it wasn't mine, though it came from me. The husky, feminine sound that clawed its way up my throat wasn't mine. I pressed a hand to my throat, attempting to trap the foreign sound there; to keep it from making the air around me feel as if it burned with the fires of Hell itself.

A woman wandered the halls, her deep ebony hair flowing to her waist as she moved as if in slow motion. She held a piece of onyx in her palm, her fingers wrapped so tightly around it that I thought it might pierce her skin. I recognized her from the photos my father had shown me, from the portraits he'd commissioned in her memory. His home hadn't been much, a cabin hidden in the woods to help protect him from the prying eyes of the Coven that would kill him if they found out he existed. But what little money he'd had, he spent on those portraits, on preserving the memory of the sister he loved more than anything.

Her eyes sparkled in a light blue. The color was unnatural, making me think of the coldest ice on the lake when it shimmered in the moonlight. There was an almost purple tint to it, the same way *my one eye tended toward the color of lilac. Her forehead was twisted into a frown, her lips parting on a silent scream. She turned to look over her shoulder, dropping the onyx at whatever she saw behind her.*

I saw nothing, stepping into the darkness of the hallway in an attempt to reach her. I followed after her as she curved around the corner, glancing over her shoulder as if she were being chased. I couldn't see anything, but I felt it.

The growl that shook the floor, that made the windows rattle in the walls.

Loralei clutched something at her hip, and it was only then that I realized what the small, black pouch must have been. It was only then that I heard the call of the bones, heard them whispering at me to come closer.

To take what was mine.

It was unassuming, looking like any tarot bag or a bag of stones and bones used for scrying. The chain that wrapped around her hip was a bright, shimmering gold that sparkled against the black of her school uniform.

"I don't have what you seek," she said into the nothingness. Her stare remained fixed at the end of the hall, her body flinching with each step that invisible force took.

I faltered, only barely catching myself with a hand pressed against the wall. The next step closer nearly took me off my feet. The air around me plunged into cold so harsh it burned my heated skin, and it was then that I could see the breath before my face.

I gasped, my breath rattling in my chest. I couldn't even see what was coming for her, could do nothing to stop it from happening all over again.

"Loralei!" I called in my panic. Her head snapped to the side sharply, that eerie blue stare landing on mine. Her eyes widened, as if she recognized me. She dropped her hand away from the bones that gave her power, standing still as she held my gaze.

"Run, Charlotte. Run!" she screamed as I stepped toward her.

It was just a dream, I reminded myself. I wasn't in my body, not truly.

A burst of red filled my vision as whatever it was that I couldn't see struck. Her chest exploded with three deep slash marks, her blood splattering all over my face. Her hand touched my arm, the warmth of her seeping out from me. Her face fell as she stared at me, as horror filled her vision. She dropped to her knees as the ground beneath her shook, as the thing came a step closer.

"Wake up, Willow," she said, her voice soft as her eyes rolled back.

Pain tore through my back, setting my skin on fire as I fought to pull her to her feet.

"Wake up!" she screamed.

The windows at the end of the hall shattered with her voice. Her panic took me, claiming me for itself. I fell as the ground shook once more, waiting for the impact on my knees.

But it never came.

I woke, gasping for breath. I bolted out of bed, barely making it to the bathroom before my stomach purged. My back burned as I shoved my hair back out of my face, the skin splitting as I curled forward. Clutching the edge of the toilet, I waited for the heaves to end.

As soon as I could, I pushed to my feet and went for the mirror above the sink. Rinsing out my mouth, I hesitated to turn to look at my spine. It had only been a dream, and the pain I felt surely had to be a figment of the fear I felt upon waking.

But my shirt clung to my skin, feeling wet as it shifted. I pulled it over my head, moving slowly as I twisted to look at it in the mirror.

Three slash marks in the odd shape of a triangle marred the ink of my tattoo, cutting through the black shading of the curving branches of the tree tattoo that crawled up my spine. Blood trickled down from them, sliding down the back of my ribcage.

I pressed my hands into the countertop, curling my fingers around the edge as I stared at the frenzied look on my face. I'd dreamt of my aunt, and she'd known my name.

Not at first, having somehow confused me for the witch who'd died centuries before she was born. I clutched my head in my hands, bending over the sink as my stomach pitched once again. It didn't make any sense. There was *no* logic to anything like this.

My bedroom door slammed as I spun to face the bathroom door, grabbing the stone soap dispenser in hand and preparing to use it as a makeshift weapon. There were no plants in the bathroom, something I would need to remedy immediately.

The hulking form of a male filled the doorway between the bedroom and the bathroom. His face was shadowed, his back cutting off all traces of the light coming from the windows behind him. My body hummed with energy, preparing for a fight.

"You're bleeding," Gray said finally, stepping forward.

Dropping the soap dispenser, I hurried to grab a towel off the rack. I wrapped it around my torso, shielding my breasts from view as he found the light switch with familiar ease.

"It's nothing. Just my period," I lied, deciding that the humiliation of openly discussing such a thing would be far better than admitting what I'd seen. There were some things that were just not normal for a witch. Being harmed by a dream was one of them. Only the Whites and Purples had the gift of sight within their bloodline.

"How am I supposed to uphold my end of the bargain if

you aren't honest with me, Witchling?" he said, his nose twitching as he sniffed the air.

"As you can see, I'm perfectly fine. Get out," I snapped, keeping my back turned away from him. I didn't want him to see the marks, not understanding what they meant. How could a dream hurt me? How could it mark me in my waking body?

"I can smell your blood. Show me," Gray ordered, stepping forward. His fingers grasped the top of the towel, as if he meant to pull it away from my body. I didn't know if the thought of being half-naked in front of him was worse than revealing the twisted injury on my back.

I wasn't sure I wanted to find out.

I let go of the towel, anyway, feeling it fall around my skin. Only his fingers grasping it held it aloft as it parted to reveal my breasts. His gaze dropped to them as his face stilled, taking in the swell of them. I *felt* the moment that gaze shifted slightly lower, grazing over my nipples and moving to my stomach. It was like a tangible thing, slithering over me like the serpent in the Garden of Eden.

"I can think of far more interesting ways to spend the night," I murmured, stepping forward.

His eyes darted to my face; his breathing carefully controlled as I touched my finger to his chest. His shirt was partially unbuttoned, revealing a thin line of skin at the top. He wore no tie, no suit jacket. Only the thin white fabric of his shirt separated me from getting to his bare skin.

I slid a single finger into the gap, brushing it over his cool flesh.

"You're playing a very dangerous game, little witch," he muttered, his face tense as he stared down at me.

I pursed my lips into a pout, a slow breath leaving me. "Promises, promises, Demon," I argued.

He moved quickly, grasping me by the elbow and turning me forward so suddenly I barely had time to catch myself on the vanity. The harshness in the movement stole the breath from my lungs, leaving me panting as I leaned forward over the sink. He shifted behind me, placing a single hand to my uninjured shoulder. He gripped it, holding me still as I fought to push back against him.

That other hand brushed my hair over my shoulder. The tenderness of the motion made my heart clench, and I bared my teeth like a hissing wildcat. I'd rather he be rough and brutal as he inspected my injury.

I'd rather outright hatred than false affection.

His hand stilled on my flesh, making goosebumps rise to the surface. "Where did you get this?" he asked. His fingers resumed their motion, touching the wounds gently and sending a flame of agony through me.

I whimpered, grasping the edge of the sink more firmly.

"In a dream," I admitted, huffing a laugh. Certain he wouldn't believe me, that he'd think I'd been attacked while I slept and was too oblivious to realize it.

"Tell me," he said instead, reaching around me to grab a clean washcloth off the counter. He ran it under warm water, wringing it mostly dry before he stood beside me and gently wiped the blood away from the wound.

I explained what I remembered, the vision of my aunt. I refused to mention the name she'd called me first, knowing that any connection to Charlotte would only call attention to myself. I lied, telling him I'd never seen the woman before in my life. I'd left off the details of the bones strapped to her hip, but I told him the truth of the creature who'd been stalking her.

Of the fact that he remained entirely unseen.

"You've seen it before," I said, turning my head to look at him.

He nodded solemnly, turning me so that I could watch as his fingers traced the marks. They'd already healed into old wounds somehow, the skin scarred instead of raw. The pain still pulsed through me as if the wounds were fresh, sensitive to the touch despite how gentle he tried to be.

"It's called the devil's eye," he explained, his voice solemn as he said the words. "It enables Him to watch you more closely."

I swallowed, looking at him over my shoulder once more as I tore my gaze away from the rough slash marks. "Well, get rid of it!"

He chuckled, but the sound held no humor whatsoever. "A Vessel cannot undo His actions," he explained, grasping my chin and turning me to face him. "But perhaps you can explain exactly what He would want with you, Witchling."

20

WILLOW

I swallowed, my body tensing as he leaned down. I couldn't tear my eyes off the side of his face as he leaned forward, touching his lips to the skin beneath the mark. Those steely eyes flashed to mine, a sudden predatory movement as he held my gaze in the mirror. His tongue slid out of his mouth slowly, the warmth of it pressing against my flesh.

I watched in horror as he dragged it up and over the mark, a slow glide of wet warmth that took the last of the blood from my skin. A shudder rolled through me when the hint of a fang sparkled in the dim lighting.

"How in the Hell should I know?" I asked, crossing my arms over my chest. "It isn't like I have Him on speed dial."

"Has anyone ever told you that mouth is going to get you into trouble one of these days?" Gray asked, touching a hand to the back of my shoulder. Pain rippled through the mark, as if it protested the touch of anyone who hadn't put it there.

"It's possible," I whispered.

That hand slid forward, curving over the top of my shoulder and wrapping around to the front of my throat. He squeezed lightly, watching goosebumps rise on my skin in response with an arrogant smirk. He leaned in, placing his mouth just beside my ear as he trailed his hand farther and snagged my bottom lip with his thumb.

"The next time you lie to me, I'm likely to make it so that you cannot speak at all."

"Good luck with that," I said, huffing a laugh against his thumb as I pulled back. It pressed my ass into his thighs, the bare skin of my back touching his chest and sending a jolt of pain through me. "Unless you intend to gag me, you're unlikely to be able to shut me up."

"You would definitely be gagging, Witchling," he growled, and the bolt that shot through me was one of shock.

Oh.

Swallowing, I forced that moment to pass and slid back into the carefully controlled persona. The seducer who would be anything, do anything, if it meant finding those bones.

"Promises, promises," I murmured, nipping at his thumb.

His responding growl rumbled in my ear, tightening things low in my stomach that I didn't even begin to understand. It shouldn't have been attractive to have him growl at the thought of gagging me on his cock. He pulled me tighter into his chest, pressing his hard length into the small of my back.

I swallowed, arching my back at the touch.

"If I bent you over the sink right now and fucked you, you'd welcome every minute of it, wouldn't you?" he asked, but he made no move to do just that.

I couldn't decide if the swoop in my belly was appreciation or disappointment when he spun me to face him, backing me toward the bare wall beside the bathtub. I didn't answer his question, couldn't find the words to respond.

I knew what I should say, knew what my body wanted me to say as I tipped my head back and stared up at him through my lashes. But I couldn't force myself to acknowledge it, couldn't give him that satisfaction, even though my duty demanded it of me.

"A girl has needs," I said, shrugging as if the person filling them was inconsequential.

His lip peeled back to reveal his fangs as he glared down at me like the problem I was.

"Love," he murmured, his voice a soft caress as he leaned forward.

His forearm rested on the wall above my head as he raised his free hand to cup my cheek with mock tenderness. It shifted to my throat once again, pushing back until my head smacked against the wall lightly. He kept his grip there, pinning me as I squirmed beneath the hold. Raising my hands, I clawed at the bare skin of his forearm.

"What did I tell you about lying to me?"

He restricted my breathing just enough that I wheezed when I tried to speak, reminding me that if we came to blows, I would lose. It wouldn't just be the opportunity to seduce him that would be lost, but I also didn't stand a chance of fighting him one-on-one without any plants around me. Whoever had decided putting witches in a building was the best way was a fucking moron, because I belonged to the woods—to the gardens and *anywhere* but here.

My only hope was the stone. I glanced at the tile floor out of the corner of my eye, dropping a single arm to guide it up.

My focus was gone in the next moment, when Gray seemed to realize what I intended. He moved quickly, my eyes snapping to his face as it crashed down on mine. His lips were on me immediately, bruising in intensity as he devoured my mouth.

His fangs brushed against my lips, tearing open the flesh as he pried me open for him. I obeyed, parting for him and letting his tongue surge inside. My hands abandoned his fore-arms, pressing against his chest. I only pushed for a moment, protesting the touch we both knew I wanted.

That I shouldn't want but would be lying to deny.

Then they curled into his shirt, grasping it and wrinkling the fabric to pull him closer. His groan came from low in his throat, filling my ear, and his body pressed tighter until I felt his cock against my stomach.

"Fuck, you're impossible," he said, pulling back just enough to mumble the words against my mouth.

I growled at him, reaching up to bury a hand in his hair. The dark, inky strands were soft in my fingers, sliding through as I gripped them harshly and dragged his mouth back to mine. Each sweep of his tongue against mine was a brand, a claim of ownership I should have fought against.

Instead, I sank deeper into his touch, pulling him where I wanted him as his body shifted. He pulled back just enough, sliding the hand at my throat down until he brushed the skin of my breast. He swallowed my startled gasp, smiling into me as he kneaded the flesh. Pressing harshly, squeezing and testing the weight of it, he chuckled as he found my nipple and ran his fingers over it.

I jolted in his grip, a strangled moan escaping me.

"Do you think any others will make you feel like this?" he asked, brushing my hardened nipple again. "Your hips are grinding on me, just begging for me to fuck you into the wall."

I resisted the urge to protest, to push him off. Especially when his hand abandoned my breast, drifting down over my stomach. I felt him against the thin fabric of my sleep shorts, pressing the jersey into me as he kicked my legs apart.

My eyes rolled back in my head as he found my pussy with expert precision, barely a whisper of a touch over my heated skin.

"Tell me to stop," he said, sinking his teeth into my bottom lip. His eyes remained open, holding mine as my breath came in a shuddering pant. "Tell me you don't want this."

My mouth parted with the need to say it, but the words wouldn't come. They couldn't, not when he pressed his hand tighter to my flesh. The cloth of my shorts rubbed against me, his fingers circling my clit slowly.

"I hate you," I muttered, pulling his hair harder.

He chuckled, pressing his mouth to mine gently as I tossed my head back. "I don't give a fuck about that. All that matters to me is how pretty you'll look writhing on my cock."

I gasped as he slipped his fingers under the edge of my shorts, the coolness of his skin touching me. There was nothing between us, nothing to separate us from the way he felt against me. He resumed his work on my clit, circling it as I lost the ability to breathe.

This was how I died.

I was going to come, and I didn't even care what that said about me.

"Fuck," I whimpered, blinding light filling the edges of my vision when he moved; his teeth grazing the side of my neck.

He stopped, his fingers stilling on my pussy.

"What are you doing?" I asked, wincing at the tiny pinch of his fangs as he bit down into my skin. He groaned at the snack, drawing my blood into his mouth as my hips moved against him.

Seeking the pressure he'd offered, searching for my pleasure.

He withdrew his teeth, his mouth redder than it had been before, and stared at me. Removing his hand from my shorts, he raised his fingers to his mouth. Those steely eyes drifted closed as he moaned, pulling them free and staring down at me.

"You can come when you tell me what I want to know."

My mouth dropped open in shock. Surely, he couldn't mean—

"Fuck you," I snapped.

I'd finish the job myself. The arrogant fucking prick. I let go of his hair, pushing against his shoulders to get him out of my way. I slid my hand over my stomach when he stepped back, slipping it into my shorts as his eyes narrowed. Arching my back, I let him see the moment I touched myself.

"Willow," he said, and the sound of my name in his voice was different. It was soft, soothing, a comfort when I wanted nothing but anger. He moved forward, grasping my wrist with his hand as I stared up at him.

The moment my eyes met his, I realized my mistake.

His pupils had bled to black, darkness consuming the blue of his stare. "From this moment until I release you, the only way you will be able to orgasm will be with me. My touch. My mouth. My cock. Your own touch will not satisfy you, nor will the touch of any other person. There is only me."

The words washed over me, cooling my skin as the compulsion sank inside of me. I reached up to touch my mother's necklace, shaking my head to deny the way the words had penetrated. "I have my amulet—"

"You also have my blood," he said, stepping back with a smirk. "Even your amulet cannot protect you from me entirely now."

I swallowed, glaring up at him as he made to leave the bathroom. "Why not just compel me to tell you the truth then?!" I demanded, watching as the black faded from his gaze. I winced as I wrapped my arms around my chest and covered my breasts from the scathing blue of his eyes.

He shrugged, tucking his hands into his pants pockets as he stared at me over his shoulder. "My way is much more fun."

21

WILLOW

I walked forward, keeping my head bowed as I followed my roommates in a line. They did the same, echoing the respect for the dead as we made our way down the steps to the front entry of Hollow's Grove. The sun seemed far too bright as we approached the bottom of the stairs, moving toward the six doors that had been thrown wide open to allow us all to funnel onto the front lawn.

The line extended around the corner, curving toward the back of the school. I'd wandered there occasionally after classes when I needed a moment to myself, and I knew that the back of the school was home to the cliffs overlooking the sea. Before we came to that though, the sprawling remnants of what had once been a beautiful, glorious flower garden separated the school from the tiny patch of land designated for burials.

Only the Greens would be buried in the earth, allowing their bodies to rot freely and the land to reclaim what belonged to it. I didn't know what magic the witch who'd died had called her own, having never had classes with the others of the Thirteen. As a legacy, I'd been strictly kept away from them, despite being brought here as one of them.

I didn't really belong to the legacies, but neither did I belong to the new students. Crystal Hollow and I had far too much history between us for me to ever be a bright-eyed first year, openly gazing upon the magic I'd been forced to keep secret. I was far too cynical for that, and I knew just how many bones the Coven kept hidden in the closets of Hollow's Grove.

I followed Della as she walked through the path; the gardens at our sides withered and dying. There was no life to be found here, and I didn't understand why no one at the school thought that unusual. To be a witch and to take no issue with the world dying around us...

It was unfathomable.

When my magic was fully restored, I'd come and make another offering. I couldn't so soon, not when I knew the garden would take it all once again. Last time, I'd been stumbling when I got up from the ground after the vines finally released me.

I suspected I wouldn't get up at all if I tried to restore the garden. The level of starvation that awaited me made me uncertain the plants would be able to stop once they started.

Della joined the circle that surrounded the freshly dug grave, the witches of Hollow's Grove standing in a single-file barrier between the grave and the rest of the school. The Vessels lingered just beyond, having come to pay their respects to the student taken too soon, but remaining far away enough to allow us to grieve our own.

I searched for Gray without meaning to, my gaze sweeping over the Vessels who all dressed so similarly. Whether it had happened before the extinction of the Hecate line or after, they'd chosen to take the color black as their own. Most wore suits day in and day out, but even those who favored more casual black clothing had dressed up for the occasion.

I found him, my body going still when I found his eyes on me. The rush of heat that filled me was indecent, making me shift on my feet as I remembered the feeling of his mouth on mine, of his hand between my legs. I'd spent most of the night seeking release, desperately trying to find it without him and praying that his compulsion wouldn't work.

All I'd done was aggravate myself, jumping into a cold shower to try to cool my overheated skin. I'd wanted to throttle him, to tear out his throat for leaving me like *that*.

Now I just wanted to fuck him, all sense of hatred disappearing from me with just his molten stare on mine. My thighs rubbed together as I shifted again, realizing what I was doing. Seeking pressure, seeking touch.

At a fucking funeral.

I shook my head, snapping myself out of it as my stare settled into a glare. He chuckled, his lips tipping up as he looked away. I let my gaze wander toward the witch to be buried, to the Covenant, who stood beside her. My mouth dropped open at the sight of the casket, of the wooden box that would separate her from the earth that needed her so desperately.

"Why is she in a casket?" I whispered, looking to Della at my side.

She turned her head to look at me slowly, her brow furrowing in confusion as a concerned smile tipped her lips up. "What do you mean, why is she in a casket? What else would she be in?" she asked.

"Greens are meant to be buried in the earth. Not in a box," I argued, my gaze snapping back to where the Covenant awaited. George found my stare, his jaw clenching as he seemed to realize just how horrified I was.

"Oh, well, she wasn't a Green. Quincy was a White," she answered, shrugging as if that explained it. My horror only grew, my eyes flashing to the box that contained a white witch. She should have been laid out upon a bed of sacred stones, allowing them to reabsorb her into the source.

"This is wrong," I whispered, and I realized that Margot and the others had started looking at me in concern.

I ignored them. Taking a step forward, I prepared to approach the Covenant. I sincerely doubted they would appreciate my interfering, but I couldn't stand there and do nothing. I couldn't watch while they kept a witch separate from her magic and her ancestors.

A hand grasped me by the elbow, pulling me back. My body seemed to recognize exactly who it was that dared to touch me, freezing in place as I looked to the spot where he'd stood only a moment before. Gray was no longer there, and as I shifted to look over my shoulder at him, I found those steely eyes staring down at me in warning.

"Not now, Witchling," he said, his voice dropping low as he tugged me back.

I tried not to show any reaction, tried not to give into the way my body reacted without thought. It was as if it knew that he was the only one who could bring me pleasure now, and it wanted to press into him and writhe like a cat.

Traitorous bitch.

"This is wrong," I said, repeating my words from earlier.

"That may be, but part of bringing change is knowing when to act and when to remain silent. You cannot restore the old ways if you piss Susannah off enough that she kills you on the spot," he said, growling his warning into my ear.

I was vaguely aware of the way the Coven's eyes came to us, watching our interaction as if it were abnormal for the two kinds to mix in the light of day.

The cover of darkness usually disguised those stolen moments.

"You cannot expect me to let them condemn her soul to this," I whispered, my heart cracking in my chest. To be unable to connect with the source and her ancestors, to suffer through a Christian burial and afterlife....

"Approach the Covenant privately, if you must, but do not be foolish enough to challenge them so publicly," he said. Even I knew the logic to his words, but my bottom lip trembled at the thought of what I would have to do.

Another scar, another stain on my soul. It may have been sold to the devil long before I was born, but that didn't mean I had to earn it myself on top of it.

"I can't do this," I said, shaking my head as my eyes burned with tears.

"You tasked me with protecting you. Let me do that," he said, releasing my arm. His hand slid down over the fabric of my deep green blazer, his fingers threading through mine until he held my hand. I stared down at it in shock, at the way we somehow fit together.

Nobody outside my mother and brother had ever held my hand before. I bit back tears at the reminder of Ash's little hand clutching mine when we'd stared down into our mother's casket not long ago, swallowing down my need to speak. Finding the bones and finding a way to get back to the brother I missed more than anything had to be my priority—even if I'd wear her soul on my conscience for the rest of my life.

My eyes traveled up over his torso and chest, back to his eyes, where he held my gaze. The burial began as George started to speak, invoking the elements that had long since turned their back on the Coven. I hoped they ignored his call, hoped he was humiliated for what he would do to the white witch who was to be buried against her nature.

They didn't, but for the strongest amongst us, the light breeze that blew against my face was a mockery of what it should have been.

The powers Charlotte had granted to the Covenant faded along with the rest of them. So what did they hope to gain by turning their backs on our ways?

A few of the Grays lifted her casket with the air, lowering her into the hole in the ground that would become her unwilling tomb. Her prison in the afterlife.

I closed my eyes and swore to find a way to make it right. I'd free her when I could. I glanced around the cemetery grounds, studying each grave marker with a new horror dawning on me.

I'd free them all.

22

WILLOW

I waved my hand in front of the Tribunal doors, smiling slightly when the mechanisms shifted and allowed me to part them. The Covenant may not allow a witch to take her place on the council that ruled our people until she completed her education, but that didn't mean the magic here did not recognize me for what I was.

More than one of those empty seats belonged to me.

I stepped through the doors as they spread, moving to the room where the Tribunal convened when they had matters to discuss. It was empty save for Susannah and George, standing at the center of the circle and discussing something quietly.

"Willow," George said, his voice far more polite than the scathing scowl I imagined Susannah leveled me with. "Is everything all right?"

"No. Everything is far from all right," I snapped. My hands clenched and unclenched at my sides, unable to contain the fury even as I *knew* this topic wasn't one I could approach with anger. Far too much was riding on making them understand.

He sighed, hanging his skull forward for a moment as he shoved his finger bones into the pockets of his black robe.

"Your mother taught you the old ways of burial, I presume?" he asked, but Susannah ignored the conversation in favor of repositioning herself. She didn't go to her throne, but moved until she stood in front of the dais, with the threat of it in the background.

As if it meant a fucking thing to me. I'd burn it to ash before I allowed her to continue to corrupt the witches of Crystal Hollow.

"George, will you give me a moment alone with my granddaughter?" she asked.

The other member of the Covenant nodded, slipping through the doors to their private space within the school.

"You're missing a few greats before that *granddaughter*," I said, my lips twisting with disgust. There was no remorse upon her face, not even a hint of an apology for what she'd done to that witch.

For what she'd taken from her.

"It hardly matters when you and I are all that remain. We are not as distant as most in our circumstance would be," she said, clasping her hands in front of her as she studied me.

"I am glad of that distance. It shames me to have any relation to you at all. What you're doing—"

"Is for the good of the Coven," she said, tipping her head to the side. It was eerie how her bones could convey so much emotion. If she had skin, I could just imagine her upper lip curling in disgust. "Something I would not expect someone your age to understand."

"How could this be for the good of the Coven? The earth is dying around you, and you're too stupid to see it! If that is happening to the earth, imagine what is happening to the crystals? To the stars and the air around us? All of those things *need* offerings. They need our bodies to be returned to them when we die. You're weakening the very people Charlotte

Hecate tasked you with protecting at all costs," I said, snapping as my eyes burned with unshed tears.

As much as I hated to cry when I was sad, the rage cries were the absolute worst. They hinted at what I assumed some perceived as weakness, when all I wanted was to commit murder.

Her chest sagged as she took a step toward me. One of those boned hands raised, touching the side of my face and cupping my cheek in a moment of appalling affection.

"You are so young. You don't understand the ways of the world yet, Willow. Let me guide you."

I laughed, taking a step back. "I will never be like you. I won't turn my back on the way magic is meant to be used the way you have."

She let her hand drop, clasping it in front of her once again. "Without the Hecate line, the Vessels have far more power than they should. We have no way to kill them, while the witches of the Coven are very mortal. They live and they die, and as we saw with the young witch last night, they're very capable of being murdered."

"But what does that have to do with starving the source? What can you possibly hope to achieve by making the witches weaker?" I asked, my frustration rising as I stared at her.

"As we weaken, so do they. They feed on us. The source sustains their vessels, but they can't access it directly. They can only touch the magic through our blood, Willow. If we no longer have that magic in our blood, then there is nothing to keep them alive," she said, and her bones clacked together as she shifted her hands. Her jaw spread in what I thought was meant to be a smile.

"But we'll no longer have magic," I whispered, stumbling back a step as her words reached me, as they penetrated the haze of my anger.

"Some of us will. Vessels are forbidden from feeding on the Tribunal. They practice the old ways in secret, to keep the masses from accessing the source so efficiently. The Tribunal remains strong because they must, and when the time comes, we will bring in a new era of witches. We will make a new bargain if we must. One that does not involve those parasites who survive off our suffering," she said, a note of wonder in her voice.

"And what happens to the rest of us when you strike that new bargain? We lose our magic?" I asked, throwing my hand to the side to gesture back to the main part of the school.

"You'll be fine, Willow. You are part of this Tribunal even if you are not yet finished with your schooling. You, or your child, will be a part of the new age of witches," she said, stepping forward to take my hands in hers. Her bones were rough from centuries of use, of being unprotected against the elements.

"This is why you've allowed your line to dwindle. All this time, you've known it doesn't matter. One is enough for you, because it's all you plan to take into your new world," I said, the breath catching in my lungs.

"And you will continue in that tradition, giving birth to a single daughter so that you never have to know the pain of losing a child," she said, pressing our hands forward. I shook out of her grip, flinching back when she touched the fabric of my shirt where it covered my stomach.

"I won't have any part of this," I whispered, taking a step away from her. "You're going to kill them, aren't you? Every last one of them. What is the point in educating them at all? Why bother?"

"Our people do not know these plans. If they were to discover them, all we would achieve is panic and rebellion. This school remains simply because it must," she explained, turning and pacing around the circle. She walked around me, her stride slow and relaxed as she shifted her hands to her spine and rested them on the curve of her pelvis.

"You made a mistake telling me," I explained, scoffing at her certainty that I wouldn't tell everyone what I knew.

That I wouldn't tell Gray.

We might have had a common goal in eliminating the Vessels, but I would never sacrifice an entire Coven to do it.

"You will tell no one, because you know as well as I do that the reality of this secret will tear this Coven in two. The Vessels will go to war with the witches, and we will not win. You'll only expedite their deaths," she said, stopping at my side. From the corner of my eye, the sun shone in the windows behind the thrones, making the dull white of her bones shine brighter. "One day, you will understand. The survival of the Coven is more important than any individual life."

"This is not an individual life!" I yelled, snapping my head to meet her stare. "This is the life of an entire Coven. This is condemning the souls of our people to Hell because you deny them their death rite."

Her hand shot forward, grasping me by the chin. The tips of her finger bones dug into my skin, sinking into the flesh as she held me still. Blood welled from where she cut me, dripping along my skin as I scowled at her.

"It is a sacrifice that must be made," she warned, her voice dropping lower as it filled with magic. She thrust her arm forward, her fingers releasing me in the same moment. I was weightless for a moment, time seeming to suspend as I watched Susannah get farther and farther from me.

My body struck the stone floor, knocking the air from my lungs as I gasped. I coughed, waiting for that breath to return as I writhed on the floor in pain.

Fuck.

I rolled over, getting my hands beneath me. The vines on the Bray throne writhed in response, looking as if they wanted to interfere. To help.

But they couldn't strike the Covenant. No magic could touch them, a gift that had been given to keep them from being struck by errant members of their Coven. Susannah's foot snuck out from beneath her robes, her toe bones catching me in the shoulder and pushing me to my back.

I wheezed as I fought for breath, feeling as if something inside of me had been broken. Pain tore through me as she placed that foot on top of my chest, pressing me down into the stone as I glared up at her.

"You will remember your place."

"I've never been very good at that," I said, my breath a raspy gurgle as moisture filled my mouth.

She removed her foot from my chest, squatting beside me as her hand wrapped around the front of my throat. Pushing down until the pressure became too much, she stared at my mouth.

"I may need you alive, but I do not need you to be awake, Willow. You would do well to remember that the next time you think to question me," she warned, those fingers clawing at my throat and tearing it open.

"I hope you burn," I rasped, raising a hand to grab her wrist.

I punched her ulna and radius, taking too much joy in the way she reared back as her bone *cracked*. Her fingers tore across the front of my throat, threatening to do more damage than I could survive. She spread them at the last moment, seeming to realize how close she was to losing the last of her bloodline.

"Did your mother tell you of the deep sleep, Willow?" she asked, cradling her cracked bone as she stared at it in confusion. It was as if she'd never been hurt, as if none had dared to strike her. "You will live, trapped within the realm of dreams, until I decide to wake you. I suppose if Iban could get past the... distasteful aspect of breeding you while you're unconscious, it would be a far simpler way to get you to do the one thing that is expected of you."

I swallowed. "You're disgusting."

"I suppose if he isn't up to the task, I can find someone else who will be. It hardly matters who the father is in the end. Your bloodline is strong enough, regardless," she said, moving toward me once more. She stared down at me as I pushed myself to sit, cradling my torso as I wrestled the pained grunt that fought to escape.

I scrambled back, attempting to put distance between us as she reached for me. I had no doubt that if she laid her hand on me, I wouldn't wake again. I would remain in slumber, and once I'd given her what she wanted, she'd get rid of me.

"Touch her again, and I will tear your skull from your spine, Susannah," Gray said, his voice deep and menacing. George stood beside him, wringing his hands in front of him as Susannah snapped her head to face them.

"George," she whispered, her voice cruel.

"You go too far in this, Susannah. This is too far," he said, glancing at Gray where he stood beside him.

The Vessel strode forward, coming to my side and glaring at my ancestor.

"She is a member of my Coven, and I will do what I want with her," she said, raising her chin as he bent down beside me.

He slid his arms beneath me, lifting me as he straightened his body.

I gasped as pain filled my torso, and the deep set to Gray's scowl made me want to wither on the spot.

"Like Hell, you will. This one is mine, and you know it as well as I do," he growled, and I was in too much pain to question those words. "Do what you want with the rest of your witches, but the next time you *touch* her, I will rain Hell upon you. You will have violated *my* right. What do you think He would do if he discovered that, Covenant?" he asked.

I watched as George nodded, pleading with his other half. "He's right, Susannah. You let your anger get the best of you. If I hadn't stopped you—"

"Shut up, George," she snapped, turning and waving a hand at Gray. "Get her out of my sight then and tell her to stay out of my way."

Gray didn't hesitate, striding for the doors of the Tribunal rooms. I laid my head on his shoulder, taking comfort for a single moment as my torso throbbed with the bite of sharp pain. He may have only intervened because of his promise to protect me, but that didn't matter now.

All that mattered for now was the fact that I was awake.

23

GRAY

*H*er arm hung limply from her body, as if it exhausted her too much to maintain her position and continue holding her ribs. I had a feeling one was broken, and I knew I had yet another fight on my hands. Given what I'd already done with the little bit of power I held over her from my blood in her body, the likelihood of Willow willingly accepting more of it would be slim.

She'd do it anyway, even if I had to pry her mouth open while she slept.

The scent of her blood appealed to me, but in the face of the pain that consumed her, I couldn't push past my rage that Susannah had harmed her long enough to think of my own hunger or desire.

One of the other Vessels moved in front of us, racing to the door to my chambers. He pulled it open, closing it behind us as I stepped into my office. I bypassed my desk and the couch, going straight for my bed.

One of the housekeepers had already been here, making my bed after I'd stepped out for the funeral service. I'd tried to keep my eye on Willow after the Grays had finished using their magic to bury the casket, but she'd slipped out the moment I let her out of my sight.

The witchling had more bravery in her pinky finger than most had in their entire body, going after the Covenant like that.

I sighed as I lowered her to the bed, dread filling me when her head lolled to the side slowly.

"Willow," I said, grasping her cheeks in my hand. I tapped my finger against her high cheekbone, waiting for her to respond. "What hurts?"

She lifted a hand, grimacing as she fought to push her blazer out of the way. I pulled her to sit, scowling when she gasped in pain. The twist to her face set everything in me on fire, making warmth fill my veins for the first time in centuries.

I'd already hated the Covenant with a passion from Hell.

Now I'd make sure that when Susannah died, it would happen very, very slowly.

I helped Willow out of the blazer, then tossed it to the side and lowered her back to the mattress. She didn't even protest the fact that I'd brought her to my own bed, laying her in my space when I could have brought her to her own room. It would have been easier in the end. Her bed was far closer to the Tribunal rooms than mine, but I needed her in my bed for this. Needed her in my space where I could keep an eye on her while she recovered.

She touched her shirt, tugging at the fabric to pull it free from the high waist of her skirt. I helped, frenzied hands tearing it free and pulling until the buttons popped down the center. They flung through the air, and she didn't fight when it revealed the black lace of her bra.

There would be little point, given I'd seen it all the night before. Touched it.

I shoved the fabric to the side, running my hand over the bruise slowly forming on her side.

"Don't touch it!" she screamed, swatting my hand away frantically. "I just need dirt. You should have brought me to the courtyard."

"What are you planning to do? Eat it? Your injury is internal, Witchling," I snapped, leaning forward to touch my lips to the swelling gently.

Willow stilled, staring down at me as I rose and brought my wrist to my mouth. I sank my fangs into it, holding it out for her as she stared at it. Indecision warred on her face, leaving no doubt that she was genuinely in pain.

I suspected she'd dislocated or broken a rib, and she knew very well how long that would take to heal otherwise.

"I already own you, Witchling. You might as well benefit from that," I said, smirking down at her as her gaze hardened into a glare. If she didn't take my blood, my compulsion would eventually work its way out of her system.

But then she'd be in pain.

She reached up with a grimace, wrapping her delicate, slender fingers around my forearm and hand. Dragging it toward her, she drew in a few deep breaths as she stared at the blood welling from the wound.

"Drink, Willow. I may be an asshole, and I will most definitely take advantage of you," I said, chuckling when her gaze snapped back to mine. "But you're safe with me. That's more than I can say of your own kind."

She swallowed, nodding softly as she lowered my wrist to her mouth. The heat of her wrapped around my skin, flooding my veins as she took a deep pull. I felt my blood leave my body; felt it slide into her mouth and felt her swallow it down.

Her grip tightened, pulling me to her more harshly as I

tossed my head back with a groan. She drank deep, taking more than she needed. I doubted it was an accident.

The Witchling was smart enough to know that the more of my blood she drank, the stronger she would be. I had the distinct feeling that the one thing Willow never wanted to be was weak. She would never allow herself to be vulnerable, and while she had to accept she would be with me now, she could go to war with others and not worry as much.

If she was going to give some of her power, she'd damn well take some of mine back.

"Clever little witch," I murmured with a laugh as she sank her little teeth into my skin surrounding the wounds. She ran her tongue over them, encouraging them to continue bleeding as she let her eyes drift closed.

Her body shifted, her rib moving beneath her skin as it snapped back into place. She let out a high-pitched whimper, continuing to drink from me through the moment of pain. With her body healed, I knew what would come next.

Euphoria.

Willow's next moan was long and low, her hips shifting on the bed as she sucked at my wrist.

"That's enough," I said, pulling my arm back. She tried to hold on to it, tried to pull it back down to her. But there was risk in taking too much, in becoming addicted to it.

I couldn't afford for her to need my blood to survive. That was a commitment I wasn't interested in.

"Settle," I said, letting my voice compel her to lie back down on the bed.

I wanted nothing more than to fulfill the craving consuming her body, to give her what I knew she so desperately desired. Especially after I'd left her wet and wanting the night before.

"Sleep, Willow," I said instead, tucking hair back from her eye.

Panic filled her eyes for a moment before they started to drift closed. She shook her head, trying to fight the compulsion off.

"No. Please," she begged as I ran gentle fingers over her forehead.

"Shhh," I said, leaning forward to touch my lips to hers gently. "You will wake in a few hours. I promise, love."

The whimper she released broke something inside of me. I'd kill the bitch for making her fear sleep.

As if her nightmares of Him weren't bad enough.

airos stepped into the room, leading some of the other Vessels into my office. I pulled the door to my bedroom closed behind me, shutting Willow's sleeping form off from prying eyes. He raised his brows at me as he caught a glimpse of *who* slept in my bed, but he didn't dare to voice the question.

"You summoned us?" Juliet asked, crossing her arms over her chest. From her position on the sofa, I had no doubt she'd gotten a good look at Willow and the way I'd covered her up carefully.

I moved to my liquor cabinet, pouring myself a tumbler of whiskey. "I've invoked *dominium*," I said, holding Juliet's stare.

She grinned, the feline expression on her face nothing but mischief. "On the Madizza girl?" she asked, pursing her lips when I glared at her.

"Yes," I said, grinding my teeth. I hated to be predictable, but they knew as well as I did just how important a role she would play in the future of Crystal Hollow.

As the last of her bloodline, she would lead the next generation on the Tribunal, and if we could manage to get rid of the Covenant...

They'd need a new Queen.

Having her on our side would work to our advantage in the conflict that had been brewing for centuries.

"Right, so she's off limits for the Reaping then," Kairos said, grinning as he shoved his hands into his pockets. The memory of Willow touching him from the back seat was like a burning flame in my blood, making me want nothing more than to rip out his throat.

Even I knew that was probably irrational, since Willow had been the one to do the touching.

I'd put an end to that now that she had more of my blood in her.

"None of the witches are to know about it," I said, taking a sip of my whiskey and watching their puzzled looks. I could understand it, because what was the point in making a claim of ownership over a witch if I didn't want the world to know she was mine?

"Why not?" Juliet asked, stepping up and taking the drink from my hand. She tossed back a sip of her own, holding my stare as she handed it back.

"She likes to play games," I said, shrugging my shoulders. "And I want to watch her be the one to squirm for once."

Juliet chuckled, shaking her head as she made her way back to the sofa. "This should be interesting."

"Who wants to place bets on how long it takes for her to rip out his throat?" Kairos asked, looking at the other Vessels in the room. While Kairos and Juliet were my closest confidantes, the others were my people in the same way the witches belonged to the Covenant.

They were my responsibility, my duty. But where Susannah Madizza was more than willing to let hers die; I would do anything to protect mine.

Even risk the wrath of the little witchling waiting in my bed.

24

WILLOW

I woke slowly, pressing up to sit. My body hummed with warmth as I looked around the empty room. The door to the bedroom was closed, the room unfamiliar except for the fuzzy haze of being brought here when I'd been in pain.

I touched a hand to my ribs, finding nothing but smooth, unblemished skin when I twisted to look at it. The memory of Gray's blood came over me quickly, making me queasy with the reality of what that might mean.

The area between my legs throbbed with need, as if the blood he'd given me had only amplified the desire he'd created in me before. I wanted to tear his throat out. I wanted to tear his clothes off.

The fact that I wasn't even sure which one I wanted more terrified me.

I swung my legs over the edge of the bed, pausing for a moment to glare down at my ruined shirt. The buttons were missing, and I found one on the floor as I looked around. With a scoff, I tugged it off my shoulders and tossed it onto the bed behind me. Making my way to his closet, I helped myself to one of his dress shirts, slipping it on over my shoulders and buttoning it slowly.

It was so long it covered my skirt entirely, so I unzipped the stiff green fabric and shoved it down my thighs. I couldn't stand to wear Susannah's house colors for another moment. It gathered at my feet, leaving me to step out of it and toss it onto the bed with my ruined shirt. With only my thigh-highs and Gray's shirt, I swallowed as I moved to the door and pried it open to peek out.

The seating area was empty, so I pulled the door open wider and stepped out. I ran my fingers over the back of the sofa as I moved, glancing at the books covering his coffee table. I wouldn't have pegged the immortal being for a reader, but there was no denying the way they were littered around his space.

"Are you looking for something in particular, Witchling?" he asked, his voice coming from the alcove where I knew his desk was. I moved toward it slowly, a flush creeping up the back of my neck as I tried to will the *need* in my body to just die already. The depth of his voice did something to me, sending a pang of want through me, which I felt with every step.

"Something sharp and pointy, preferably," I said as I strode toward the alcove. I touched my hand to the wall as I curved around it, feeling the moment his gaze settled on me.

He dropped his pen to the desk, leaning back in his chair as he stared at me. "Are you sure about that? Helping yourself to my shirt, I would be inclined to say you're looking for something to gag on."

My mouth dropped open, an incredulous laugh tearing free from my throat. Of all the things he could have said...

That was the last thing I expected.

He grinned as he stood from his chair, stepping around the

edge of the desk to approach me. He stopped in front of me, making no move to touch me.

"How are you feeling?" he asked, his forehead pinching as if he were genuinely concerned.

I swallowed, my discomfort growing beneath the weight of that gaze. Only the bargain, I reminded myself. He needed me to stay alive and to do his job to keep me safe, or there would be consequences for him.

It was nothing more than the bargain.

"Better," I whispered, my voice raw.

He reached behind him, plucking a tumbler off his desk and handing it to me. I took a delicate sip of the amber liquid, trying to let it bolster me.

"Water would have been more appropriate if you're nursing me back to health."

Gray shrugged, taking the tumbler and turning it in his grip. He made sure to take a sip from the exact same place I had, the intimacy of the intention behind that making me squirm.

"You look healthy enough to me," he said, smirking as he set it on top of the desk.

I shifted on my feet, feeling uncomfortable. "Thank you. For coming for me. For keeping her from..." I trailed off, unable to finish the thought. It was horrific to think of what she might have done if Gray hadn't come when he had.

"I'll always come for you, Witchling," he said, holding my stare for a moment.

Those blue eyes glimmered with something that felt like *more*, stealing the breath from my lungs for a suspended moment in time. The gold seemed to flash; the twisted connection between us pulling taut.

Then he ruined it, turning his stare away and touching the

underside of my chin. "Can't have you being the one to give me orders, now, can I?"

I grimaced, the reminder serving its purpose. Grounding me in the reality.

Love wasn't in the cards for me. Not with a witch, and definitely not with a Vessel. We could and would work together, but this was nothing more than a business arrangement between two people who hated each other.

Even if we wanted to rip one another's clothes off.

I moved around him, approaching his desk and putting him behind me. Drawing in a few deep breaths to steady myself without that piercing stare on mine, I fiddled with the paperweight on his desk. The black gem was somehow translucent, and the face of a woman stared back at me as I lifted it.

Her face was blurred, and I couldn't see the details as Gray reached around me and set it back on the desk. I whirled, spinning on him and shaking off the dread the sight of that woman filled me with. The makeshift crown upon her head was a twisted, gnarled thing, with birch branches sweeping across her head like antlers.

"Susannah isn't going to let me bring us back to the old ways without a fight. We'll need to avoid her notice for a while," I admitted, wondering how far Gray's protection would actually go.

"That sounds familiar," he said, crossing his arms over his chest. He stared down at me with a raised brow, reminding me of the warning he'd issued at the gravesite.

"You were right, okay? I should have listened to you. You know her better than I do," I mumbled, twisting my lips.

"That looked absolutely painful," he muttered, rolling his eyes to the side. "But I'm glad if nothing else, this has put us on the same page. Do what you must to work toward your end goal, but don't endanger yourself in the process."

"We should discuss strategy. I'm sure you have thoughts about the best way to go about this," I said, watching as he strode around his desk and left me there. He bent over a piece of paper, picking up his pen and scribbling a note for himself as if I were a bother.

"Love, I don't give the first shit about the politics of the Coven. I don't care how they choose to practice. If they want to waste the gift they were given, then they deserve to lose it," he said, a slow smile spreading across his face as my stomach dropped. Nausea churned in it as I tipped my head to the side, my eyes drifting closed in my confusion.

"But our bargain—" I broke off, a shuddering gasp leaving me as his steely stare met mine when I opened my eyes. "You never cared about the magic, did you?"

The white of his teeth glinted as he ran his tongue over his fang. "I got what I wanted out of our bargain," he said, evading the question entirely. His eyes dropped down my body, that feeling of nausea in my gut so at odds with the pressure between my legs. Even now, with the unrelenting rage building in me, I couldn't push it away.

"You fucking asshole!" I screamed, grabbing the black paperweight off his desk. I threw it, aiming for his stupid, handsome face. My body moved more quickly than I expected, the paperweight flying through the air too quickly for me to track.

I had only a moment of shock as it sped toward his face, and he twisted out of its path only *just* in time for it to skim over his shoulder. Crashing into the portrait of Lucifer behind him, it shattered into shards of glass on the credenza below the portrait, cutting a seam through the center of the canvas.

For a moment, everything was still. Gray's attention

snagged on that paperweight on the floor, remaining there as I fumbled for what to do. For what to say. I wouldn't apologize when he'd manipulated me so thoroughly.

But could I blame him? I'd been so convinced I had the upper hand that I hadn't thought it through. I hadn't considered that he may not have the same goals as I did. The fault was mine entirely, but I still hated him for it.

He turned to face me, his body moving so painfully slowly that I counted my breaths before his stare landed on me once again. His face was so carefully controlled, and somehow, I thought that might be worse than his rage.

I blinked.

He was gone.

My breath rattled in my lungs, and I pursed my lips together as I turned my head slowly. Looking over my shoulder. I didn't dare move, didn't dare to give him any reason to think I'd run. The hair on the back of my neck rose, and in this moment, I knew he was the predator and I was the prey.

His hand wrapped around my nape, shoving me forward as he appeared at my side. His other hand swept everything off his desk with a growl, sending it clattering to the floor with a crash I suspected everyone in Hollow's Grove heard.

He shoved me toward the desk, bending me forward so harshly that I only just managed to catch myself with my hands and keep my face from smacking against the wood.

"Thorne!" I said, wincing when he pushed harder and shoved my cheek against it. He kept me pinned there, a low rumble vibrating in his chest.

"That is not my name. Not to you," he warned, holding me still as I fought, pushing against his grip.

He leaned his body over mine, the fabric of his slacks rubbing against the bare skin of my thighs and my ass where his shirt had ridden up in the scuffle. His lips touched my cheek, his eyes so close to mine that it felt like nothing existed but him. His mouth brushed my skin as he spoke, sending a shiver through me.

"I think you've forgotten what I am, Witchling."

"A mistake I won't make again, you fucking—" I said, glaring at him as my nostrils flared with my anger. He was too fucking strong, keeping me pinned still without any effort on his part. I could exhaust myself, and he wouldn't even break a sweat.

"I tolerate your mouth because you *amuse* me, Willow. Tread carefully, or you just might cease to be amusing," he said, his voice stern as he pulled back slightly. He stared down at me, keeping me held still as I swallowed my retort. "I am a demon," he growled, holding my gaze with blue eyes that seemed to shine from within. "I may be trapped within a body that resembles a man, but you would be a fool to mistake me for one. I am not human, and I will not behave as one."

"There is a difference between expecting you to be human and expecting you not to lie to me," I said, sinking my teeth into the inside of my cheek in an attempt to keep some of the venom from my voice.

"When have I lied to you?" he asked, his head tipping to the side with genuine curiosity.

"You said I was safe with you!" I hissed, struggling against his grip to prove my point.

"Are you hurt?" he asked, his voice a soft murmur.

I considered his words, analyzing my body from my fingers to my toes. In spite of his harsh treatment and the speed with which he'd moved me to the desk, I didn't think I'd so much as bumped against it. I greatly doubted there would be so much as a bruise on me the next day.

"Or are you wet?" he asked, and the hand that didn't pin

me at the nape touched my bare hip. I halted against the desk, wincing as his fingers slid over the swell of my ass.

He cupped a single cheek in his palm, gripping it and digging his fingertips into it as I fought back my strangled whimper.

"Fuck you."

"I do believe that's what you want," he said, his laughter sliding over my skin and making me feel too warm. The mixture of desire and rage burning in me was almost too much to handle, leaving me gasping on his desk as he leaned over me once again. "Do you want to come, Witchling?"

"I want you to *release* me," I snarled, rearing back against his hand. I barely managed to push up at all before he shoved me back down, flattening my cheek against the desk.

"*That* is not going to happen," he said, the smirk in his voice making me seethe. I searched for plants in his room, for anything I could use against him. I didn't suspect it would end well, but it didn't matter.

There were none.

I raised my foot, slamming it down upon the stone with a grunt. It cracked beneath the force of my heel, my magic echoing through it as the floor beneath us shook.

He slapped my ass lightly, sending a tiny jolt of sharp heat through me. The swell of my ass cheek shook lightly when he struck it.

"That was expensive."

"Of course you would know how much it cost. You're older than dirt!" I scoffed.

"Tell me you don't want me, and I'll let you go," he murmured, sliding his hand from the fleshy part of my ass to where I bent over. He slid it between my legs, brushing his thumb over the lace of my thong where it covered my pussy.

I moaned, my hips moving to seek out more of the pressure. There was no controlling it, no containing the surge of pleasure that spiraled through me. He'd edged me so efficiently and left me wanting for days. My body wanted the release it was owed.

"I am going to cut off your dick and feed it to you," I threatened when he stopped, shifting his hand to the inside of my thigh once more. It horrified me to feel how slick my skin was, how wet I'd become the moment he touched me.

The moment he put the fear of the devil in me after I'd thrown that paperweight.

There was something seriously fucking wrong with me.

"That would be very foolish, since my cock is the only one your pretty little cunt can find pleasure in," he said, his laughter coating my skin as he shoved the fabric of his shirt up farther. Leaning forward, he trailed his mouth up the bare skin of my spine, tracing the trunk of my tree tattoo with his tongue.

"What do you want from me?" I whimpered, every touch of his lips or tongue sending a pulse of want straight to my pussy.

He chuckled against my spine, slipping his free hand between my legs once more and shoving my panties to the side so that he could touch bare skin. A single finger found my entrance, sliding into me slowly and stroking over a spot within me that made my eyes roll back. Grinning into my back, he ran his fang over the curve of my hip.

"Beg."

"What?" I asked, my mouth going dry. He couldn't be fucking serious.

"Beg me to make you come. If you expect me to get on my knees for you, then you'd better be ready to ask me for it, Witchling," he growled, stroking my clit with his thumb while his finger made slow, smooth slides in and out of me.

"Gray," I mumbled, faltering for any other words. I couldn't give him that. Even in my desperation, even knowing it was what I was *meant* to be doing. Vessels couldn't love, but they could feel desire. They could feel convenience and attraction.

They could trust the woman they fucked and leave her unaccompanied in their office.

"Give me the words," he ordered.

"Please release me, and I'll do it myself," I growled in spite of myself.

His chuckle was a bastardization of humor. It was the brutal reality that I didn't think he ever intended to release me. Even when he was done with me, he'd probably keep the compulsion on me for the sick satisfaction that I would never again be able to find pleasure.

With myself. With anyone.

And it would be he who filled my fantasies. The only man who could make me come.

"Where's the fun in that?" he asked, squeezing his hand at the back of my neck. "Beg me to make you come."

I whimpered when he added a second finger to me, the slow twist of them inside me absolutely torturous. He gave just enough to torment me, his careful control both admirable and terrifying.

"Please," I whispered, hating the word as soon as it left my mouth.

"Please what, Witchling? Please stop?" he asked, drawing a strangled sob from me.

"Please make me come, Gray," I whimpered, my body going slack against the desk. I gave up, having given the only thing I hadn't wanted to sacrifice.

He was silent for a moment, his hand stilling between my legs before he released my neck, and the ability to move was suddenly mine once again. I pushed off the desk, feeling his hand slide down my spine to press into the small of my back.

"Lie down and grab the edge of the desk. Now, Willow," he ordered, and his body left mine. The air felt too warm in the absence of his touch, but I did as he'd commanded.

Lowering myself to the desk, I rested my cheek against it the way he'd held me before. Stretching up with both hands, I grasped the edge of the desk on the other side. His fingers hooked into the fabric of my thong on either side, dragging it down over my ass and thighs and helping me step out of it. He slapped his palm down on the inside of my thigh, making me jolt.

"Spread your legs for me."

I swallowed, letting my eyes drift closed as I obeyed. I watched from the corner of my eye as his form blurred, lowering to the floor behind me.

"Oh God," I whimpered when the heat of his gaze settled on the bare flesh between my legs.

He slid a single hand against me, cupping my pussy and working his thumb in and out of me. "God has nothing to do with the things I'm going to do to you, Witchling," he said, leaning forward.

His breath touched my heated flesh, sending a wave of pleasure through me. I waited for the moment his mouth touched me, waited for him to deliver on his promise.

He shifted to the inside of my thigh instead, placing a delicate kiss against it. His lips spread wide, his teeth sinking into the skin on the back of my thigh as I gasped.

The pain was instant and all-consuming, drawing out the pleasure he'd tormented me with. The sharp bite only lasted a moment, and then something else took its place.

I moaned, pushing back against his mouth as the fire went straight to my belly. As it curled and writhed inside of me, finding a home. His ragged groan drove me forward, my fingers clutching the edge as if my life depended on it. I drifted through the haze of pleasure, losing track of the space around me as he drank from me.

"Gray," I whimpered, feeling something crack in my hands.

He pulled his fangs free, the wet heat of his mouth coasting over my flesh. The moment his lips touched mine, I was lost.

Nothing existed but the brand of his mouth on me. But the heat of his tongue sliding through me. He pressed his face into my flesh, and there was nothing teasing in the way he devoured me. He ate like a man starved, like I was his last meal on earth.

"Fuck," I groaned, resisting the urge to writhe on his tongue. "Don't stop. Please don't stop."

Moaning into me, he proceeded to give me what I wanted. His tongue found my clit, circling it slowly and bringing me to the edge. He kept me there, his careful, masterful strokes driving me insane.

"Gray!" I shrieked, losing myself to the pleasure that lingered just out of reach.

It was so close I could taste it.

He pressed his tongue flat against me, the shallow, firm sweeps of it against me finally driving me over the edge. I went lax against the desk, my grip releasing as I cried out. White flashed behind my eyes as they closed, filling my vision with nothing but light so bright I thought I might never see the dark again.

My breath came in deep, shuddering pants when I snapped back to reality, feeling the firmness of the desk against me. Gray rose to his feet behind me, helping to peel me off the wood. He said nothing as he spun me to sit on the edge, staring down at me as if he could see inside my very soul.

He couldn't, because if he could, he'd have killed me already. The Vessels might have liked Charlotte, but they wouldn't like a random witch who could unmake them and had been raised to hate them all.

"You broke my desk," he said finally, his chuckle drawing a smile from me.

I turned to look at the cracked wood where I'd gripped it, shrugging as I wondered what other skills his blood would give me. "Be grateful it wasn't your face."

He smiled, running his thumb over my lip. I tasted myself on his skin, still trying to catch my breath.

"Go get some rest," he said, stepping back and moving to his chair. I stepped away, taking the reprieve to gather myself. "But Willow?" he called out as I approached the door. I turned to face him, pretending my heart wasn't pounding in my chest. "The next time we see each other, it will be you on your knees."

I held his gaze, trying to cling to the pleasure that left me satiated. "Don't fuck with my energy, demon," I said, turning and leaving his office.

That sounded like a tomorrow problem.

25

WILLOW

I was avoiding him.

He knew it. I knew it. I was fairly certain the entire school knew it at this point. Two days had passed since he'd put me out of my misery in his office, and I refused to so much as think about him.

About the way he'd felt breathing into me.

"Tomorrow night, we will have our first Reaping," Susannah said as she paced at the front of the room. Iban sat beside me, his flirty smile doing nothing to quell the rising panic within me.

Of all the things I'd known about Hollow's Grove before coming here, the Reaping had been the one that terrified me most. It shouldn't have mattered now that Gray had fed from me multiple times, but somehow it did. I couldn't avoid him if he was coming to my room at night.

"As part of the bargain between our kinds, witches were required to provide blood to us in order to sustain our physical forms. This is an aspect that has been nourished and held as sacred through all the centuries of difficulties between us," Gray said, his hands shoved into his pockets as he leaned against the doorway behind us. The classroom they'd chosen was larger than normal, accommodating all the seventy odd students in attendance.

I swallowed when Iban took my rising fear of being unable to avoid Gray as discomfort with the feeding itself. He placed his hand on my knee, squeezing it reassuringly. "It isn't that bad," he whispered, giving me no choice but to smile at him. I ignored Gray's glare when it settled on my face, pretending he didn't exist.

That seemed to be my pattern now.

"You mean they feed on students? I assumed they fed on people in town," one of the other witches said. I recognized her as one of the remaining eleven other new students, someone who had been pointed out to me after the burial of the witch who'd died.

"The Vessels you see at Hollow's Grove are assigned to the school. They remain here, and as such, they feed off who they please while they're within these walls. Only the underaged are off limits, according to the bargain," Susannah explained.

"If a Vessel has been assigned to you for this Reaping, you will find a red mark on your bedroom door when you return from your classes tomorrow evening. If not, you will be required to remain in your quarters regardless starting at eight. If you've never participated in a Reaping, someone will assist you with making preparations if you're chosen," George continued, his voice far more sympathetic as the new students exchanged worried glances. "There's nothing to fear. Should you wish it, the feeding can be quite quick and painless."

I swallowed as I glanced at Iban. "When will they share the pairs with us?" I asked, watching as his lips pursed.

"What do you mean?" he asked, tipping his head to the side.

"The Vessel who has chosen us to be his feeder for the year. When do we find out who it will be?"

The shock on Iban's face did nothing to abate my rising panic. "There hasn't been a pair bond in decades, Willow. They stopped doing them after the massacre fifty years ago," he whispered, leaning into my side as he spoke.

I felt Gray's stare on my back, as if the bastard wasn't satisfied with the knowledge that I would never be able to enjoy being with Iban. Distance would be the only way to placate him, but I'd be damned if I gave him the satisfaction.

"What are you talking about?" My mother had attended the University after the massacre. She'd never hinted that it wasn't the way any longer, that they'd strayed from the original way to handle the Reaping. "Once a week, the Vessel who chose us comes to feed."

"Once a week, the Vessel who is assigned to us feeds, but it's a different one of them every time. They did it to avoid witches and Vessels forming unnatural relationships with each other," he explained, shrugging his shoulders.

"A different one every week?" I asked, feeling like the breath had been stolen from my lungs. It shouldn't have mattered. If one Vessel fed from me, that was surely enough. They were all the same, all monsters hidden in human skin crafted from the earth.

Except it would make it that much more difficult for me to use Gray's possessiveness to my advantage. It would be less time I could spend getting him addicted to me, my blood, my body. Not to mention, it meant Gray would be feeding from another witch. I growled beneath my breath, shaking my head and smiling when Iban looked at me in shock.

Fuck.

*T*he red mark on my door stole the breath from my lungs. I should have known that I would have the misfortune of being chosen in the first week, but I'd hoped...

I didn't know what I'd hoped.

"It's not so bad," Della said, letting herself into my room. She went to the bed, picking up the light gray, floor-length slip that had been left on top of the bedspread. "And it can be pleasant if you want."

She moved the thin silk one to the side, revealing a short slip of lace. "Why are there two?" I asked, sitting on the edge of the bed.

"You wear this one," she said, picking up the lacey one and holding it to her body as she spun. "If you're open to feeding more carnal desires."

"If I'm open to letting the Vessel fuck me?" I asked, huffing out a breath. I didn't even know who it would be.

Della shrugged her shoulders, picking up the silk night-gown and handing it to me at whatever she saw on my face. "You don't have to love someone to fuck him. You don't even have to like him."

"How am I supposed to make the decision of whether or not I want him? I don't even know who will walk through that door," I said, sighing as I stood and shoved my blazer off my shoulders. I folded it and placed it on top of my dresser, letting my fingers drop to the bow at my throat as I unknotted it.

"You won't ever know who he was, and I think that's some of the appeal of it. It's a night of fun, no consequences for tomorrow because you won't even know his name," she said with a laugh. "Are you more attracted to women? I just assumed you were into men because of the way you flirt with Iban. If you like women too, I can tell Headmaster Thorne. There are a few female Vessels who prefer female company."

"No, it's not that. But witches hate the Vessels, so why would they allow Vessels to touch them?" I asked, thinking about how I'd desperately wanted to avoid the forbidden aspect. How I'd feared the judgment if I'd allowed a Vessel to touch me intimately.

It seemed more witches were willing to allow it than I'd expected, just under the cover of darkness and the secrecy of the Reaping.

"Spoken like a woman who has never had hate sex," she laughed, standing and helping me unbutton my shirt. I didn't protest the odd intimacy of it or the fact that it left my bra open to her view when she finished. It felt like taking care of me, like the closest thing I'd ever had to friendship when she tucked a strand of hair behind my ear.

It made me feel younger than I was, than I'd ever been allowed to be.

I thought of Gray's hands on me, of his mouth devouring me as if he couldn't decide if he hated me or wanted to live with his face between my legs.

I suspected this concept of hate sex had merit.

"Not quite sex," I said as the realization hit me.

Della grinned, understanding lighting her face. We both knew that someone had touched me with less than good intentions, that he'd taken more than I should have allowed.

That I'd liked it.

"No one but us has to know. I'll help you get ready, and your secret is safe with me if you choose to put on the lace. There's no guarantee he'll take what you've offered, but either way, that secret is yours to keep," she said, stepping away as I pulled my shirt off and tossed it to the hamper in the corner. My skirt and socks followed as I shoved them down my legs, leaving me in my bra and underwear as I reached for the silk nightgown.

As tempting as it was to give another Vessel what Gray thought was his, it would undo years of preparation. Years of my father's insistence that keeping myself untouched would drive a Vessel to the point of obsession.

Especially if I bled the first time.

I froze, the fabric scrunching in my hand as it clenched into a fist. "Do the Vessels often reject offers?" I asked, dread rising in my throat. I tried to swallow around it, feeling like grave dirt filled my lungs suddenly.

"Not in my experience," she said, studying my face too closely.

All Vessels fed on the Reaping. That much I knew. If there were no pair bonds—if Gray was not the one who came to me that night—would he be with another? Even just the thought of him feeding from someone else made me want to tear out his throat.

Shit.

I wasn't supposed to care about that. He wasn't mine, and he never would be.

Fuck. Fuck. Fuck.

I dropped the silken nightgown, my hand hovering over the lace one for a moment as I considered. The petty, vindictive part of me wanted to let whoever it was who came through my door take it all. I wanted to give what had been meant to be Gray's away, showing him how little he mattered.

The witches may never know, but I had no doubt Gray would be able to smell me on another male. He'd know exactly what I'd done, and it would serve him fucking right.

I swallowed, shoving that part of me down, and picked up the silk gown.

"Maybe next time," Della said, smiling kindly. "The first time is overwhelming. I think that was the right choice for tonight."

I tugged on the fabric, pulling it overhead and letting it settle on my curves. It hugged every line and groove in my body, fitting like a second skin as if it was made for me.

"There will be plenty of time for me to partake in the other pleasures," I said, shoving down the part of me that cared.

"Bra and underwear off," she said, her lips twisting and nose scrunching. "Those are the rules. Regardless of which clothes..."

"That's disgusting," I muttered, but I reached behind my back and unhooked my bra.

My breasts dropped without the support, the fabric clinging to them and leaving *nothing* to the imagination in the silk that was semi-transparent. Shimmying my underwear down my legs, I tossed them to the side and moved to the center of the room when I was ready.

"You have two options. I can either secure you to the bed or the hook," she said, pointing above my head. Sure enough, hanging from the ceiling was the tiniest of hooks I hadn't noticed.

"Secure me?" I asked, watching as she went to the closet. She pulled a pair of padded cuffs from the top shelf, coming toward me as she took my hands in hers. Wrapping each of my wrists in one of them, she moved slowly, giving me time to adjust to the feeling of cushioned leather against my skin.

When each of my wrists was wrapped, she hooked the cuffs together with tiny latches so that they were stuck together in front of me. "This can't be necessary," I said, my eyes widening when she went to the closet again. She came back with a chain, feeding it through the loops in the leather until she wrapped it around my wrists.

"You can't be allowed to see him," she said, letting the chain drop to the floor. She held a piece of cloth in front of my face, the meaning clear as I swallowed.

"No," I said, shaking my head. "I refuse to be tied up and blindfolded."

She sighed, taking my bound hands in hers. The warmth of her skin penetrated the sudden chill that had taken me, bringing me back to the one place I didn't want to go.

The one place I swore I would do anything to avoid.

My chest heaved, the panic coming swift and suddenly. I couldn't breathe. Darkness closed in around the edges of my vision.

"Please. Please don't," I begged, shaking my head from side to side.

Della froze, her face twisting as she realized something was wrong. "Willow, I have to. If I don't, they'll force you. Do you understand me? This is not optional."

I whimpered, looking between my two options as I fought for the ability to breathe. "I can't..."

"I'll get Headmaster Thorne," she said suddenly, sighing as she looked at me. "Maybe he can make a special accommodation if he sees you himself."

"No!" I screamed, making her freeze in place. "The hook. Just do it," I said, trying to still the trembling in my fingers. My jaw ached with how harshly I gritted my teeth, with the way I clenched to try to keep the panic at bay.

The pain helped. It always brought me back to the present.

Della grabbed a control from the closet, pushing a button until the hook lowered itself in front of me. I stared at it as she twisted the red fabric, twisting it and layering it until I was certain I wouldn't be able to see through it. Until I knew all that would remain was the darkness that never seemed to end.

"Are you sure?" she asked, reaching up with a single hand.

I hadn't realized I was crying until her finger slid through the wetness on my cheek, brushing it away with a gentleness I didn't deserve. I sniffed back the others, shutting out the shame.

I nodded, letting my eyes drift closed as she covered my eyes with the fabric. The moment it touched my skin, my eyes flung open. They found nothing but pitch, eternal black. Nothing but the void of all light and life.

Like being buried alive.

I whimpered, pinching my eyes closed again and trying to convince myself it was only the back of my eyelids. That I wasn't there all over again.

I was at Hollow's Grove. My father couldn't touch me.

Couldn't punish me when I disobeyed him on the weekends he brought me to his cabin.

Della raised my wrists to the hook, looping the chain over it. Only the clanking of them filled my ears over the sound of my own harsh, ragged breathing.

I felt when she stepped away. The chain rose, dragging me up onto my toes as my arms pulled tight over my head.

"It will be over soon, Willow," she said, her footsteps fading away.

Then she was gone, and I was alone again.

Alone in my own personal Hell.

26

GRAY

She waited, suspended from the ceiling.

A single breath in. A single breath out.

All I could hear was her racing heart as it filled the room. I stepped in, watching as she flinched from the sound of my footsteps. Branches scraped over the window outside, making her spin her head in the other direction.

She squirmed where the other witch had helped her string herself up, and I could just imagine the ache that had built in her shoulders. I'd kept her waiting, wanting her dread and anticipation to simmer in her blood before I came to her.

It made it taste all the sweeter.

She'd lost sight of what the Vessels were, of who we were meant to be. She needed the reminder of what I was capable of and what I was not. A Vessel could never love her. She'd never be anything more than a convenience and a toy.

She swallowed loudly, struggling as her toes slipped out from under her. She gasped, her breath coming in deep, shuddering breaths as her mouth dropped open in panic.

What the Hell?

I took another step toward her, watching as her body went

perfectly still. I resisted the urge to speak, keeping my voice silent because of the knowledge that she would recognize it. Even though I wanted to comfort her, to calm her racing heart, I knew that once I spoke, the game would be over.

And I so very much wanted to play.

The blindfold remained tightly fastened around her head despite her best efforts. I stepped up behind her, letting her feel the weight of my presence. She managed to get her feet beneath her once again, pressing up into her hands just slightly and taking some weight off her shoulders.

I rested a hand on her hip, my fingers gently stroking over the silken fabric as she stilled. It pleased me that she hadn't chosen the lace nightgown, refusing to allow a stranger to take what was mine. It didn't matter to me that I would have been the one to fuck her, despite her intent.

Her plan to give her body to another would have been enough to make me punish her.

I wanted her as obsessed with me as I was with her. It would be the perfect karma for the way she'd slithered beneath the surface of what made me, making herself at home in my soul.

Her breath raced, wheezing out of her lungs as she headed toward a full-blown panic attack. "Just get it over with," she growled, trying even now to regain some of the control I'd taken. Her heart throbbed in tune with her words — pounding so hard and fast that I felt it in her hip.

I wrapped my hand around the front of her body, pressing my palm into the bare skin of her chest and feeling her pulse. Her heartbeat.

Her body shook, trembling with fear of that which she could not see.

In the time I'd known Willow, I had only seen her afraid in the moments when the Covenant threatened to put her into the deep sleep. Whatever had caused this fear, I vowed to learn the cause.

A woman like Willow was not meant to be afraid.

My other hand rose from her hip as I moved beside her, leaning into her arm as I trailed delicate fingers up her spine. I traced the addictive tree tattoo there, tickling over the trunk through the silk until the fabric ended. My touch shifted to bare skin, her warmth seeping inside me in spite of the distinctive chill to her.

She sighed, releasing a slow breath. Her next inhale shuddered, her lungs filling completely finally. Sweeping her hair to the side, I revealed a shoulder and her nape as I curved my body around to her back and removed my hand from her chest.

I buried my fingers in her hair, tugging her head back firmly as she gasped. I trailed my nose over her jaw for a moment, offering her a single moment of affection and trying to shove away the remnants of her panic.

Of the fear I didn't understand.

She'd been fed from before. She'd given blood before.

None of it made sense, but I knew without a doubt I would do whatever it took to get to the bottom of it.

Using my hand in her hair, I guided her head to the side. Twisting it to give me a better angle to reach her neck. My breath wafted over her skin, sending a shiver through her body. My fangs trailed over her skin for a moment.

Taunting. Teasing.

I sunk them into her, the sweet taste of her covering my tongue. I drank as she went lax in my grip, moaning her pleasure.

Pleasure I wouldn't allow her to reach when she thought I was someone else. I bit down harder, incapable of controlling my anger at her being aroused with someone else. *This* was the reminder I'd wanted.

All witches were the same, and only good for one thing.

The more of her blood filled me, the more I felt renewed.

Awakened, somehow, and I never wanted it to end.

 he witch wrung her hands as she stepped into the open door. She reached up, knocking on the doorjamb as if I wasn't already looking at her.

"You asked for me, Headmaster?" Della asked, her nerves pulsing off her.

"Close the door and take a seat, Miss Tethys," I said, returning my attention to the paper in front of me. The conversation at hand would require delicacy, and I knew I needed to tread lightly if I wanted to have any chance of not revealing myself to the witches.

Only Susannah knew of my *dominium* over Willow and the fact that none of the others would be feeding on her until I relinquished my claim on her. I'd hoped to watch Willow squirm, to torment her and make her realize she wasn't above feeling pleasure from the very creatures she hated.

I wanted to know if it was purely me who made her react so viscerally, or if she solely had a high sex drive and needed contact. "I want you to tell me about what happened last night."

The witch took her seat, her face paling as she looked at her lap and continued to wring her hands. "I-I fulfilled my duty in the Reaping, Headmaster. I swear, I did what was expected of me."

"Not with you. With Miss Madizza. The Vessel who fed

from her indicated she was distressed beyond what he deemed normal for a first Reaping," I explained, dropping my pen and leaning back in my chair. Della swallowed, her eyes pinching closed. "As Headmaster, it's my duty to make sure he didn't do anything that crossed any lines. If he frightened her—"

"No. No, I don't think it was the Vessel at all," she said, sitting up straighter. I watched indecision war on her face, watched her debate whether or not she should tell me what she knew. "She asked me not to say anything, but Willow was distressed when she saw the cuffs, even more so when she realized she would be blindfolded."

"Did you explain the process to her? Surely if she'd understood..." I trailed off, letting my words hang unspoken.

"I did. She knew what was going to happen. I don't think there's anything anyone could have done to calm her, Headmaster," she said, glancing off to the side. She sank her teeth into her bottom lip. "I've never seen anyone so afraid."

Everything in me stilled. By the time I'd reached her, her fear had coated the room. It had left a distinctive chill in the room, as if Willow had tried to summon the grave to swallow her whole. Such things were impossible, but that didn't stop me from pausing before I'd entered the room.

The distinctive taste of magic in the air had been unmistakable, but there'd been very little plant life for Willow to summon to her aid.

"Willow Madizza?" I asked, feigning ignorance to get her to tell me more.

"I know. She's always fearless. Seeing her like that..." She trailed off, turning back to face me slowly. "I think something happened to her. Something horrible."

The pen snapped in my hand, and Della's eyes widened as ink spilled onto the pages atop my desk. "See what you can find out for me."

"I... What?" she asked, her mouth dropping open in shock. "Surely you can't be asking me to spy on my friend and report back to you? If something did happen, her trauma should be hers to share."

"The students of this school are my responsibility, Miss Tethys. If there is something I need to know about to make special accommodations for future Reapings with Miss Madizza, then I'd like to be informed, and I do not think I can trust her to be honest," I said, standing from my desk. I moved toward the door, watching as she hurried to gather her pack of books and sling it over her shoulder to follow.

"You know she doesn't like the dark, and she doesn't like being restrained. Isn't that enough?" she asked, reaching out to touch a hand to my forearm. "Please. Let her keep her secrets." The fact that she'd dared to touch me spoke to her desperation to help Willow, and I realized it wasn't just my skin the witchling had worked her way beneath.

She'd found a friend, a true one from the looks of it, when I'd thought such things would be impossible at Hollow's Grove.

I shrugged off her touch, making my way back to my desk and nodding in dismissal.

"There can be no secrets in Crystal Hollow."

27

I crooked my finger twice, summoning Iban forward. He shook his head from side to side, a youthful, disbelieving smile reminding me of just how young he was.

How young *we* were, and the Choice he'd been forced to make before he was old enough to understand the implications of it.

"Do you ever regret it?" I asked, dodging backward as he lunged for me. His hands wrapped around air, finding the spot where I'd stood only a moment before completely empty. Slamming the side of my arm down on his back, I used his momentum against him.

My push made him spiral, his arms flailing a little as he fought for his balance, and he spun to look at me. All around the grounds in front of the school, other students did the same. Witches paired off with witches, Vessels observing primarily but interacting when they thought they would be well received.

"Sometimes," he said, shrugging his shoulders as if it didn't matter.

I supposed in a way it didn't, given that nothing anyone did could ever change it. I hoped he at least found what he was looking for one day, but the fact that he'd chosen the ability to bear children over having magic when Susannah intended to allow them all to die anyway…

I sighed, spinning and aiming a kick directly for his face as he rushed me. He stopped just in time, my leg raised in the air so that the sole of my sneaker was only inches from his nose. He grinned, touching the bare skin of my ankle where it peeked out from beneath the black leggings I'd donned for the day.

The fabric was thin, hugging my curves flawlessly. There was no gap between my thighs, and I gloried in the feeling of pants that I'd been denied since arriving in Crystal Hollow. I'd gotten far too used to rubbing deodorant on the inside of my thighs every morning to prevent the chafing burn that happened when I had to walk from one side of the school to the other too many times in one day.

I pulled my foot out of his grip, tipping my head to the side and giving him a look that communicated he needed to focus. He smiled unapologetically as I stepped back, squaring my posture and readying for the next mock attack.

"Do you think you're doing her any favors?" Gray asked, stepping up beside Iban.

"Stop it," I snapped, glaring at him from the corner of my eye.

He raised a brow at me in mocking condescension, and I just waited for him to voice the words that made his lips tip into a smirk.

I could hear them as if he'd spoken them; feel them hanging between us.

That's not what you were saying when my mouth was on your pussy.

I swallowed, turning my gaze away and raising my hands

into fists. I waited for Iban to regroup himself after the interruption, raising his own hands and stepping toward me. He moved slower than I knew he was capable, the eyes supervising every move he made making him nervous.

"There's a murderer in this school," Gray said, his voice dropping to a low seethe as he placed a hand on Iban's shoulder and shoved him away. The way the others around us stilled at the reminder of the word, at the reminder that there were twelve of us who were very vulnerable. "If you aren't going to take her safety seriously, then let her fight with someone who will."

"You?" Iban asked, and the challenge in those words wasn't lost on me. It was an acknowledgement of everything Gray should have worked harder to hide, knowing that a relationship between us should have been kept a secret.

Gray ignored Iban, turning to me more fully and spreading his feet until he stood shoulder-width apart. It was the first time I'd seen him out of a suit in the light of day. His black sweatpants hinted at the deep lines of muscle in his thighs, and his black t-shirt was so fitted that everyone knew just how broad his shoulders and chest were.

He didn't so much as raise a hand at me as he quirked his brow, waiting for me to strike.

"I'm not very likely to be doing the attacking," I murmured, watching as his laughter began in his stomach. His chest shook with the force of it as he bowed his head forward, his eyes drifting closed.

"Have you fucking met you?" he asked, his breath a deep wheeze that drew a laugh even from Iban as he watched our interaction.

"Rude," I snapped, crossing my arms over my chest. I was far too aware of the all-too-curious stare of the other man who wanted to fuck me, not trusting anyone in this school as far as

I could throw them. Iban was sweet, and I suspected he had the best intentions at the end of the day.

But that didn't mean Susannah hadn't already wrapped her bones around him.

I hadn't been able to shake her words when she'd been ready to put me into the deep sleep, that Iban could be convinced to visit me. I wasn't so sure, because at the end of the day, I suspected his vision of a family involved a wife and not someone who slept eternally and left him to raise a child on his own.

Gray moved quickly, his body crossing the distance between us. I barely had time to uncross my arms before the flat of his palm slammed into my chest.

I fell back to the ground, the wind knocking out of me as I forced myself to get my hands beneath me and pushed to my feet in a swift jump.

"Again, *rude,*" I said, rolling my neck from side to side and trying to make my body go loose.

I couldn't be distracted by Iban's watchful stare, not if I wanted to survive a spar with a Vessel *mostly* unscathed.

"There's my favorite witchling," Gray murmured, and the praise sparked something warm in me.

My stomach rolled over itself, leaving me feeling vulnerable and exposed for a moment. I shook it off when Gray swung a leg for my feet, giving me just enough time to jump over it before his fist aimed for my face.

It skimmed my cheek as I turned my head, narrowly avoiding the strike. I glared at him as I moved, stepping closer to him. My arms were so much shorter than his, which seemed endless, forcing me to get farther into his space.

He could and would grab me, but he wouldn't have the ability to land a hit with the same momentum. His arms swung for me, trying to wrap around my back as I drew in a deep breath and dropped to my knees.

I might have made a snarky comment about how he'd been right that I'd be on my knees next if I hadn't needed to hurry. I cocked back my arm, delivering a sharp jab to his stomach and aiming for his spleen. I wasn't even sure Vessels had organs, but it seemed like it would be worth a shot.

My knees struck the dirt, and I flattened my palms together. After sliding them between his legs, I spread them wide and tucked them behind his knees, then *pulled*. Gray's legs bent forward. I hurried to get my hands free before they became trapped, spinning to my feet and raising a leg.

The roundhouse connected with the side of his face, knocking his head to the side. He caught my ankle and used it to twist my body. My other leg left the ground, leaving me to spin in the air as I fell to the ground. The moment my back struck the earth, I wheezed and attempted to get to my feet once again.

"Fuck," I groaned, pressing a hand to my chest.

Gray closed the distance, crawling over my prone body to straddle my hips and glare down at me. Blood welled at the corner of his mouth, and it gave me a moment of pride to know that I'd at least injured him before he knocked me on my ass.

He stared down at me, seeming entirely unconcerned with the way the others around us whispered as he reached for my wrists. I punched him in the face, spreading the gash on his lip as he smiled and finally caught me, pinning my hands to the ground next to my head.

I barely resisted the urge to spit in his face.

"Hate me all you want, Witchling. I'm trying to keep you alive," he said, cutting off my words as he leaned forward. "You're not human. So stop fighting like one."

I swallowed, not having reached for my magic once during our spar. I assumed that was normal, but as I glanced around, the other students seemed to call theirs to their aid as they moved.

My father had taught me to fight. My father—who did not possess even an inkling of magic in his veins.

I swallowed, nodding in agreement for once. I couldn't argue with what we both knew was true. He released me finally, getting to his feet and leaving me sprawled on the ground.

"Get up," he muttered, squaring himself all over again.

I pushed to my feet much more slowly, focusing on my breathing and dropping into that place my mother had taught me to touch. To stroke and nourish. The magic of the earth flowed through my veins. Their voices spoke in my ear; all I had to do was listen.

My eyes drifted closed as I touched what remained of life around me. Gray stared at me when I opened my eyes, giving me the moment I needed to ready myself.

I lunged first this time, striking toward him as I aimed for his face. He sidestepped as I pulled on the grass with my magic, encouraging it to grow and extend. When he moved, the grass wrapped around his feet, holding him still as I tried again.

He evaded even still, his speed far too fast for me to even consider matching. It was *impossible* to get to him in a one on one, and my frustration grew.

"You're a witch, Willow. So be a fucking witch and work in tandem with your magic."

I growled, reaching for the dirt as he broke free from the blades of grass and caught me around the waist. His hands pressed into my stomach, lifting me from the ground as he flung me backward. The earth rose up to meet me this time, catching me and cradling me as I sprawled on my back.

The bastard flicked a piece of dirt off his shirt, staring down at me and making my blood boil.

"Again."

I went again.

28

WILLOW

I was going to fucking kill him. In his sleep, preferably, when he couldn't fight back. I lowered myself into the bathtub later that night, wincing as the scalding water touched my sore muscles. Everything hurt, a deep throbbing ache that I hadn't felt for years now.

My father's best efforts had stopped being productive when I'd reached my teen years, quickly outmatching him, and he'd had to focus my training in other ways. With other opponents, trapped in a ring where he could place bets on whether I'd win or lose and make money off my attempts.

He bet against me more often than not. Some of the greatest joys in my life came from those days when I clawed my way out of the ring, my body broken and bleeding, in time to watch him hand a wad of cash to the man who organized those fights.

By that point, the earth answered my call when I needed healing. My magic hadn't fully awakened until sixteen, but it still recognized me and the blood that dripped upon the earth as I stumbled toward my father's car.

My injuries would disappear; nothing for my mother to

see. My father's threats toward my brother always rang in my ears when I didn't tell her exactly what happened, keeping me quiet. She never knew the depths he would go for his vengeance, never knew exactly what he'd planned.

She envisioned a quiet search for the bones. A silent rebellion that would be over as quickly as it began, and then I could come home after claiming what was mine.

She'd loved my father, even if he never cared for her.

I rested my head against the back of the tub, my hands playing with the surface of the water softly. Bubbles ran over my skin, the tingling, popping feeling of them nearly enough to distract me from the feeling of someone watching me as my eyes drifted closed.

My gaze darted open immediately, and I sat up straight in the tub. There was no sign of anyone in the bath with me, and I swallowed as I sank lower into the water once more.

Willlloooowwwwwww.

I sat up straight all over again, water sloshing as I grabbed the edge of the tub. Branches scraped against the window outside, startling me as I spun to glance at it. Silence reigned, claiming the bathroom as I held perfectly still.

Willlllooowwwwwww.

I swallowed, raising a hand to clutch at my mother's amulet. The voice continued, a slow, drawn-out murmur that barely resonated with words. There was something serpentine about it, something slow and slithering as it sank inside me. It started at my toes, tingling over me like a lover's caress.

I reached into the water with my free hand, panicking as I felt my legs and tried to find the source of the touch. But I was alone, the tub empty save for my body and the bubbles on the surface.

Come to me, witchhhhh.

I pinched my eyes closed, leaning back against the tub as

the force of that voice hit my belly. It crawled over me, and I could have sworn if I'd allowed my eyes to open, I'd stare into the face of a monster.

My other hand covered my amulet, focusing my will on the crystal that protected me from compulsion. That protected me from the call of whatever creature tried to summon me from my bath.

"It's not real," I said, trying to reassure myself as I clutched that amulet.

The voice stopped, giving me a reprieve of silence. I waited several moments for it to return, for it to sink into my head all over again.

Nothing came.

I opened one eye slowly, peering out cautiously. The bathroom remained empty, and my lungs heaved with relief as my other eye opened. I sat in the stillness of the bath, wondering if I'd imagined the entire thing. If my exhaustion had taken a new life or if it was just the school itself.

If the ghosts of Hollow's Grove had come to take me to the grave.

I swallowed, gathering my bar of soap into my hands and working it into a lather. I whispered words in Latin, warming the lavender within the bar to help soothe the chill that had covered my skin in goosebumps in spite of the hot water.

The door to the bathroom burst open, Gray's frantic face filling my vision as I shrieked. I plunged myself beneath the surface of the water, keeping only my head above it.

"What is wrong with you?!"

"Are you hurt?" he asked, his relieved sigh making my fingers twitch.

"I'm just sore from earlier," I said, my brow furrowing. I didn't want to think about what had sent him rushing into my room at this time of night. "What's wrong?"

"Get out," he said, grabbing the towel off the rack beside the tub. He dropped it onto the sink vanity, reached into the tub, and grabbed me beneath my arms when I didn't move quickly enough.

"Gray!" I protested, smacking his hands away when he set me on my feet on the floor. He paused, glancing down my body and taking in what he hadn't seen. He'd seen it in bits and pieces, particularly the prime real estate, but I refused to cower or hide as his gaze swept over my body.

"Fuck," he grunted, shaking his head and reaching for the towel as he gave me one for my hair.

I worked to dry the length of it, shaking it and wincing at the mess it would be the next day with such harsh treatment.

He ran the towel over my shoulders with rushed strokes, dragging it lower over the rest of my body as I tried not to focus on the fact that I was naked with him.

Naked, and we weren't...

I swallowed. "What's going on?"

"There's been another murder," Gray answered, catching my gaze as the towel froze on my skin. My heart throbbed, pulsing in my chest as I thought about the voice I'd heard.

Calling to *me*.

"Gray," I whispered, catching his arm as he turned away. My mouth dropped open silently, the words getting caught in my throat. I couldn't risk telling him about the voice. What if it had something to do with my bloodline?

He pulled away when I said nothing more, heading for the door to my bedroom. I wrapped the towel around my body and followed, tugging on the pajama shorts and t-shirt that he set out for me.

"There's something you need to see," he explained, taking my hand and guiding me to the halls outside my room.

Following behind him, I tried to shove down my rising

dread. Students milled in the hall, giving me a passing glance before it darted away at the glare Gray gave them. We hurried down the stairs, taking them as quickly as I dared without risking falling on my face.

My wet hair clung to the side of my face, chilling me to the bone as Gray guided me to the doors. The crowd that surrounded his body had formed in the exact spot Gray and I had sparred earlier in the day, where both our blood had spilled on the ground by the end of the training session.

I didn't recognize the witch on the ground, but whoever had killed him had cut his throat. Blood covered the grass. The plants ignored it, as it hadn't been given willingly. I swallowed as the crowd parted, revealing the stone wall of the school behind them.

Blood covered the stone, wedged into the crevices and dripping down the smoother parts of the surface.

Two.

I swallowed, staring at the words as my horror mounted. Gray had wanted me to see it; he'd dragged me here so that I could see the message written in blood.

"Are they counting their victims?" I asked, shoving the panic down in favor of rationale.

Any normal person would need answers. It was a natural assumption, and it still could have been accurate. I swallowed, hoping that was the case. My stare moved away from the body, sweeping over the crowd of observers studying not the body but me. Glaring at my hands as if I was the one who'd cut his throat.

"Before Charlotte Hecate was torn apart and her pieces scattered, she foretold a prophecy of the daughter of two," Susannah said, stepping up beside me. She looked down into my eyes, and I felt the sweeping analysis of that stare.

My breath caught in my lungs, and I held it there, forcing

myself to hold her stare. I hadn't been around the Covenant since she'd tried to force me into a deep sleep, and I hoped that the last interaction would cover any of my nerves about this conversation.

This was far too close to home.

"What kind of prophecy?" I asked.

I barely knew anything about it, barely understood a single piece of what I was supposedly destined to do. All my father had said was that I needed the bones, that they needed to be returned to our bloodline.

What happened after I found them was a mystery. One I hoped would become clear once I connected with the other half of my magic.

"I hardly think that's relevant today. The Covenant has done everything in its power to prevent it from coming to pass," Gray said, scoffing as my blood chilled.

"I should think you've played some part in that," Susannah snapped, finally turning her attention away from me.

I sighed, a tiny bit of my relief slipping loose, allowing Gray to take the focus off me.

"Of course. I have hunted down every male witch who tried to escape making the Choice on your behalf, Covenant." He fiddled with his nails as if the topic of murdering male witches meant little to him.

I swallowed.

Not every one.

Running my hands over my face, I tried to steer clear of this conversation. But there was one thing I couldn't ignore.

The opportunity to find out the information I'd been denied all my life. "What kind of prophecy?" I asked.

"Charlotte foretold of a witch born between two bloodlines who would restore what had been lost to time," Susannah said, clasping her hands in front of her.

"What does that even mean?" I asked, glancing at Gray.

He shrugged. "All manner of things have been lost to time. It could have been anything. Charlotte was... troubled toward the end of her life. The way of things often left her deeply unsettled," he answered, taking my arm despite the watchful eye of the Covenant. She didn't seem surprised by the intimate touch as he led me away, heading back toward the school.

We entered through one of the six doors, my feet somehow functioning when I felt like the world had been tilted on its axis.

"Willow, wait!" Della called, following behind us. She caught up with us, walking beside us as Gray led me to my room. She swallowed as she cut in front of us, glancing at Gray and seeming to consider before she continued. "Did you hear it?"

"Hear what?" I asked, my hands clenching.

I didn't miss the way Gray's stare dropped to where my arm was looped through his, studying the tension in my body. He was too observant for his own good, and if I hadn't needed him to find the bones, I'd have been far better off if he simply ceased to be.

Even if the thought of it made my heart hurt in a way I refused to acknowledge. He was my enemy, and when I found the bones, I would send his soul back to Hell where it belonged.

That was how it had to be.

"I heard something calling your name," she said, swallowing as she looked at Gray. "I think it wanted you to be next."

I dug my nails into Gray's skin, forcing a smile. "I thought I was hearing things," I said, admitting it when left with no other choice. To deny it would just seem odd, would only raise his suspicions, given that I hadn't been the only one to hear the call. "It felt like compulsion."

Gray tensed, a low growl rumbling in his chest.

Della nodded, clutching her own amulet as she looked at Gray. "It did. I followed it. I worried..." She swallowed, hanging her head forward. "I found him, but whoever killed him was gone by the time I got there."

"Who else heard this voice?" Gray asked, glancing back at the small group that stared at me intently. I swallowed, dreading what was coming.

"I don't know," Della admitted, but there was no doubt in my mind that others had heard it call my name. The way they looked at me... They knew it should have been my body lying in the dirt.

"At least they won't think I'm the killer now," I said, trying to grasp at the silver lining.

"Don't tell anyone about this, just in case, Miss Tethys," Gray said, holding her gaze intently. "Until we know who we can trust, we need to keep this to ourselves."

"You suspect someone?" she asked.

He nodded. "None of the Vessels do anything without my knowledge. I can attest to the whereabouts of each of them tonight."

"So it wasn't one of them. But who else could use compulsion?" she asked.

"The prophecy referred to a daughter of two. If one of those lines happened to be the Hecate line... that witch could compel if she managed the impossible and found Charlotte's bones," he said, but my brow furrowed.

That wasn't possible. Because it certainly hadn't been me who lured the witch from his bed.

I didn't speak a word.

29

WILLOW

I walked through the halls, unable to find any sort of rest despite the midnight hour. I knew without a doubt that the odds were great it wasn't safe for me to be walking through the abandoned halls, but as I dragged my hand over the stone walls of the school, I couldn't seem to force myself to care.

There was something so peaceful about the halls being empty, something soothing and calming about thinking of my aunt following that same path all those years ago.

Had my dream of her been real? Had it been the exact moment of her death that I'd somehow dream-walked into?

The Hecate line had been known for prophecy and metaphysical magic far more elusive than the more tangible magics of the elements the other lines favored. The cosmic witches focused on divination even more intensely, but the ways they channeled the stars to tell them the stories of the future were far different from the Hecate way of hearing whispers from the ghosts of our ancestors.

From the bones of Charlotte herself.

But I didn't yet have the bones, had no connection to Charlotte aside from my distant, removed blood that was just as far removed as the Covenant. But whereas my relation to Susannah filled me with some of my greatest shame, the connection to the brave witch who had started it all was my source of pride.

The image of her walking through the forest at night filled me with a sudden rush, her deep auburn hair blowing in the wind as her cloak fluttered about at her feet. She was younger than I'd imagined. Something dark glimmered in the distance in front of her. The figure of a man waited for her at the edge of the trees, and the magic pulsing off him was dark.

Stained with death and decay, he held out a hand for the young witch.

She spun, and her eyes connected with mine in a moment of shock. It was the same feeling I'd had when Loralei stared at me and spoke. Even though Charlotte didn't speak a word, she nodded briefly once before she stepped into the embrace of an eternal darkness. It choked out the light, flooding the hallways that both surrounded me and didn't all at once. The sconces lining the halls flickered out, the lightbulbs within them bursting. The sound of glass striking the stone floor jolted me out of the illusion.

I gasped for breath, feeling as if I'd only just returned to my body. My skin felt strange, suddenly foreign, rather than the home that had housed my soul for the entirety of my existence.

For a moment, I'd been weightless. Drifting and free, separated from the flesh and bone that tied me to this plane.

Figures stepped around the corner at the end of the hallway, and I felt a moment of panic that the devil from my vision had seen me. That he'd followed me through the memory of Charlotte and had come to take me, to claim what he'd marked as his. I reached behind me, touching gentle fingers to the marks on my shoulder through the t-shirt I'd tugged on before leaving my room.

Even though I didn't trust Gray, I was far better off with him being the sole keeper of that knowledge. No one else needed to know that the devil's eye marred my shoulder.

"Madizza?" one of the men said as he stepped up.

I didn't recognize him from the legacies I'd spent most of my time with during classes, and a quick glance at the two girls and two boys who accompanied him confirmed that I didn't know any of them either. The one who'd spoken glared at me, and I swallowed as I prepared for whatever argument was coming.

One of the other guys whispered, his voice low, drawn out, and mocking. "Helloooo, Willoowwww."

"That's me," I said, forcing a smile even as my unease grew. They spread through the hall, surrounding me as they moved, and a chill skittered up my spine.

"Looking for your next victim?" one of the girls asked.

I turned my stare to her, my brow furrowing as I pursed my lips.

"She's not the killer, Demi. She's the one who should be dead. Not Shawn," the first witch said.

"Or maybe she's just trying to throw us off her trail," Demi said, raising a brow as she sneered at me.

"I'm not the one doing this. Just because I'm a Madizza, that doesn't mean I'm safe from whatever this is. I'm one of the thirteen, all the same as you," I answered, thinking back to the bodies of the two students who had already died. I wished more than anything that there was something I could do to stop the killings, and maybe the best way for me to move forward was to refocus on finding the bones.

To stop delaying what I needed to do. Stop antagonizing the headmaster and make myself malleable.

Become whatever he wanted me to be.

"You expect us to believe you have nothing to do with it? Your blood rejuvenated the courtyard, and the first body was found there within days. You bled on the ground outside today and now Bash is dead too; his body just conveniently left there? You're at the center of fucking everything that has gone wrong here," she said, her voice rising as the flat of her palm struck me across the cheek.

My face turned with the force of it, and I raised a hand to touch the blood that welled at the corner of my lip.

"I'm not going to fight you," I said, shaking my head as one of her friends raised his hands, ready to defend her.

"What are you? Afraid?" the other girl asked.

"Yes," I said, breathing evenly. "But not of you."

Her friend struck forward, sinking his fist into my gut and knocking the breath out of me. "Then fight, bitch."

"You spelled witch wrong," I argued, forcing my hands to stay still at my sides.

My magic tried to rise within me, but I rolled my neck to the side and inhaled, keeping it locked within my chest and refusing to let it crack the stones of the school with my anger.

"I am afraid of whatever is killing us. That's why I'm not going to fight you."

Another punch to my stomach, followed by one that struck my nose. It crunched in my face. Blood burst from it and dripped down over my lips. Pain made my head throb, but it was *nothing* compared to what I'd already endured at far more vicious hands.

"Because you'll just kill us instead?" He sneered.

"Because I know how terrified you are," I said, my voice more nasally than normal. My blood stained my teeth as I spoke, the metallic taste filling my mouth. "And I understand what fear can make us do."

Someone punched me in the lower back, sending me sprawling to my hands and knees as sharp pain tore through my torso. A foot connected with my ribs, driving into me so swiftly that I sputtered, gasping for breath as I collapsed onto the floor.

Worse. I'd been through worse, I reminded myself. Pinching my eyes closed and curling up on my side, I pulled my legs against my chest to protect as many of my vital organs as I could.

One of the men reached down, grasping me by the hair.

"You should leave before he finds out what you did," I said, shoving down bile as he glared down at me.

"Vessel loving bitch," he snarled. "You're so fucking loyal to him, and he follows you around like a puppy, doesn't he? But where was he during the Reaping, Willow?"

"Are you finished?" I asked, feigning disinterest, even though the reminder was like a stab to the heart. It hurt more than any of the physical wounds they'd managed to inflict, serving as the reminder I needed.

Gray could and would have my body. But he would never have my heart.

Because he didn't have one to give me in return.

"Yeah, we're done," he said, pulling my head away from the floor with his hold on my hair. He slammed it back against the stone, making my vision swim for a moment.

Then it went dark.

I crawled up the steps, taking them one at a time as my body fought to pull itself up. I couldn't quite get to my feet, using the railing at the side to help me when I finally reached the top. His room was closer than the earth at the bottom, and I knew I was going to regret the choice when he hunted them down and killed them all the next day.

Why would he bother? That nagging voice in the back of my mind needed to shut the fuck up, needing to keep out of my business.

I let go of the railing, sprawling across the floor in front of his door. I was shocked to find he hadn't already felt my pain, that his blood in me hadn't been enough to alert him to what happened. Maybe he'd hoped they would finish the job and he wouldn't be held responsible because of our bargain. Even with that condemning thought dancing in my head, I pulled myself toward his room, seeking the one place I felt even remotely safe.

I didn't want to think about that.

I pulled myself to his door, slumping against it and raising my arm just high enough to knock on it as firmly as I could manage. Sleep pulsed at the edge of my vision, trying to pull me under as I waited.

"Willow," he said, but his voice didn't come from behind the door. It came from behind me, his footsteps quick as he darted down from the stairway that curved ever higher into the upper levels. "I've been looking everywhere for you."

He knelt in front of me, touching his fingers to my nose and wincing. My eyes drifted closed, the darkness trying to swallow me whole all over again. His deep sigh was half a rumble, a growl that seemed to echo through the halls. "Fucking Hell," he muttered, reaching down and gathering me into his arms.

"Had nowhere else to go," I mumbled, leaning against his chest as he pulled me to my feet long enough to get the door open. He shuffled me in, closing it behind him before he smoothly lifted me into his arms. "Think we've been here before." My laugh was humorless as he brought me to his bed, laying me atop the surface.

He didn't answer, bringing his wrist to his mouth and biting it as he swam in and out of a fuzzy circle. "Drink," he said, offering it to me. I hesitated, and I could see him just enough to watch as he rolled his eyes. "I think it's time you acknowledge that it is too late to save yourself from me, love."

I opened, nausea swirling in my gut as he pressed his wrist to my mouth tightly. He shifted, bringing it to me and letting his blood pour in. I screamed around him as my nose shifted, healing with a snap.

"Who?" he asked, staring down at me as I drank.

The haze began to lift, leaving me all-too-aware of the rage simmering behind those steely eyes. I swallowed down more of his blood, moaning as it became something else. He pulled his wrist back, depriving me of taking more and more, until I could no longer tell what blood was his and what was mine.

"It doesn't matter," I said, shaking my head as I grabbed him by the front of his black shirt. I tugged him toward me, letting him taste the mix of his blood and mine. He groaned, pulling back with a shake of the head.

"It matters to me. Who did this? Was it Susannah?" he asked, helping me sit up. He guided me out of the bed, bringing me to the bathroom as he stripped my shirt over my head.

I giggled, feeling like my limbs were far too light in the aftermath of his blood. I raised one to touch his nose, poking it teasingly.

"Are you going to fuck me, Headmaster?"

"Fucking Hell, Willow," he grunted, pulling my shorts down my thighs. I was naked without them, leaving me nude in front of him for the second time in one night. "Someone just tried to kill you."

"If that was what they wanted, I'd be dead," I said, leaning into him. My naked breasts pressed against his shirt, the soft fabric of it making my nipples pebble. He growled as if he felt it, the hint of fangs peeking out. "You've had me naked twice, and somehow I am still unfucked."

"Unfucked?" he asked, the barest hint of a smile spreading his lips as he reached into his shower and turned on the water. He turned me to face the shower stall, pushing me forward until I stepped beneath the spray.

The water tinted pink as I let it wash over my face, running down the drain with a color I didn't want to consider. "Mhmm," I hummed, running my hands over my body as he watched. I smiled as his eyes followed my hands as I worked the body wash into a lather and rubbed it on my breasts.

"Get clean," he said, his voice dropping lower. "You'll be safe here until I get back."

"Where are you going?" I asked, trying not to think of how genuine my pout was. I hated the idea of being ignored, of not being given the attention I wanted when I so rarely wanted anything.

It was easier not to want, but I wanted *him*.

"To look for anyone who looks like they got into a war with a hellcat," he said, turning to the bathroom door.

"You won't find them," I said, calling after him.

He froze, spinning to pin me with a glare. "Why wouldn't I? I think you'll find I'm quite resourceful, and there's no corner of this school I do not know."

I paused, running conditioner through my hair before I answered. "You won't find them because I didn't fight."

"Them? More than one person *beat the fucking shit out of you*, and you didn't fight?" he asked, the sudden stillness in his body enough to chase away the remnants of being blood drunk.

"Not every fight is worth fighting," I whispered, running my fingers through my hair as I stood beneath the spray.

"You could have been killed," he said, his face twisting with something that felt too much like recognition.

I turned away, staring at the tiled shower as I prepared to lay the darkest part of me open and raw. It was a calculated choice, a strategy. I closed my eyes tightly.

But that didn't make it any less true.

"And if I was? What difference would it have made?" Silence arched between us as I opened my eyes slowly, meeting the storm waging in his eyes with a twist of my lips as I fought back the burn of tears. "The only person who would care is—"

Gray closed the distance between us, stepping into the shower and backing me into the wall. Water beat down on his head, slicking his dark hair to his skin as his eyes sparked with anger.

"I. Would. Care."

My heart thumped in my chest, the conviction in those words almost enough to make me believe them. If only it were possible.

"Gray," I murmured, shaking my head as he grasped my chin and raised my gaze back to his.

That hand slid to cup my jaw, his fingers grazing the side of my neck. "You fight. Every moment of every day, you fight. Because that is who you are," he whispered, dropping his forehead to mine.

"What happens when I'm tired of fighting?" I asked, trying to ignore the pool of tears threatening to fall. Hoping the water from the shower would wash them away before he could notice.

His face softened, his lips touching mine in a kiss that was so much more delicate than any other. "Then you let me do it for you."

*G*ray laid me on the bed, his clothes dripping all over the floor as he tended to me first. Helping me shift beneath the blankets, he didn't seem bothered by the fact that I was naked in his sheets as he turned away and strode into the bathroom.

I stared at the ceiling as my fingers clutched the blanket to my chest, feeling more laid bare than I'd allowed in... longer than I could remember. I'd had Ash before, had the innocent love of my little brother to keep me motivated.

I still did, in a way. Still had the knowledge that what I did would give him a better life in the end to push me forward. But I couldn't shake the sinking feeling in my gut. The one that questioned if I was really better than any of the people of the Coven whom I'd claimed to hate.

Gray was an asshole. He was infuriating and brought out the absolute worst in me.

But he was also the first person I'd turned to when I was hurt, and even I couldn't convince myself it had been because of the bargain between us.

My hair was damp against the pillow, the sheets soft

against my skin. I lay in the bed of the man who was meant to be my enemy, who, according to the plan my father had decided for me before I'd been born, I would send back to Hell and never see again once I found the bones.

My nostrils flared as I threw back the blankets, swinging my legs over the edge. I hurried to his dresser, grabbing one of his shirts and pulling it over my head in a hurry. It hung around my hips, drowning me in a way that I didn't let myself stop to appreciate.

I grasped the handle of the door to his bedroom, turning the knob and hauling it open in my haste to get away. I couldn't breathe, the sudden suffocation of all my conflicting feelings hitting me straight in the chest.

My heart twisted, my breathing stalling. The door pulled out of my hand, slamming shut as I whirled to face the man who'd stepped out of the bathroom to find me attempting to flee. He'd stripped off his clothes, the lines of corded, well-trained muscle tensing and relaxing as he dropped the towel he'd used to dry his hair to the floor. Another towel was tied around his waist, and I swallowed as I pressed my back into the door behind me.

"Going somewhere, love?" he asked, taking slow, measured steps toward me. Even with the predatory way he watched me, he dropped his outstretched hand to his side.

"How did you do that?" I asked, my eyes widening in realization. We were still alone in the room, no sign of any witches I hadn't seen before to close the door.

He smiled slowly, his fangs gleaming at the corner of his mouth. "One of the reasons the Covenant decided we could no longer pair bond with witches was because of the addiction it created and the secret relationships it encouraged between our kinds," he said, reiterating the words Iban had told me before. "But that wasn't the only reason."

"Why else did they end the pair bonds?" I asked, swallowing as he finally reached me.

He pushed a wet strand of hair back from where it had plastered itself to my face, staring down at me intently. "Because if a Vessel feeds from the same witch repeatedly, if it is that one witch's blood exclusively that flows through veins, we get the magic that goes with it. Not the same as the witch possesses, but enough for little tricks."

"But during the Reaping..." I sighed, my brow twisting with confusion. He'd fed on someone else then, while another Vessel took my blood for his dinner.

"You think I would allow anyone but me to touch you?" he asked, chuckling as he slid his hand to my nape. He trailed his fingers over the tree there, the touch so similar to the man who'd fed from me that realization dawned.

"You asshole!" I shrieked, placing my hands on his chest and shoving him back.

The cold malice of his laughter spread through the room, raising the hair on my arms as he leaned away from me and grasped my chin between two fingers. "Careful, love. You just might come close to admitting you wanted it to be me."

"Fuck you," I rasped, slumping against the door. I'd been panicking, struggling with my feelings for him, and he'd been playing games with me the entire time.

"You're so focused on the Reaping that you haven't even stopped to consider the greater concern, have you?" he asked, leaning down to touch his mouth to mine. He paused there, steely eyes staring at me as his fang touched my lip when he smirked. "I can feel your magic flowing through me—even the faintest whisper of what you cannot touch."

I froze, my body going still as I stared up at him in horror. I swallowed as he wrapped his palm around the front of my throat—shoving me into the door and pinning me there. I struggled against his grasp, the terror clawing at me making me frantic as I scratched his arms with my nails.

"Gray, please—"

He reached up, wiping a terrified tear from my face and ignoring the way I fought against him.

"I've known exactly what you are for quite some time, Witchling."

31

WILLOW

I couldn't breathe. Even though his grip wasn't tight on my throat, there was no air in my lungs. I stretched out with my magic in a panic, reaching for the trees outside the windows.

"No," Gray said, the simple command rocking through me as he forced me to hold his gaze. The compulsion slithered inside me, shutting down the flow of magic where it began.

"Just kill me and get it over with then," I wheezed, sinking my nails into his skin. His blood welled beneath them, staining my fingertips. He tipped his head to the side as he bared his teeth at me, but there was no force behind the gesture.

If I didn't know better, I'd have thought he *liked* it when I bled him.

"If I wanted you dead, I'd have killed you already," he said, leaning forward to rub his nose against the length of mine. The affection of that moment while he held me pinned to the door was too much, shoving past that horrible numbness that had spread at the realization that I'd been doomed before I ever even began.

I would never stand a chance at finding the bones now.

I raised my leg, stomping my heel down onto his bare foot in my rage.

"That hurt," he growled, glaring down at me as he readjusted his stance. Meeting that glare with one of my own, I spit in his face.

The splash of moisture struck him in the cheek, and his gaze shuttered as everything in him stilled. He reached up with his free hand, gathering the shirt I'd thrown on in my haste to escape, and used it to wipe his cheek clean.

One moment, I was pressed against the door.

The next, I lay on my back.

The mattress was firm against my spine. Nausea swirled in my stomach at the sheer speed that Gray had moved us. There had been nothing but a blur—his hand at my throat, lifting my weight from the floor before he threw me to the bed.

"That was rude," he growled, shoving my legs apart as I kicked at him. Maneuvering his hips between my thighs, I thanked everything that was holy for the fabric of his towel separating us.

"If you aren't going to kill me, then get the fuck off me," I snapped, struggling beneath him. "You lied to me!"

"I don't think you're in any place to make judgments about my dishonesty. What exactly did you have planned for me after you found the bones, love?" he asked, his fingers squeezing my throat as if he needed the help to get my attention.

I let my eyes drift closed, my brow twisting with the pain of having to admit what I never wanted to think about. "I didn't want to do it," I said, my voice sounding far more hollow than I cared for.

"Do what exactly, Witchling? What was your plan for me?" he asked, shaking me by that grip on my throat.

I opened my eyes just enough to peer up at his blazing eyes of steel, at the storm that raged within him.

"I was going to Unmake you. All of you," I admitted, my bottom lip trembling.

Gray released my throat, rising to his knees as he straddled my waist. Something in his face reminded me of devastation, and if he'd been capable of feeling such a thing, I might have believed it.

"But you didn't want to," he said, his voice a quiet murmur.

I couldn't decide if his rage still existed, if it lingered beneath the surface, or if he'd entered that place of disbelief where even rage couldn't touch us.

"I wouldn't have hesitated with any of the others," I admitted, shrugging my shoulders. Getting rid of them was a means to an end, a way to free the Coven from the deal it had made and the Vessels that trapped us within it. "But you..."

"You expect me to believe that?" he scoffed, staring down at me as if he saw me for the first time. "You've been after my cock since you got here. Did you think I was hiding the bones there?"

I pushed up onto my elbows, staring up at him and shaking my head. "That's not—it might have started that way, but it wasn't. *Fuck*." I groaned, dragging my hands over my face.

"You can't even say it, can you?" he asked, placing his hand on the bed beside my head. He leaned over me, curling his fingers into the neckline of the t-shirt I wore. "You're in love with me, Willow Hecate. *Say it.*"

The name I'd never been allowed to use struck a chord within me, the *rightness* of it simmering in my blood.

"I *hate* you," I snarled instead of giving him the answer he wanted. His blood made him more able to *feel* my feelings, but he was wrong.

He had to be *wrong*.

His resounding growl thrummed through me, bringing my body to life as his mouth crashed down onto mine. It was a clash of lips and tongue, of teeth and violence, as he devoured my mouth as if it were the blood he needed to survive. My lip cut on his fangs, providing him with that very sustenance a moment later.

"Whatever helps you sleep at night," he muttered against my mouth. "I'll help you find the bones, but I expect something in return."

His other hand went to the collar of the shirt, and he tore it down the center as cold air kissed my flesh. I gasped when he pressed his nude form and all his skin against mine, reaching between us to unknot the towel wrapped around his waist and shove it out of the way.

I groaned the moment his cock touched me, sliding against me and dragging a moan from him too.

"Fuck, you're already wet. At least your greedy little cunt is ready to admit it wants me."

He drew back slowly, the glide of him over my flesh making everything inside of me tense.

"Gray," I said. I couldn't find the words to make him stop without embarrassing myself.

The head of him notched against my entrance, and he shoved forward in a harsh, swift drive that tore me in two. I curled forward, touching my forehead to his as my hips tried to recoil. White hot pain spread through me, drawing a strangled whimper from me as Gray froze.

He pulled his head away from mine, staring down into my pained face as his realization dawned. "Why didn't you tell me?" he asked.

Because *that* would have been a fun conversation. *My*

father thought I'd have a better chance of seducing you if I was a virgin.

Okay.

"It's fine," I said through a strangled breath, lowering myself back to the bed and trying to ignore the way my body clenched around him—trying to shove him out. "Just give me a minute to—"

He pulled out. The sudden emptiness of my body came as a shock. He grasped a thigh in each hand, his fingers pressing into the soft flesh as he spread them wide and stared down at the space between my legs. I studied him, the reverence on his face as he watched me.

"You're bleeding," he said, sliding himself down the bed until his face was centered just above my pussy. He sprawled on his stomach, his beautiful face staring up at me as he touched his tongue to my center and dragged it through my flesh.

He groaned into me, the vibration of that sound making a wave of pleasure spread through me.

"Do you know what happens to a witch in the Coven on her sixteenth birthday?" he asked, his eyes drifting closed as he slid his tongue into my entrance and fucked me with it.

Finding any traces of the blood from losing my virginity.

"No," I said, but I had a feeling I wouldn't like it. I had a feeling my father had either unknowingly or willingly set me up for something that would be more dangerous than I realized.

"There is magic in blood and sex, some of the most potent that exists. On their sixteenth birthday, a female witch is forced to choose a partner to give herself to. A witch wouldn't dare risk her first time being with a Vessel," he said, dragging another slow, torturous swipe of his tongue through me.

I froze as he crawled up my body, prowling over me. He

slid into me in one smooth movement, taking his time and moving slowly as he reclaimed the space that he'd made his own. He pulled back slowly when he met resistance, working the rest of his length into me bit by bit.

"Why not?" I asked, sliding my hands around to his back.

I winced when he found the newly tender tissue, working his way through it even as I gasped.

"If there is magic in blood, imagine what kind of magic resides in blood that can only be given *once*? It forms a bond, an *obsession*, between the Vessel and his witch," he said, snapping his hips forward and burying himself to the hilt.

I whimpered, my body feeling too full as he lingered there. One of my hands dropped between us, pushing against his hips lightly to get him to pull away just a bit until I adjusted to the discomfort.

He didn't.

"You made a mistake, Willow," he said, finally pulling back to give me a reprieve. He pushed back in slowly the next moment, taking away the short-lived relief. "I will *never* stop wanting to be inside you now."

I whimpered, my nails digging into the bare skin of his hip. He was impossibly hard against my hand, all lean, solid muscle that flexed and relaxed with each roll of his hips. His groan rattled in my ear as he dropped his weight against me, holding himself off just enough not to crush me.

A distant sort of pleasure lingered out of reach, the uncomfortable feeling inside me too much of a distraction for me to grasp it.

Gray's eyes met mine as he continued his relentless, slow glides in and out of me. I knew he was taking his time, taking me more slowly than he'd intended when he'd shoved himself into me in his rage.

"Relax," he murmured, the compulsion of those words

sliding over my skin. My body reacted instantly, my muscles going lax. He seemed to get even farther inside of me, another tiny press as he moaned. "That's it. You'll get used to the way I feel inside you."

I whimpered as he leaned forward, dragging his fangs over my neck. He sank them in, taking my blood in a feeding that I suspected was more for my benefit than his. The pain of his bite faded quickly, allowing that thick, pulsing pleasure to spread from my neck and down through my torso. It reached inside me, stroking that distant pleasure that I couldn't grasp and bringing it to the surface.

"Gray," I murmured, my voice trailing off as pleasure swallowed the words.

He bit down harder. My legs tightened around his hips, holding him tightly against me as my orgasm built and swelled, pulling me beneath the surface while he continued to fuck me. The warmth of his release filled me as he groaned into my neck, pulling his fangs free and licking my blood from my skin.

I fell into the darkness in the wake of blinding light, sleep pulling me under while Gray was still inside me.

J shook my head as I stared out the window at the grounds below, keeping my eyes firmly attached to the blood dripping from Willow's palm. She held a knife in her other hand, squeezing her fingers into the cut she'd made so that her blood flowed freely onto the dying plants.

It had been all I could do to control my instincts and allow her to leave my room at all. I'd let her rest and then woken her up with my cock between her legs. Whatever soreness she felt from the night before was easy to chase away with a single bite, until she'd all but writhed in my lap when I brought her into the office area and guided her to ride me on the sofa.

I wanted her scent to fill my office. I wanted all who stepped in here to smell her on me and around me.

I wanted my claim to be *known* now that Willow herself knew I'd fed from her on the night of the first Reaping. She might not have known I'd already claimed *dominium* over her, but that was hardly relevant.

The curious little witchling wouldn't even know what that was, despite the knowledge her mother had instilled her with.

Kairos stepped into my space. "You needed me?" he asked,

forcing me to turn my stare away from the window finally to meet his gaze.

"I have to go into town for a while today," I said, crooking a finger and summoning him to the window. "I want you to keep a very close eye on her. For your sake, though, I do not suggest letting her know you're watching."

"Does she have the bones already?" he asked, his shocked expression turning toward me. We didn't speak of them often, aside from when I'd informed my people that a Hecate witch had returned to Crystal Hollow.

"Not yet," I said, blowing out a breath as I considered the lengths she'd been willing to go to find them. What she'd still be willing to do. "That doesn't mean she won't maim us both if she thinks I gave her a babysitter."

He chuckled beneath his breath, and I had the distinct feeling he wasn't taking me seriously enough. He'd find out soon enough if he didn't believe me.

Willow would make a snack out of him if he underestimated her, but I didn't think he'd doubt her abilities. Not after what he'd seen her do the day we went to collect her.

"How long do you think you'll be gone?" Kairos asked as I watched Willow through the window once again.

It shouldn't have infuriated me that she pressed her knife into her open wound, peeling off any dried blood that had slowed the flow. I might have healed her from the attack the night before, but I'd also fed from her.

More than I should have, if I were being honest.

"A few hours at most," I answered.

Willow stumbled over a tree root as she dripped her blood upon the ground, her lips moving in the faintest hint of a spell as she moved. The plants behind her blossomed, fresh greenery sprouting and flowers blooming in a wave of life. She stopped, tucking her knife into the sheath she'd strapped to her thigh at some point after leaving me an hour ago. Kneeling at the side of the walkway, she held out her palm and allowed a small pool of blood to gather in it.

I watched as the plants swayed toward her, a single leaf touching the surface of the blood as it drank. She ran a delicate finger over the rosebud that bloomed as she watched, and the irony of the moment wasn't lost on me.

Willow was the last of the Hecate witches—the intended keeper of the bones and a necromancer of great power if she could find them. But *life* followed her everywhere she went, drawn to her in a way I couldn't remember any of the previous Madizzas inciting.

"It's fascinating, really. Watching the way she interacts with the plants," Kairos observed, his head tipping to the side. I growled, turning my attention away from my witchling to give the Vessel a warning even he couldn't ignore. He rolled his eyes. "Not like that. She's life, but she's also death. There's never been a witch like her. The things she's capable of..."

He swallowed, and I realized the man wouldn't underestimate Willow. The fear he held for her was healthy, his eyes widening when Willow raised a hand, and the rosebush grew taller. The vines extended, lengthening as the plant shot toward the building and climbed up an abandoned trellis. Willow stood, raising her stare to the window where we watched her as those roses came to a stop just below the windowsill.

Point taken.

I turned away from the window, guiding Kairos to give her the distance she required. She could have her privacy for now.

It would take time for Willow to come to terms with what we were to one another, for the depths of the obsession she'd only intensified by giving me her virginity. By the time she understood, it would be too late for her.

"Someone hurt her last night. I expect Juliet will have an answer for me when I return," I said, accepting his nod as affirmation. Willow might not be willing to condemn those who had done it.

But I certainly fucking would.

33

WILLOW

G ray stepped away from the window finally, giving me a reprieve from the feeling of his eyes on me. I'd come out to the gardens to be alone for a few moments, to sink myself into the only thing that made sense to me.

Nature was constant. It ebbed and flowed, but the force of it always lingered in the earth, waiting for something to draw it to the surface.

Waiting for someone to love it so it could meet its full potential.

The rose bush dipped a stem into the dirt, a single leaf forming a cup as it scooped up a bit of dirt. Raising it to my hand, it dropped the dirt into my open palm and let it heal the wound I'd created to give them new life.

"*Bene facis,*" I murmured, running the tip of my pointer finger over the sharp edge of the leaflet.

I rose to my feet, smiling as I backed away from the portion of the garden I'd already brought back. I wouldn't allow Susannah's machinations to pollute the earth to continue. I'd do whatever I could to preserve that which was truly innocent in her crimes. I walked through the gardens, losing track of time as I allowed my thoughts to wander. I didn't know what last night meant for the future of my duty, if I would be able to find the bones if Gray helped me as he said he would.

And what if he did? Would I turn around and Unmake him after?

I stared toward the school, swaying toward the stones of the building and running my fingers over the abrasive surface. There was evil and corruption within those walls. That couldn't be denied.

But there was also Della, with the kindness and compassion she'd shown me when I'd lost my shit the night of the Reaping. She'd been far more patient than she needed to be, never pressing me for more information to appease her curiosity.

She'd been a friend when I needed one the most.

There was Iban, with his quiet steadfastness and flirtation. Iban, who was so determined to find the love of his life that he'd given up a huge part of who he was.

Margot, who had suffered and didn't like to be touched, but no one had ever taught her that just because her magic was rooted in desire didn't mean she had to participate in it.

There was corruption, but there were also decent people who didn't know any better or understand the consequences the Coven would cause.

My neck prickled, forcing me to spin back to face the path. The hair on my arms rose, alerting me to something approaching that I didn't understand. I'd never had those senses before coming to Crystal Hollow.

I'd never felt things coming or seen the past in my dreams. I wondered if it was the proximity to the bones, if even them being somewhere closer was enough to bring my abilities to the surface to some extent.

Not the physical, but the internal magic.

The bones of half the Covenant approached as if I'd summoned her with my thoughts. There was something so tense in the set of her jaw that my skin crawled.

"Susannah," I said cautiously. I hadn't forgotten what she'd done the last time we'd been alone.

What she'd threatened to do.

But these gardens were my territory, and the roses swayed into the path and blocked her from reaching me.

"I've no intention of hurting you today, Willow," Susannah said, as if I was an insufferable problem that she intended to rid herself of.

"Then what do you want?" I asked, waving a hand.

The roses retracted back into their garden beds, staying ready if Susannah chose to change her mind. My blood was so fresh here, they would defend me even without my request.

"I knew there was something wrong about you the moment I saw you," she said, her eyes dropping to the fresh puncture wounds on my neck. There was a set on either side, one from last night and one from this morning, and she shoved her hand into her pocket as she made a disgusted sigh.

"Likewise," I said, smiling sweetly. "Though I think yours is probably a little more obvious. Bag of bones and all."

"It took me too long to decide why you looked so familiar, even though you look nothing like Flora did," she said, pulling her hand from her pocket slowly.

I swallowed, my eyes dropping to the picture she held in her hands. It was in black and white, but the face of a woman stared back at me as she held it out for me to take. It was a face I'd seen far too often in my father's cabin.

One I'd seen in my dream.

One that he hated to see staring back at him when he looked at me.

"You're the spitting image of Loralei, girl," she said, her voice dropping low as she spoke the words. "Your aunt, if I assume correctly?"

"I don't know what you're talking about," I said, shaking my head in denial. "I've never met this woman."

"Of course you haven't," Susannah scoffed. "She was murdered within these walls long before you were born. That doesn't mean you don't know exactly what she is."

I dropped my hand, letting the picture fall to my side as I considered my options. It wouldn't take much to find my father now that she knew what she was looking for. There had to be records of his birth *somewhere*, and all things hidden could be found once someone knew what to look for.

"And what do you intend to do with that knowledge? Kill me?" I asked, staring my potential death in the face. I looped a finger in a circle, rousing the plants beside me. They pulled back, preparing to strike if they needed to defend me.

"You are the last of my bloodline. Surely you must know that I would do anything to preserve that," Susannah said, hanging her head forward. She pinched her brow between two finger bones. "Leave. Leave this place and never return. Ward yourself so that even the Covenant and Alaric cannot find you. I will allow you to live out of loyalty to the blood we share, but you cannot remain here."

A few weeks prior, the offer would have been everything I wanted. I'd attempted to fulfill my duty and failed, but I'd done what I could. She'd given me permission to leave, to go to Ash and live out our lives free of the Coven.

And yet...

"Where are the bones, Susannah?" I asked, staring her in the face. It was the closest thing she would get to a confession from me, the acknowledgement that I was searching for something only a Hecate would care about.

Susannah laughed, the sound vibrating against her rib bones awkwardly. A chill ran up my spine. I didn't want to consider what it was that she found entertaining in all of this. I glanced at the rosebush at my side, swallowing as she took a step toward me.

"Foolish girl, your lover has had them all this time. Surely you know that and that's why you allowed him to touch you. Why you've let him take such liberties."

My heart jolted at the certainty in her voice. In the way she was so confident in her assertion. I couldn't be positive if she was lying to trick me, but I felt like I couldn't breathe past the sudden pressure in my chest.

"You're wrong," I said, forcing myself to laugh off the pain. "Gray knows what I am. He said he would help me find the bones. He would have given them to me if he had them."

Susannah stilled, her skull going slack as the traces of amusement faded from her bones. "He knows?" The closest thing I'd ever heard to fear filled the tremor in that voice as she closed the distance between us, clutching my hands in her grip. "Hell's sake, Willow. Listen to me. If you only ever listen to one thing I tell you, let it be this. Run. Run and do not ever come back," she ordered, wincing as the thorny vines of the roses wrapped around her bones and pulled her arm back away from me.

"Why would I run? The Vessels loved Charlotte for what she was to them," I said, laughing in the face of her terror. I couldn't shake that sinking feeling in my gut, no matter how hard I tried, not even when the roses wrapped around Susannah's waist and she didn't fight.

"All that I have done, the choice male witches are forced to make, has been to keep him from getting his hands on *you*," she said as the rosebush dragged her toward the ground.

I didn't command them to stop; I couldn't. Not when I didn't believe she'd allow me to live.

Not when she knew who I was.

"You're not making any sense," I said, shaking my head in denial.

"Those bones are not worth what you will unleash if you stay here. You don't know him, Willow. The bargain swore those of us who do to secrecy," she said, something that resembled a strangled sob leaving her as the rose bush dragged her to the fresh dirt in the garden bed. It pulled her to the surface, snapping her bones as I winced. She lay in a heap of bones as the flowers and thorns wrapped around her, pulling her into the earth.

She disappeared bit by bit, the plants dragging her below.

"I won't unleash anything. I just want to do what's right."

"Your destiny is not to do what is right. Your destiny is to destroy us all." Susannah gave me one last horrified look before her skull started to fade into the dirt.

The rosebush shifted to cover the grave where it had buried the Covenant alive, leaving me blinking at it in shock. My bottom lip trembled as I stood, looking back toward the doors to the school.

I took a step, determined to ask Gray what she'd meant.

I stopped.

She hadn't fought. She was the *Covenant,* and plants or not, she could have easily escaped. She hadn't wanted to, not if...

Run.

I looked away from the school, turning my body toward the woods surrounding Hollow's Grove.

Casting one last glance over my shoulder and heaving a deep breath to calm my panic, I ran.

uck. I hated running.

I wheezed as I bent forward, placing my hands on my knees and trying to get a deep breath in. I couldn't function on so little oxygen.

Couldn't *think*.

What could Gray have hoped to achieve by lying to me about the bones? By keeping them from me? If Susannah was telling me to run, there had to be more to it than just the simple reality of him wanting to prevent me from finding them. That fear in her voice had sunk inside my skin, slithering beneath the surface like an insidious menace.

But instead of doubting what she'd said, I was left with the growing, dawning realization that something was wrong. That I'd missed something that had been staring me in the face.

A howl cut through the woods, raising the hair on my arms. Susannah had been willing to let me flee, to let me attempt to escape the fate waiting for me in Crystal Hollow.

Because she'd known the odds of me surviving were minimal. *Creatures far worse than witches call these woods home.*

I swallowed, heaving a sigh and spreading my feet

shoulder width apart. Letting my magic loose was always like releasing a breath, like releasing a tiny sigh of that power into the world and molding it to my will.

I grasped my knife from the sheath, slashing it across each of my palms quickly before returning the blade slowly. My blood dripped onto the forest floor, the sound of it echoing in the silence around me. There were no noises as the beasts hidden here stalked me, keeping quiet as I listened for them.

I inhaled, filling my lungs with air and the feeling of the woods around me. I exhaled, blowing a long, steady breath into the trees. They answered, the forest itself seeming to shift as trees swayed to the side, showing me a path through to the border where it met the outskirts of Salem.

The beasts were to my right, their footsteps thudding against the ground and vibrating against my soul where I'd connected to the trees. I took off at a run even as my calves burned, taking the path the forest had revealed and refusing to look over my shoulder to see if they would catch me.

The ground helped, rising and falling to give me momentum beneath my feet as I kept breathing. Each sigh let loose a little more of that power that I kept trapped within my skin, until the air around me seemed charged with it.

Never had I surrounded myself so thoroughly, had I released so much of it into the earth and the air. A creek bed came up before me, and there wasn't enough time to stop—to slow myself before I would stumble into it. A tree in front of me shifted, swinging a branch toward me just in time for me to grab it.

Bark dug into my skin, drawing blood that paid the debt between us as the branch swung forward and flung me over the creek.

I flailed in mid-air, my legs continuing to run even though there was no ground beneath my feet for a few moments suspended in time. I gasped as I struck the ground, rolling myself forward and popping up onto aching legs the next moment. The howls of the beasts stalking me came even closer, and I realized it wouldn't be enough.

Even with the forest aiding me, I would never outrun them. Not with the way they were gaining on me, and hiding wasn't an option when they could scent the trail of blood I'd left behind. When they could feel the magic in the air and know that something that didn't belong was here.

I kept running, pushing for the boundary. My only hope was to reach the end of the woods by some miracle.

The creature that prowled out in front of me was straight from my worst imaginings. Long, gangly limbs covered in gray, mottled skin. It walked on all fours, the head of a wolf resting atop its shoulders even though the hind legs were far more similar to a human's than an animal.

I skidded to a stop in the dirt, looking over my shoulder as the rest of the group emerged from the trees behind me. Their chests were muscled and covered in hair, the hair on their backs so long that it disguised the curvature of their spine. The creature's fingers were long, the black nails at the end even longer than the teeth that sparkled in the dim light of the forest as the one in front of me opened his jowls and growled as he stood up to full height.

Standing on just his hind legs, he was at least a foot taller than me. I swallowed, tugging my knife free from the sheath and keeping it at my side.

I waited, sinking into the place where I felt the earth communicate with me. Where I felt each and every shift of the creatures' feet in the dirt and dying leaves.

The one in front of me leapt forward, landing on his front legs as he raced toward me. I spun, throwing my knife at him. I didn't pause to listen for his whimper of pain before I ducked low and tucked myself beneath his body, vaulting to my feet on the other side as he crashed into the others.

Gathering my bleeding hands in front of my body, I watched and waited for the three still standing to move. The one with my knife in his chest lay on the ground. One of his companions sniffed the wound, then bared his teeth at me.

The next bolted forward, and I shoved my arms in front of my body. Crossing them, I muttered beneath my breath as the trees followed. A thick, sturdy branch from each side of the clearing surrounding us followed suit, crossing to wrap around one of the beast's front legs on the opposite side.

I squeezed my hands together as the creature tripped. The branches tightened as they wound tighter around his limbs. I pinched my eyes tightly closed in regret when he came closer still, stopping just in front of me when the branches held tight.

"*Lacrima,*" I whispered, wrenching my arms apart.

The branches pulled quickly, uncrossing and tearing the animal's legs from its body. Its howl of pain filled the woods.

My bottom lip trembled, hating the death and violence as the ground soaked up the monster's blood. Taking the sacrifice I'd offered, even if it was not my blood that fed it. The next beast pounced in my moment of distraction, and I flung myself backward as fast as I could to avoid the swipe of claws.

Burning pain cut through my cheek, narrowly missing my eye as three talons tore through my flesh. My fingers worked in front of me, tying knots in the branches like a net. My back struck the earth finally, the creature's jowl only a few breaths from my face when the branches slid between us and connected, forming a barrier as they shoved him back.

He sprang up quickly, lunging at the branches and tearing at them with teeth and claws. I turned and sprinted into the woods.

My face throbbed, and my hands began to clot. I'd given

too much, and my body moved more sluggishly than it should have. That breath that had seemed so easy to exhale before was impossible to reign back in, the magic wanting the freedom it had been denied for so many years.

I gasped as I tried to pull it back as I ran, needing the extra energy within me to get my legs to move. The magic tickled my skin, a taunt and a tease as I winced back from the feeling.

Something struck my back, knocking me flat on my face in the dirt. I rolled quickly, staring up at the beast as he prowled around me and moved his body over mine.

His legs were so tall that even as he stood over me on all fours, there was no contact between us. His deep, dark eyes glared down at me, his teeth bared and dripping saliva on my face as he brought his mouth close to my face. His breath stunk of rotten meat. The stench grew stronger as he opened his jaw.

He drew his head back ever so slightly, his mouth parting. I squeezed my eyes shut and waited for the end. I dug my fingers into the earth below me, seeking reassurance in my final moments and waited for the pain of teeth sinking into my face.

Pain that never came.

The beast yelped. My eyes flew open. Hands grabbed the creature by the mouth, one holding his upper jaw and the other grasping the bottom. I stared straight into his throat. He'd come so incredibly close to biting me.

The hands holding the creature pulled, a roar filling the air as the beast's jaw separated, snapping as it broke. The hands ripped and tore until blood burst from the creature like an explosion. It covered me, raining down on me. I blinked through it and shuddered on the ground.

I pushed up to my elbows, staring at what remained of the

creature as the man holding him tore him straight down the middle, severing his body from head to groin into two halves.

He discarded the halves to the ground in a pile of mutilated flesh, those steely blue eyes rising to meet my shocked stare.

Fuck.

35

GRAY

I spun away from Willow as the last of the wolves leapt up behind me. Thrusting my arm forward, I drove it into the creature's chest and stopped him with my other hand on his mouth. Grasping his snout in my grip, I pinned it closed with a growl of my own as I leaned in to show my teeth.

"*Mine,*" I snarled.

I held its gaze as I yanked my hand free from his chest, taking his heart with me and dropping both the dead body and still pumping flesh to the forest floor. Willow moved behind me, getting to her feet.

I spun just in time to see her staring down at the piles of remains in horror. She stepped over the gore from the one I'd torn in half, and I couldn't decide if she was approaching me or moving away—putting distance between us.

The last werewolf had a knife in its chest, but it pushed to its feet and lunged for Willow, anyway. I closed the distance between us quickly, grabbing it out of midair by its throat and tearing it out. Willow's arms were covered in even more blood by the time I dropped it to the ground. I lifted a hand to wipe the creature's blood from the side of my face.

"Gray," she murmured as I narrowed my rage-filled stare on her. I adjusted my suit, taking another step toward her as she backed away slowly.

"*What. Were. You. Thinking*?" I asked, enunciating the words slowly. I extended a hand, touching the wounds on her cheek.

"I..." She trailed off, and for once, she seemed to not have any words.

She pulled out of my grip slowly, dropping to her knees and collecting a handful of dirt. She pressed it into the slash marks, letting her magic heal her. I watched as the skin knit itself back together.

Something about her choice to use dirt rather than my blood set me on edge.

"You could have been killed," I growled, reaching down to take her hand. Guiding her back toward the school, I watched from the corner of my eye as Willow glanced behind her and to the boundary with Salem.

"How many of those things are there?" she asked, looking over her shoulder. Searching for more of them, I realized. A bit of the tension consuming my chest eased.

"I haven't exactly taken a census," I said, tucking her into my side. Her steps were slow and measured, as if walking took all the energy from her.

"What are they?" she asked.

I sighed as I scooped her into my arms. She wrapped her arms around my neck, but the movement and contact were far more hesitant. As if she wasn't sure how to touch me, when she'd never hesitated to put her hands on me in the past.

To torment and tease.

I'd saved her fucking life, and she acted like I was the monster.

"The Cursed," I said, turning my stare down to those odd, mismatched eyes. She was such a unique conundrum, my witch of two bloodlines.

Someone I had spent a very, very long time waiting for.

"Who cursed them?" Willow asked, swallowing as she held my stare. I leaned forward, running my nose against the side of hers in an effort to soothe her. She was jumpy, jolting back from the contact instead of allowing me to offer her comfort.

"Charlotte Hecate," I answered, glaring at what remained of the monsters she'd created in her first moments of power. "When she first made her deal with Him, she had no ability to control the magic she suddenly had. There were men from Salem village chasing her through the woods, trying to hunt her down so they could imprison and ultimately hang her. The original Cursed were those men, and I imagine they can sense her blood in you."

"I never understood how the witch trials even began before Charlotte's deal," Willow said, gazing out at the woods as I carried her back to Hollow's Grove. I hadn't even arrived in town when Kairos called to inform me that he'd seen Willow race into the woods as if her life depended on it.

"The fear of ignorant men is a powerful thing. Charlotte decided if they were going to kill her for practicing witchcraft even though she was innocent, then she was going to do the very thing they accused her of," I answered, staring off into the woods as I thought of the way Charlotte had recalled her life experiences. "She made them eat their words and their convictions."

Willow opened her mouth, preparing to ask the next question that she hoped would distract me. "I—"

"How long do you intend to avoid answering my questions? What were you doing in the woods in the first place, Willow?" I asked, watching as she pinched her eyes closed.

Silence.

"Susannah cornered me in the gardens. She knows what I am, Gray," she said finally, and everything in me stilled.

Well, that changed things significantly. I didn't respond to her as we approached the front doors of Hollow's Grove. I'd ask more when my witchling was safely tucked into my office, with no plants to answer her call.

36

WILLOW

I stepped out of Gray's bedroom after showering, dressed in the clothes he had fetched from my room for me. I tried not to think about the way he'd found homes for the spare sets in his drawers and his closet, hinting at the number of nights he expected me to spend here.

I caught a glimpse of myself in the mirror as I walked past the dresser, prodding at the bite marks on each side of my neck. The lacy bralette I wore beneath an off-shoulder black sweater did nothing to disguise them, leaving them open to view. I had a feeling it was intentional, since Gray had chosen what to leave out and what to pack away.

He wasn't in the bedroom, giving me a few moments to contemplate my next move. Ending up back here after running was the worst-case scenario. He would know something was wrong, and I didn't know how much I could lie and insinuate that I'd been afraid of Susannah when she didn't turn up after our altercation.

Fuck. Fuck. Fuck.

I moved to the door, pulling it open and stepping into the sitting area. There was no sign of Gray on the sofa, so I ducked my head low and kept my gaze fixated on the floor in front of me. Making my way to the door to the hallway, I considered my options for escape.

The woods weren't an option, clearly.

"Where are you sneaking off to?" he asked, stopping me as I approached the door.

I dropped the hand that had started to reach for the doorknob, letting it fall to my side as I turned to face him at his desk with a sad, pathetic smile I knew would do nothing to appease his curiosity.

"I was just going to go grab something to eat," I said, picking at my fingers with the hand that stayed by my side. My hand rubbed against the fabric of my leggings, and I fought to still the motion. "Do you want me to bring you anything?"

"I hardly think you're in any position to give me the only nourishment I'm interested in right now," he said, the smirk that transformed his face playful. Something in it didn't reach his eyes in the same way it normally would have, and I couldn't decide if what had changed was him or just my perception of him. "Sit, please. I have something I'd like to discuss with you first."

I smiled, pursing my lips as I took the seat in front of his desk. He stood from his seat the moment my ass touched the chair, walking around to my side and leaning against the desk. He'd stripped off his suit jacket, but his white shirt was still stained with the blood of the werewolves he'd slaughtered. He didn't seem to mind as he undid his cufflinks, rolling his sleeves up to reveal his forearms.

"Ooo... we're using good manners. Am I in trouble?" I asked, forcing a playful smile to my face.

He stared at me with the slightest of smirks, a tiny huff of humorless breath escaping him as he saw right through my bullshit.

"That depends. Do you want me to punish you, Witch-ling?" he asked, reaching down to grip the edge of his desk. His grip tightened until the wood groaned, and I shifted in my chair.

"Am I going to enjoy it?" I asked, my breath shuddering with fake laughter.

He tipped his head to the side as he watched me, releasing the desk with a single hand to pick up the knife he must have taken from the werewolf I'd thrown it at. He toyed with the blade, using it to poke the thumb of his other hand. Blood welled from the wound, and he reached forward to drag it over my lip. I swallowed, resisting the urge to lick my lips.

"Why wouldn't you?" he asked.

I swallowed, choking on my laughter. "You're holding a knife," I said pointedly, my gaze dropping to the sharp, pointy thing I very much feared would be heading for my heart soon enough.

He chuckled, placing it on the desk behind him as he leaned toward me. "When have I ever hurt you? We both know I'm far more likely to bend you over this desk and fuck you until you cannot *breathe*. Maybe then you will understand the fear I felt when Kairos informed me you'd gone into the woods," he growled, his voice dropping lower as all pretense of civility dropped off his face. That guarded mask of humanity that he so carefully wore fled, revealing the brutal monster waiting beneath his skin.

"Is that the part I would enjoy?" I asked, placing my hands in my lap.

He studied the motion, the reserved action that was supposed to be how I'd behaved during the entirety of our seduction. According to my father, men preferred subservient, quiet women.

Then there was me.

Gray sighed, leaning forward with a hand on each arm of the chair I sat in. He moved fluidly, his body sliding through the space between us until he stood, leaning into my face as I sat back fully. He bent at the waist, caging me into my seat until all I could see was him.

"Would you like to find out, love?"

I swallowed, drawing my bottom lip between my teeth. I couldn't function with him so close, with the way his gaze examined every corner of my face, as if he could see inside me.

See the doubt Susannah had planted.

"What did she say to you?" he asked when I didn't respond.

I couldn't find the words to answer his sexual advances, because even though it made things clench low in my stomach, my brain wasn't quite as on board with the idea.

"She came to me with a portrait of my aunt. She knew who I was," I said, swallowing as I gave him just enough of the truth to attempt to disguise my deception.

"And how did that lead to you making the incredibly stupid decision to go into the woods on your own?" he asked, the steel of his eyes glimmering coldly.

"She told me she would allow me to live if I left Hollow's Grove and never came back. I didn't want to come here in the first place. Why would I hesitate to leave?" I asked.

"If Susannah wanted you to leave the school, why wouldn't she have arranged for someone to drive you to town?" Gray asked.

I swallowed as I tried to think of what I could say to that. It hadn't even occurred to me that she might have arranged transport for me if I hadn't been in the process of burying her alive.

"Maybe she didn't want me to survive, and letting those things take care of me in the woods was a way to not get her hands dirty," I said, echoing the same thoughts I'd already had on my own. There was something so tragic about thinking the only family I had would dispose of me like that.

Tragic, but unsurprising.

"Hmmm." Gray straightened, releasing the arms of the chair. "Kairos," he called. The door to Gray's office opened as if the other man had been lurking on the other side, waiting for Gray to summon him. Kairos stepped in, shoving his hands into his pockets as he observed us. "Tell me what you saw."

Kairos glanced at me, and there was an apology in that stare as he winced, turning to hold Gray's inquisitive look. "Susannah followed Willow into the gardens. A few moments later, Willow sprinted into the woods."

"And what of Susannah? Where is she now?" Gray asked, settling his deep stare on me.

My thoughts raced, my palms sweating as I picked at my fingers in my lap.

"Why were you watching me?" I asked, turning to look at Kairos over my shoulder more fully.

"Because I asked him to. I protect what is mine, even if it means preventing you from making stupid fucking decisions that threaten your own safety," Gray snapped, leveling me with a glare that I swore could have made anyone wither on the spot.

"Bring Susannah to me. I want to know exactly what she said to Willow in that garden. Clearly, I am not going to get the truth from my witchling," he said, ordering Kairos to do his bidding.

The other man shifted on his feet, and my eyes drifted closed. I knew what was coming next.

"That's the problem, though. Nobody can find Susannah. She never left the gardens from what I saw," Kairos said.

The weight of his gaze on the side of my face made me

want to shrink back inside myself. There was a moment of silence, a beat and a pause where nobody dared to speak or move.

Gray's stunned laughter broke it, and he reached down to run the back of his knuckles over my cheek. "Devious little witch," he muttered, finally grasping me by my chin and forcing my gaze up to his. "You really are so fucking beautiful, even when you lie through your teeth."

"I haven't lied," I argued, jerking back from his touch. "Susannah told me to leave Hollow's Grove. I left because I was afraid of what she would do to me if I did not."

"And you didn't once consider coming to me for help. I wonder why that might be," Gray murmured, dropping his hand away from my face. "Search in the dirt of the garden beds." The order went to Kairos, who nodded with wide eyes and retreated from the room.

The moment the door closed behind him, Gray released a slow, steady sigh. The air tinged with something dark, my skin crawling as he stepped around the edge of his desk.

"It really is a shame. I'd hoped to hold on to these until everything was ready so it would be less traumatic for you."

He approached the portrait of Lucifer Morningstar, slipping his fingers beneath the edge to pull it away from the wall. It swung out on hinges, revealing the metal of a safe behind it. Everything in me sat up straighter, my swallow getting stuck in my throat. Gray touched his hand to the safe, allowing the biometric technology to recognize all his fingerprints. The lock clicked open, and Gray didn't so much as glance back at me as the runes carved into the metal glowed. He grasped the handle, swinging the door open.

I couldn't breathe.

My lungs filled with raw, unfiltered power the moment the safe opened, and I could barely see through the haze of black as he reached into the safe and pulled something free. I gasped for breath, curling over myself as pain tore my insides in two, as my stomach cramped, and things felt like they shifted within me to make room for the new magic.

For what I'd never been able to touch.

Gray turned away from the safe, holding the unsuspecting velvet bag in his hand. It was the deepest black, the fabric smooth as he ran his finger over the surface of it.

The bones woke up. They rose to answer his call as my back bowed and then straightened.

"You've had them all this time," I gasped, running my hand over my arm as he stepped around the desk. I'd wanted the bones; thought they were the key to completing my destiny.

Now I couldn't wait to get away from them.

I pushed to my feet, swaying beneath the power trying to draw me in and consume me. I stepped around the arm of the chair as Gray's voice lashed out like a whip.

"Sit down, Willow," he ordered, the compulsion in his voice forcing me back to my chair.

He held out the bones for me, watching and waiting for me to take them in my grip. Despite a lifetime of training for this moment, I didn't want them.

I didn't want to aid in whatever he had planned, and with the way his blue eyes bore down on me, there was no doubt that it was something.

Something bad.

"Take the bones, Witchling," he said.

My hand rose as if it would take them in spite of my desires, but I forced my fingers to curl into my palm. Refusing to touch them, to take them on his terms.

"No," I said, gasping as I fought his compulsion and shook my head. It took everything in me to fight it, to keep my hand away from the bag. "I want no part in this."

"Your entire life has been a part of this," he murmured softly, reaching out with his free hand to tuck a strand of hair behind my ear. It was wet, and it was only then that I realized I was sweating with the effort of denying the bones.

Of refusing to allow them to make their home with me.

"Then I guess it's time I make a new one for myself," I grunted.

Gray smiled, a humorless, twisted thing filled with pity. "I have waited a very long time for you, and my patience grows thin. You will accept the bones one way or another."

"I don't want them anymore. Not until you tell me the truth," I said, laying my hands atop the arms of the chair. I grabbed onto the wood, digging my nails into it with the force of resisting the call.

"What you want does not matter. They've chosen you," he said, opening the top of the bag and staring into it. The soft, pulsing light of faint purple that illuminated his face would live in my nightmares for an eternity.

He snapped out with his free hand, grabbing me by the hair and tugging my head back. My neck arched back, my arms flailing as I tried to find a part of him to scratch.

"Gray!" I protested, struggling as he shoved the weight of something eternal into my chest.

I rasped, power flooding my chest as the bones rose from the bag. He held the soft velvet against my skin, allowing the bones to shift and mold themselves as they climbed around my neck. I squeezed my eyes closed, fighting the burning pain that they brought. It was like nothing I'd ever known before, like being remade and reborn as they snapped and tumbled, the click-clack of bones bumping against one another as they settled into the shape of a necklace and *stayed*.

I reached up, tugging at the bones and trying to remove them. My aunt hadn't worn them as a necklace when I'd seen her, and my mother had never mentioned anything of the sort when she spoke of the bag the Hecate witches had been known to carry.

"Why?" I wheezed when the bones wouldn't budge. I didn't understand.

Gray leaned forward, touching his mouth to the corner of my lips gently. "Because you will be the last of the Hecate line and the magic in those bones will die with you, my love."

37

WILLOW

*H*e released his grip on my hair, stepping back and staring down at the bone necklace he'd forced on me. I raised tentative fingers to touch them, wincing back from the feeling they created within me. My earth magic felt like life, like new growth and spring. This felt like the slow decay of autumn, like the death of all nature.

I pushed to my feet, heading for the mirror next to the doorway so that I could look at the bones slung around my neck. They were the finger bones of my ancestors, of the witches who had come before me. They dangled as if tied by an invisible chain, draping themselves in a single layer along my skin.

"You're beautiful," Gray said, approaching my side as if he intended to step into the mirror with me. There was no reflection of him in the glass, his Vessel not existing even as his hand touched my shoulder.

The faint purple of my eye seemed to glow in the same way the bones had when he'd opened the bag. I swallowed, grasping one of the bones and trying to pull it away from my neck.

Gray stepped away finally, going back to the portrait behind his desk and closing his safe. I tried not to think of what other treasures might exist within there, what he might be hiding from the world.

Kairos shoved open the door as he stepped into the office. "We found her. The plants didn't want to let her go, but—"

I reached out with my hand, laying it on the bare skin of his neck.

The magic of the bones reached out immediately, spreading through my veins. He froze, his eyes wild as he looked down at me in horror, his gaze settling on the bones around my neck.

"Release him, Witchling," Gray said, taking a step toward me. Fury rose in me as his compulsion slid over my skin, never seeming to sink inside me and force me to obey as I turned my glare back to him.

I didn't so much as glance at Kairos as I let that magic spread through the Vessel, Unmaking the very fabric that had woven him together. His body slipped, melting away. Gray's jaw clenched.

When I turned my gaze back to Kairos, all that remained was a puddle of muddy earth on the floor, what my ancestor had given to lend to his creation.

"That was unnecessary. Look at the mess you've made," Gray said, pinching the bridge of his nose.

He approached me, closing the distance between us and slamming my back into the door. I fought to find bare skin, touching his face and using it to press him away from me as he lunged with his teeth ready.

His fang pierced my hand, but I willed that magic into my palm to Unmake him. Smiling into my grip, Gray drew his tongue over the wound he'd created and pulled my blood into his body once again.

"There's so much of your blood in me, Witchling. You cannot Unmake me, because those bones recognize me as part of you."

The inside of my head roared like the wind in the trees, rustling the branches of my mind as I made the connections. The first time we'd met, he'd fed from me. He'd taken from me every chance he got.

"Is that what all this was about?" I asked, gesturing between us.

As if his betrayal with the bones wasn't enough, the thought that he'd been using me, allowing me to think I was seducing him all along, just so he could have my blood in his veins, somehow made it worse.

"No, Witchling," he said, guiding my hand away from his face finally. He pressed his body into mine, staring down at me with a cruel smirk. "You were a very unexpected surprise."

I flinched into the wall at my back, desperately seeking distance between us as he raised his hand and toyed with the bones around my neck.

"Take them off," I ordered. A tiny spark arched between him and the bone, burning the flesh from his finger as he pulled it away.

"I'm afraid I couldn't do that even if I wanted to. They're tied to your life now, and I definitely want you to stay alive," Gray said. He ducked in front of me, taking a step back as he bent at the waist. His shoulder pressed into my stomach, and he hefted me over until I stared at the ground behind him.

"Put me down!" I shrieked, kicking at him, but his arm lay flat across the back of my thighs and held me as still as possible.

The bones clattered around my neck, touching my jaw and making me hope they would somehow fall off, but the magic that held them fastened to me refused to release me.

He stepped through the open door. "I do not suggest you allow her to touch you unless you want to return to the mud from whence you came," he said, barking the order at the Vessel who waited in the hall. "Have Susannah brought to the Tribunal room and tell Juliet to fetch the missing pieces."

"I—okay," the other man muttered, racing off to play errand boy.

I grabbed at Gray's dress shirt, untucking it from his pants and sliding my hand into it so I could drag my nails across his skin as he walked down the stairs. He jostled me on his shoulder, whistling calmly as he made his way toward the Tribunal.

"I really wish you hadn't taken my knife," I muttered, hatred lacing my voice. Gray spun on the stair landing, adjusting me on his shoulder as he hurried down the rest of the stairs. "You're awfully chipper for someone who just had all his plans ruined."

"Ruined?" he scoffed, reaching the bottom of the steps. "All Susannah did was force me to work on a tighter timeline. Believe it or not, I was trying to be kind to you."

He set me to my feet, taking my hand in his and guiding me through the darkened halls.

"By lying to me? Hiding my birthright from me?" I asked, tugging back on his grip. He was relentless, his hold like a cage I couldn't escape.

"Yes," he said, turning to level me with a steely stare that danced with something like twisted delight. "I am furious that things had to happen this way, because you will not walk away without hating me for what I am about to do."

I swallowed, forcing my feet to still. He dragged me over the stones, stopping and turning an exasperated sigh to me.

"Then don't do it. There's still time to decide to do the right thing."

"The right thing," Gray scoffed, looking at the window

where moonlight shone in. The hall to the Tribunal room was empty, the doors thrown open wide in a way I'd never seen at the end of it. "You mean like Susannah's plan to allow the witches to die out and make way for a new era?"

"I never said that was right," I snapped. "What is it with the people of Crystal Hollow and being determined to destroy everything you've built here? It could have been a haven, instead it's a curse."

"Crystal Hollow was always just a stepping stone to getting what I needed," Gray said, guiding me into the door to the Tribunal. George was pacing in the center of the circle, walking back and forth as he muttered to himself.

"I get the distinct impression a lot of things fall into that category," I muttered.

George turned to face us finally. His jaw fell open when he found the bones around my neck, and it was readily apparent that Susannah hadn't shared her epiphany about me.

"Willow..."

Gray came up behind me, wrapping his arm around my waist and pulling me in close as he ran the back of his knuckles along my jaw and nuzzled into my hair.

"A lot of things do," he agreed, his words a soft caress despite the pain they brought me. "But never you, Witchling. You're the key to everything. You're exactly what I've been waiting for all these years."

He touched the flat of his palm to the bones where they touched my chest. The edges sharpened by time pressed into my skin, drawing blood as they scraped me.

"Willow!" George protested, taking a single step toward me.

He froze in place, and Gray raised his other hand to face his palm toward the half of the Covenant. George fell to his knees beneath the weight of the pure, dark power Gray sent toward him.

"Only a Hecate can Unmake a Vessel, and only a child of Charlotte can end the corruption of the Covenant she trusted her people with," Gray said, flinging his hand toward George.

The skeletal figure flew into the wall at his back, his bones clattering against the stone and remaining pinned there even after Gray released me.

"You touched my magic," I whispered, raising a hand to touch the bones.

It was unheard of for anyone to be able to channel what wasn't in their blood, leaving me to sputter as Gray found the center of the circle in the Tribunal. But my magic was in my blood—the same blood that filled his Vessel. He lifted a hatch in the tile, shoving the floor out of the way to reveal something beneath it.

"Where did you think Charlotte *got* her magic?" he asked, squatting down to examine the mirror on the ground. It reflected the ceiling, curving in a circle with the head of a woman at the top. I recognized her immediately.

From the paperweight I'd thrown at Gray.

"What is that?" I asked, staring at the mirror and trying to decide my next move. I had the distinct impression running was in my best interest but knew I wouldn't get far until there was something to distract Gray.

The Vessel Gray had sent to get Susannah came scurrying into the room, dragging the brittle, broken bones of the other half of the Covenant behind him. She groaned and whimpered, her skeletal form slowly working to repair itself.

I had a feeling she'd been better off buried alive.

I swallowed, stepping toward her. Gray's hand grabbed my wrist, standing smoothly as he held my gaze. I watched from the corner of my eye as he used the darkness, twisting it into a mass of knots and using it to tie Susannah's bones back together. He flung her toward the wall beside George, suspending her from the ceiling as the Vessel who'd brought her dropped two items onto the floor next to the mirror.

I stared at them, my heart beating wildly as I tried to determine what they were. Tried to make sense of what I was seeing.

A heart.

The deep bluish-purple flesh should have been rotted by now if it was what I suspected. I gagged, horror dawning along with my realization. The piece of flesh beside it was less identifiable, but I couldn't stop my hand from trembling where Gray held me.

"It's a liver," he said, answering my silent question.

Two.

A heart and a liver.

I swallowed back bile, blood roaring in my ears. "What have you done?"

38

WILLOW

I hadn't thought to ask if something had been taken from the second victim. It hadn't seemed relevant when he lay there dead and...

Hell.

I tore my eyes off the organs lying discarded upon the floor, wincing when Gray tucked his fingers beneath my chin and raised my stare to meet his.

"Why?" I asked, searching his gaze for any sign of remorse. "You—that night when you came to my bathroom. You seemed worried for me."

"I have had centuries of practice lying to naïve little girls just like you," he murmured, the words striking me in the chest and causing a deeper ache to bloom.

Juliet came into the room, another Vessel at her side as they shuffled the ten remaining new students into the space. Gray was quick to bend down, taking the discarded organs in hand and placing them on top of the mirror on the floor. The female Vessel compelled the new students into a circle surrounding us, raising goosebumps all over my flesh.

"What are you doing?" I asked, holding her stare.

The humorous woman I'd met in the car on the way back from my mother's house was gone, her mouth set into a stern line as she went about her business and maintained her compulsion.

Gray stepped away from me, approaching the first of the witches. The girl cowered, flinching back even though her feet wouldn't allow her to move as Gray held out his hand. Juliet happily slipped a knife into his hand, and he turned to hold my gaze as he dragged it slowly across the young witch's throat.

"No!" I screamed, running forward.

Gray raised a hand, catching me around the front of the throat and holding me pinned there even as I struggled against his grip. The strength he possessed, the sheer power in that hold... He'd allowed me to think I stood a chance.

My feet left the ground as he lifted me, stepping to the side as the witch fell to the floor with a thump.

"Brain," he said callously, and to my horror, Juliet nodded, bending down beside the felled witch to gather the body part.

"Why?" I rasped, clawing at Gray's hand where he held me still. I watched in horror as he dragged his blade across another throat, uncaring for the life he ended. I *felt* the soul leave, *felt* the life end and death claim it.

My fingers tingled, magic that I didn't know how to use yet coursing through them. Gray felt it spark against his skin, smirking at me as he stepped to the side and moved onto the next witch.

"Are you going to come out and play with me, Little Necromancer?" he murmured, smiling cruelly.

His expert cuts across throats ceased to matter. They stopped existing as I focused in on that heated stare and felt nothing but hatred for the man who had deceived me. For the murderer who would kill my own kind.

"Your aunt was one of the few who couldn't be compelled, not with those bones attached to her hip. The way she screamed lives on in my dreams."

Silence roared in my head, deafening and drowning out the subtle whimpers of the few witches he hadn't killed. Another throat, another slit.

"What did you just say?" I asked, the emptiness in my chest spreading ever wider.

"Your aunt screamed when I cut her throat before she could ever lay a hand on me to Unmake me," he repeated. He watched his knife cut across the next throat, allowing it to move much more slowly. Letting the witch feel every piece of skin sever before death finally claimed him.

I recognized him as one of the ones who had attacked me that night, and the fact that he seemed to get extra attention from Gray should have come as a shock.

"Why? She was a Hecate witch. Why would you kill her?" I asked, the breath rushing out of me. None of it made any sense. None of it added up.

Gray cut the last witch's throat, walking me backward toward the mirror at the center. He stopped just beside it as Juliet continued to gather the organs from the bodies that littered the Tribunal room floor in a circle.

He released me, letting me fall to my knees in a heap as I stared up at him.

"Every moment Loralei spent with the Coven was a threat to her brother's existence. I couldn't risk the Covenant learning the truth of his birth. Not before he met your mother and contributed to you."

He reached down, grabbing me and pulling me to my feet in front of him. "Bleed them," he said, raising a single hand to point at where the Covenant hung suspended. They'd not spoken a single word, watching in unnatural silence that led me to believe they couldn't speak.

"They're nothing but bones. They cannot be bled," I answered, shaking my head.

"Then I guess you will just have to give them flesh first," he said, touching a pinky finger to the edge of one of the bones on my neck. That inky, dark magic snapped out, lashing forward toward Susannah like a whip. It wrapped around her bones, drawing her closer to us as Gray slid his fingers into mine and entwined them. "Take what you are owed, Witchling."

"No," I said, shaking my head in protest. "I won't be like you. I won't be like them."

Gray tucked my hair behind my ear, leaning in to whisper against my skin. "I think you'll find you will, whether you like it or not. Please do not make me force your hand. We both know you will hate me for it, and neither of us want that."

"Speak for yourself, Headmaster," I snapped, jerking away from his touch.

He sighed into the side of my neck. "You disappoint me, Willow. Remember this moment when you cannot bear to look at me come morning. I didn't want to have to do this." He touched his mouth to my temple in something that seemed close to pity. "Bring him," he said, turning to look at one of the other Vessels.

He hadn't been able to compel Lorelai because of the bones. He couldn't compel me any longer either, I realized.

"Bring who?" I asked, glancing around the room. I tried to think of who he might have to hurt me, who he might think he could use to force me to become a monster like him.

Iban.

I stared at the door that led to the halls, watching for any sign of the male witch who had become one of the closest things I had to a friend. In spite of the fact that I suspected he didn't approve of what he assumed was happening between Gray and me, he hadn't judged me for it.

My heart sunk, dropping into my stomach as two figures strode into the Tribunal room. My father's face was twisted with arrogance as he guided the small figure at his side. His knife lingered just in front of Ash's throat as everything in me stilled.

"No."

"Do as you're told, and I promise you nothing will happen to your brother," he said, running his nose along my cheek.

I gasped, breath evading me as my father took up his place at the side of the room. Ash's gaze held mine, the terror in his brown eyes hardening something inside me that I'd sworn I'd always keep soft.

Killing the ember of life within me and turning it to rot and decay.

"I will kill you for this," I growled at my father, my jaw tensing as I rolled my neck.

"Don't worry, baby girl. You won't live long enough to make good on that threat," he said, his laugh coating my skin.

Gray touched a hand to the bone necklace, drawing my attention back to him with a ragged gasp. He leaned in, whispering in my ear as he smiled. "Do what you're told, and I'll let you kill him and raise him as many times as it takes for you to work out that anger."

"And what about the hatred I feel for you? Do I get to kill you, too?" I asked, wincing when he stepped behind me and wrapped his arms around my waist once again.

He held me, that dark magic that existed within him drawing mine to the surface. He covered my hand with his, raising my palm to face Susannah. Her bones had started to heal, forming back into her original shape just enough that I could make out the horror on her face.

Her bones covered with raw, bloodied flesh as the magic sprang forward in dark tendrils. It wrapped around her as Gray raised his knife to my palm and slashed the skin. My blood dripped down, the dark tendrils swallowing it as it grew.

Susannah's eye sockets filled with opaque flesh, muscles wrapping around her leg bones. Gray raised my other hand toward George, doing the same as life once again filled his features. Reversing the rot that claimed a body was disgusting work; their bodies a mess of blood and gore and organs.

When it seemed like Susannah would fill out with skin finally, Gray tore my hands down and severed the magic. The freshly grown flesh melted from their bodies, dropping to the ground as liquid. The thick, viscous blood slid across the floor, gathering in a pool just on top of the mirror and filling the space between the pile of organs.

George shook his head as the last of his flesh faded, leaving him as nothing but bones again. They sparkled for just a moment as he turned to face his other half, the Covenant reaching toward one another.

The tips of their finger bones just brushed against one another—the barest of touches—and the Covenant exploded into bone dust. I stared in horror at the space they'd once occupied, only turning my attention away when Gray spun me to face him.

His eyes were on mine as he placed his hand on top of one of my shoulders, steadying me against the panic I felt. Not knowing what he was doing, what was next, was almost too much to bear. The tip of his blade pressed into my stomach, pushing forward slowly as he held me still.

I gasped as it cut me open, sliding into my skin.

"I'm sorry," he whispered, touching his forehead to mine

as he pushed the blade into the hilt. I wheezed, gasping for breath as the white hot burning consumed me. "It will be over soon."

The betrayal hurt almost as much as the knife. It felt as if it punctured a hole in my heart that would never heal. I stared up at him as tears streamed down my cheeks, whimpering in pain as he dragged the blade up and made the wound bigger.

I couldn't breathe.

"Gray," I mumbled, swaying on my feet as he pulled the knife free and tossed it to the side.

"I didn't expect to regret this part," he said, slipping his fingers into the hole he'd created in my stomach.

I pulled against his grip, tears streaming down my face as Ash screamed from the side of the room. Gray held my gaze as his hand filled the chasm the knife had made, grasping onto something and pulling it free slowly.

The fabric he pulled from my abdomen was stained with blood, wrapped around something curved and narrow. He sank his teeth into his wrist, pressing the wounds to my mouth and offering me the blood I needed to heal.

To heal the wound he'd inflicted.

Because he'd fucking *stabbed* me.

I struggled, pulling away as my hands covered my stomach and tried to stem the bleeding. "What is that?" I asked, staring at the rune covered fabric in horror. The symbols were painted in black, standing out sharply against the bright red of my blood. Gray continued to shove his wrist against my mouth, forcing me to drink more and waiting until my stomach healed before he answered my question.

Unwrapping the fabric, he held up a single rib bone and smiled.

"Blood and bones," he said, turning back to face the pile of organs and blood. He held up the rib, and I watched from behind him in horror as the blood formed a vortex. It swirled around in a circle, getting taller and taller, but staying within the confines of the mirror. Gray glanced back at me once more, cocking back his arm as if he meant to throw the rib.

"No!" I screamed, taking a single step toward him just as he tossed the rib into that storm.

It absorbed it, a flash of purple light erupting through the space. The blood drained to the ground, evaporating and revealing the form of a woman standing on the surface of the mirror. She wore a dress of dark fabric so shiny it looked like liquid.

Her face was tipped toward the ceiling, her chin angling down slowly as I stared at her in shock. Her hair was the same auburn tinted ebony.

She opened her eyes slowly, a spark of pale purple shining out from each. She smiled, the expression softening the harsh lines of her face.

"Hello, Willow."

39

WILLOW

I gaped as I stared at the woman, as the remnants of the Covenant's blood dripped from the silk of her gown. She touched Gray's arm as she passed, squeezing him with a familiarity that made everything in me freeze solid. She didn't linger as she passed him, her slow, steady strides crossing the distance between us until she stopped just in front of me.

A single youthful hand raised to my face, cupping my cheek as she stared down at me and smiled.

"I don't understand," I whispered, glancing over her shoulder to where Gray watched our interaction intently.

"But I think you do," the woman said, dropping her hand from my face and stroking a finger over the necklace of bones as she lowered it to take my hands in hers.

I paused, staring into those ageless eyes that seemed to see inside of me—that seemed to understand me in ways no one else did or would. I couldn't explain the connection, or the way the weight of that stare made something inside me rattle.

"Charlotte?" I asked, my gaze dropping to her teeth as her smile broadened.

She nodded, squeezing my hands as I gaped at her. I didn't understand what resurrecting Charlotte Hecate meant or why it was so important, but she turned to face my father with a glare before I could ask any further questions.

"You swore you'd bring back my sister!" he shouted, his face mottled and angry as he leveled that glare at Gray. The Vessel was unimpressed, cleaning beneath his nails with the dagger he'd since picked up from the floor as if he feared I may try to stick him with the pointy end.

I would, determined to repay that *favor*.

Charlotte advanced on my father, that slow gait of hers eerie and terrifying as she raised a single hand. My father gasped for breath, releasing the knife he'd held to Ash's throat and grasping his own as he clawed at his skin. As he tried to free himself from the witch who was suffocating him without ever laying a hand upon him.

"Only the worst kind of man would harm his own daughter," Charlotte said.

Ash bolted from my father's side, running into the center of the Tribunal circle. I dropped to my knees on the tile as he slammed into my chest, knocking me back onto the balls of my feet as I curled him into my arms.

"Low," he murmured, loud sobs wracking his little body.

"Shhh," I whispered, forcing a fake smile to my face. Even knowing he couldn't see it, that he'd buried himself in my chest too fiercely, it felt like an important act. "It's going to be all right. I promise you'll be all right."

I squeezed him tightly as I watched Charlotte approach my father. She stomped her foot on the floor of the Tribunal room, and the stones and tiles separated beneath her. The pit that opened between her and my father was small and cramped, and she stepped around it to grab him by the back of his shirt.

"Let us see how you like living in the darkness," she growled and tossed him into the hole.

He screamed as she waved her hand over the pit, clawing at the dirt that fell back in and slid to surround him. The stone and tiles repaired themselves in a slow wave, spreading across the top of the hole until there were no signs of damage.

Charlotte had buried my father in the ground beneath the school, and as her gaze came to mine and she raised her chin, I understood.

She knew. She knew what I had suffered when I disappointed him. Knew of the little coffin-shaped alcove he kept off the corner of his basement, where the only way out was through a locked door at my feet.

She knew the way dirt trickled through the cracks in the wood to touch my face, knew the way the darkness had settled itself inside my soul.

I swallowed, standing as she approached. Ash fastened himself to my legs, wrapping his arms around them tightly and refusing to let go. I didn't speak a word of what Charlotte knew as she approached, that understanding arching between us as she rested a gentle hand atop my brother's head and lowered herself in front of him.

"Juliet will take you back to your father now, Bug," she said.

I shook my head, wrapping my arm more tightly over his shoulder and pressing him into me. Charlotte's gaze was sympathetic and sad as she looked up at me.

"Don't make me say goodbye again," I begged.

"This goodbye is not forever, just for the moment," she said, looking at the Vessel over my shoulder. Juliet stepped up, holding out a hand for Ash as I looked down at him and shook my head again.

"I can't," I whispered.

Charlotte rose in front of me, taking my face in her hands and brushing her thumb through the tears that had gathered beneath my eyes. "You've not yet fulfilled your destiny, my darling. It is not safe for him here until you do."

I closed my eyes, turning my face down to press my lips into the top of Ash's head.

"No, Low," he begged, pleading as Juliet took his hand and tugged him gently away.

"I love you," I said, my nostrils flaring as I tried to fight the sob rising in my throat. As I tried to control the endless flood of tears that came with the overwhelming emotions. "I will always protect you, even if I'm the one that you need to be protected from."

"Low!" he screamed, latching on to my hand as Juliet pulled him into her arms.

She was gentle with him, wrapping him up as if he were as precious to her as he was to me. We shared a look, and she nodded her understanding as if she'd heard my words.

If anything happened to him, I would Unmake her Vessel and trap her demon in a circle to play with for weeks.

Ash's fingers slipped through mine when I didn't hold on to him the same way, and I felt every bit of his skin slide against mine.

"I assumed I'd already played my part in bringing you back," I said, the melancholy of my voice sounding odd even to me. It wasn't natural for me to feel so hollow, for the emptiness that I kept trapped within the well inside me to rise up and swallow me whole.

But what had been the point?

My entire life had been to find the bones, and I didn't even know *why*.

"I am not your destiny," she said, taking my hand in hers. She guided me back to the mirror on the ground, and we stared down at our reflections in the glass. "I am merely a gift from your husband so that you can survive what comes next."

She touched her free hand to the top of my shoulder, pushing me to my knees in front of the mirror as I blinked at her reflection in confusion.

"I-I don't have a husband," I said, trying to ignore the way her responding smile raised all the hair on the back of my neck.

She slipped her fingers beneath the edge of my sweater, tugging the fabric to the side so that the devil's eye was visible. She pressed her finger into the center of the mark pointedly, leaning forward to meet my stare in the mirror. "This mark would say otherwise."

I swallowed, following her path as she came around to the opposite side of the mirror and kneeling to face me. "I have so many questions. I don't understand any of this. That bone wasn't mine. How did it—"

"I put it there on the night you were born," Gray answered, coming to stand behind me. He touched his finger to the devil's eye, bringing that sharp sting of pain to the surface. "A long time ago, Charlotte asked me to make sure she would always be with you."

"I—but *why*? None of this makes any sense," I asked as Charlotte took my hands in hers from across the mirror.

"You were the price of my bargain, Willow," she said, rubbing her thumbs over the back of my hands.

"The Vessels were the price of the bargain," I argued.

"The Vessels were a distraction. They were my way of trying to limit the ability the demons had to hurt people by forcing them to stay local to the Coven. They were never the price the devil demanded for the magic he gave me. That was always you," Charlotte said, shaking her head sadly. "Only the daughter of two bloodlines, of two magics, can open the seal."

I stared down at the mirror, at the face of the woman carved into the stone surrounding the glass. "Why is your face on the mirror?" I asked, and something in my own words was doubtful. Something in me had started trying to connect the dots and put the pieces together.

"Look again. That is not *my* face, my love," she said, confirming my rising horror. Gray came up to stand behind me, a solid presence at my spine as Charlotte guided my hands to linger just above the glass.

The woman in the stone stared back at me, the features of her face so familiar that I'd seen them every day. The dress and crown she wore were like nothing I'd ever seen, and I hadn't made the connection in the context.

But she was me, carved into stone—Devil only knew how many years before I'd been born.

Charlotte pressed my hand into the glass, following it with the second as I tried to understand what was happening. Pain exploded through the ends of my fingers, burning as if I'd stuck my hands into the flames of Hell itself. My tentative touch straightened, the glass pulling me from the other side as Charlotte covered my hands with hers.

"Whatever you do, do not let go until I tell you," she said, her face twisted with the same pain that consumed me. Flames spread up my arms, leaving my skin unmarked, but the pain that twisted my body was no different. "You'll die if you do."

The mirror shattered beneath my hands, glass falling into an endless pit below us. It went on for eternity, fading into darkness as it dropped. A single light shone through, spreading through the chasm as magic spread. A spiral set of stairs appeared slowly, step by step, as it lowered into that growing pit. Only when the light of them touched the bottom did my horror at what I was looking at truly hit.

"Then let me die," I said, pulling on my hands. Even though the glass was gone, it wouldn't release me.

"You must live. You must live because you are the only hope of fixing what I have done," Charlotte said, her voice horrified as the first of the creatures placed his foot on the bottom step. "I'm so sorry."

He was almost human-like as he turned his shocking red eyes up to me, ascending the stairs slowly. The wings of a bat curved around his shoulders, draping and nearly dragging against the ground as he climbed. I didn't know why he didn't just fly, but I swallowed as I tried yet again to let go of the magic opening the pits of Hell to earth.

Beelzebub crested the top of the stairs, thrusting a hand up onto the floor of the Tribunal room and pulling himself out with a roll of his neck. The leathery texture of his wing brushed against my cheek as he emerged, stepping forward so that the one who followed on his heel had room to move.

Satanus followed behind him, his body larger than the winged being who had come before. His chest was broader than two men combined, his body taller than any I'd seen. He shrank slightly as he pulled himself up from the pits, but the horns atop his head set him apart, anyway.

Leviathan came next, carrying the end of some kind of cot behind him. The fingers he'd wrapped around the post he carried were long, spindly things with too much webbing between the fingers. The talons there were monstrous, like something pulled from the depths. But it was the sleeping figure upon the cot that stole the breath from my lungs.

Facedown upon it, the open, weeping wounds where wings should have been were an identical match for the portrait in Gray's office. He didn't move, his chest didn't rise or fall, even as Belphegor carried the other end of the cot. They maneuvered Lucifer up and out of the pits. The male form lying sprawled on the cot in front of me was dead, entirely devoid of life.

But the devil couldn't die.

"Why is he like that? Why isn't he moving?" I asked Charlotte, refusing to look into the pits and watch as the remaining of the seven archdemons of Hell made their way for the hole between realms.

The one I'd opened when I broke the seal.

She smiled sadly, holding my horrified stare with a soft expression.

"Oh, sweetheart, because His soul is already here."

40

WILLOW

*M*ammon and Asmodeus emerged from the pit as I stared at Charlotte, trying to make sense of her words. Her lips pressed into a thin line as Gray dropped his hand to my shoulder, brushing his touch against the mark of the devil's eye on my skin. I jolted, pressing forward to get away from the touch, as I spun to look at him over my shoulder.

Those steely eyes held no apology as he watched me, as he watched understanding dawn on me. "You once asked me my true name," he said, the cruelty in those words sinking into my gut. "Are you ready for the answer yet, wife?"

I turned forward, staring at Charlotte as my jaw set tight, and my teeth clenched together.

No.

Charlotte smiled again, squeezing her fingers over my hands. "It's time to let go now," she said, staring down into the pit below. Lesser demons climbed up the stairs, rallying to the surface now that the archdemons weren't there to fight them off. The souls of the damned would spread across the earth if I didn't let go of the magic, but I didn't know how.

Charlotte's legs evaporated into mist slowly, blowing away even though there was no wind within the Tribunal room.

"I don't know how," I said, shaking my head. More and more of her vanished, until she was nothing but arms and a head and neck floating in the air.

All the sacrifice to bring her back, and she faded into the magic of the mirror.

"Please don't go," I begged, latching on to the one kindness. On to the one person who would help me.

I didn't know how I was so certain she would, given everything that had been taken to bring her here in the first place. Only that she would.

"I'm always with you," she said. She raised her hand from mine, her flesh fading to dust.

"No," I said, staring at the other hand as she lifted it finally.

"Now, Willow!" she screamed.

I grimaced as I pulled at my hands with all my strength. The seal held me tight. My scream echoed along with hers as Gray wrapped his arms around my waist. He yanked me back, tearing my hands from the glass as it reformed.

Charlotte faded away, smiling peacefully as she became ashes on the wind.

I scrambled away from Gray's touch, staring at the repaired glass of the mirror and finding only my own reflection in it. The bones around my neck rattled as if they felt her leaving, drawing a strangled sob from me that I couldn't seem to suppress.

I tucked my knees beneath my body, curling my torso over them and squeezing tightly. I didn't dare to look behind me, to look at the seven monsters I'd set free upon the world.

The first of them stepped up beside me, holding out a hand that I ignored.

"Come, Willow," Gray said. The steely command in that voice brought my rage to the surface burning away my horror.

"I will *never* forgive you for this," I seethed, ignoring his offered hand.

"You will," he said softly, running his knuckles down the side of my cheek and drawing my attention to him. "In time, you'll realize just how fleeting human life is. How little it matters. When everyone you know has died and lies rotting in the earth, you and I will remain. You will find that anything can be forgiven, if given the time for memory to fade."

"I'm human. I will die like all the rest," I said, pushing to my feet and ignoring his outstretched hand.

"You will not remain that way for long," he said, reaching down to take my hand.

I couldn't think about the promise in those words, about what they meant for my future, as he guided me toward the cot where Lucifer slept. They'd turned him to his back since carrying him out of Hell, his sleeping face visible as we approached his side.

He wore nothing but a simple pair of black pants slung around his hips, and my eyes tracked over the gleaming, sweat-glistened muscles of his torso to rest upon his face more fully. His shoulders were broader than his tapered waist.

His face was familiar, as if Gray's Vessel had been molded to his likeness. It dashed any hope I had of escaping the truth staring me in the face.

That I'd fucked the goddamn devil himself.

I swallowed, covering my mouth with my hand and ignoring the six other archdemons who surrounded us.

What the Vessel hadn't been able to do was accurately capture the ethereal beauty of the archdemon in front of me. It hadn't been able to express the presence he held, even in his unconscious state.

Gray took my hand, placing it against his chest. I realized he'd unbuttoned his shirt, giving me bare skin to touch.

"Put me back," he said, the words both an order and a request as he gazed down at his body.

I tugged my hand back. "Are you out of your fucking mind? No," I snapped, wincing when he crushed my hand to his chest and my bones ground together.

"Over a dozen have already died today," he said, sweeping his hand out to gesture to the mostly empty Tribunal room. The bodies of the witches still lined the floor, but there was no sign of my father, the Covenant, or Charlotte to mark the deaths that had occurred. "How many more do you think I will add to that in order to get you to do what you're told?"

"Please, Gray," I murmured, even if the name felt wrong. Like I was still lying to myself.

That wasn't his name.

"I cannot love you in this form," he said, his voice softening as he took my other hand in his and rested it atop the chest of his other body. His true body. "But I can in my own. Let me love you as you deserve, Witchling."

I scoffed, not believing for a moment that he cared about *that.* Whatever he hoped to gain from having his body back had nothing to do with me.

Still, my eyes drifted closed as the magic of the bones called, arching between my fingers and spreading through my body. I couldn't bear to watch as they did what they'd been created for, only hoping it would save lives to give him what he wanted.

Gray crumpled at my side, his Vessel falling to the floor as my eyes flew open. I turned to look down at the body on the cot, waiting for the moment life returned.

His chest expanded with his first breath.

And Lucifer the Morningstar opened his golden eyes.

. . .

*T*he end...for now.

The Cursed is coming August 23, 2023.

Pre-Order Now.

Or if you can't wait until then, continue the story chapter by chapter on Kindle Vella. Read now.

Desperate for more of Gray & Willow? Download the sneak peek into The Cursed, book two of the Coven of Bones series, including an alternate POV of the night Loralei Hecate died.

Get it here.

ALSO BY ADELAIDE FORREST

Adelaide Forrest writing fantasy romance as Harper L. Woods:

The Of Flesh & Bone Series

What Lies Beyond the Veil

What Hunts Inside the Shadows

What Lurks Between the Fates

The Coven

Adelaide Forrest writing dark romance:

Please heed the trigger warnings for each book.

BELLANDI WORLD SYNDICATE UNIVERSE

Bellandi Crime Syndicate Series

Bloodied Hands

Forgivable Sins

Grieved Loss

Shielded Wrongs

Scarred Regrets

Bellandi Crime Syndicate Volume One

Massacred Dreams Series

Dreams of the Vengeful

Dreams of the Deadly

Beauty in Lies Series

Until Tomorrow Comes

Until Forever Ends

Until Retribution Burns

Until Death Do Us Part

Beauty in Lies Boxed Set

OTHER DARK ROMANCE
Black Heart Romance Presents Heaven & Hell

Wrong

ROMANTIC SUSPENSE NOVELLAS
The Men of Mount Awe Series

Deliver Me from Evil

Kings of Conquest - Cowritten with Lyric Cox

Claiming His Princess

Stealing His Princess

Printed in Great Britain
by Amazon

19853475R00174